1 MONTH OF
FREE
READING

at

www.ForgottenBooks.com

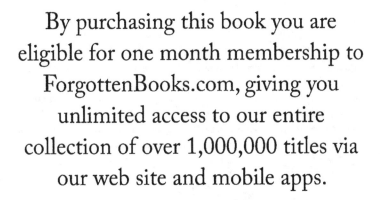

By purchasing this book you are eligible for one month membership to ForgottenBooks.com, giving you unlimited access to our entire collection of over 1,000,000 titles via our web site and mobile apps.

To claim your free month visit:
www.forgottenbooks.com/free539703

ISBN 978-0-484-58276-6
PIBN 10539703

MY GRANDMOTHER'S GUESTS

AND

THEIR TALES.

MY GRANDMOTHER'S GUESTS

AND

THEIR TALES.

BY HENRY SLINGSBY.

" I should be, sir, the merriest here,
But that I have ne'er a story of my own
Worth telling at this time."

The Maid's Tragedy.

IN TWO VOLUMES.

VOL. II.

LONDON:

JAMES ROBINS AND CO. IVY LANE, PATERNOSTER ROW;
AND JOSEPH ROBINS, JUN. AND CO. LOWER
ORMOND QUAY, DUBLIN.

———

1825.

MY GRANDMOTHER'S GUESTS,

AND THEIR TALES.

THE party being assembled on the following evening, my grandmother proposed that the tales should begin without delay.

" I make this suggestion," said the old lady, " in order that our gossiping may not interfere with the pleasure we hope to derive from the stories we are to listen to; and I do it at this moment in particular, because Harry, whose turn it is to begin next, is very fond of cheating us of a quarter of an hour if he can."

" At least I do not deserve that reproach on the present occasion," said Harry, "for I have taken the trouble to transcribe my tale, so that it is a matter of indifference to me when I begin. You, my dear madam," said he to the old lady, " objected to one story because there was not a real ghost in it: I have endeavored, as far as I could, to accommodate your taste, by introducing a demon in my story, and that is worth half a dozen ghosts. Elizabeth too, I think, complained that there was no love in the same story: I have contrived a pair of *inamorati* in this, who, I hope, will please her."

" Let me advise you, then," said Elizabeth, " for your own sake, to begin. If you go on in this way, you may raise expectations which it will, perhaps, be difficult for you to satisfy."

" Thanks for your caution," said Harry; and, opening his manuscript, he began to read.

THE MAGIC MIRROR.

The Student's second Tale.

> ——————————— I tell thee
> There's not a pulse beats in the human frame
> That is not governed by the stars above us :
> The blood that fills our veins, in all its ebb
> And flow, is swayed by them as certainly
> As are the restless tides of the salt sea
> By the resplendent moon.
>
> FROM A MS. DRAMA, BY H. NEELE, ESQ.

THE MAGIC MIRROR.

A COLLEGE is the place of all others where profligacy most plentifully abounds; and, perhaps, of all the colleges in the world, that of Göttingen is the most famous in this respect. We can, upon occasion, furnish some very tolerable specimens of dissolute, idle, roaring youngsters from Oxford and Cambridge; but the most notorious of our Mohawks must blush at his insignificance when compared with a real thorough-bred German Bursche. In the single article of drinking he would put to shame even the master and fellows of Trinity; and, for vulgarity, blasphemy, and profaneness, all St. John's could not match him.

It is, perhaps, natural that young men, who find themselves thrown together in a society where every restraint is taken off, (and such is a college life,) should indulge in all the riot of

youthful blood and unripe reason. Their occupation is always at their own choice. A very
little study will enable them to go through the
ordinary exercises; while temptations of all
kinds, and the influence of example, are constantly persuading them to do exactly that which
they ought not to do. Often these excesses, indulged in early life, entail upon their victims
years of misfortune, penury, or disgrace;—sometimes even more disastrous results have been
known to come of them; and it is an instance
of the latter description that has furnished the
story you are about to hear. It was related to
me by an officer in the service of the King of
Prussia, with whom I travelled from Geneva to
Basle in the course of the last year. The conversation happening to turn on the state of the
German universities, he told me this story. I
am quite sure he believed in the truth of every
syllable that he uttered. He began, as well as I
recollect, in this manner:—

It was early in the last century, on the eve of
an All-hallows Day, that a set of riotous young
men, the greater part of whom were students of
the university of Göttingen, were seated round
the table of a public tavern near the college.
The bottles had circulated so rapidly that many
of the boon companions were lying beneath the
table, joining in the revels only by an occasional
half-uttered imprecation or a loud snore. By

slow degrees the party dwindled away. The
drawers carried off such of the roysterers as
could not walk, and such as could reeled home
to their beds. It was eleven o'clock; one so-
litary waiter lay sleeping upon a chair in the
corner of the room; and of the late noisy and
numerous company there were but two left
whose brains had resisted the stupifying effect
of their debauch. One of them was Leopold
Von Desterreich, a student; the other was a
captain in a regiment of Jägers, then quartered
in the town : his name was Schwartzwald.

In the whole university there was not any
young man who kept up the true character of a
collegian with a more assiduous perseverance
than Leopold Von Desterreich. He was the
only son of a too-indulgent mother; his follies
and faults were not only overlooked, but his
purse was so amply supplied that he had the
means—and, to persons of his age, the inclination is never wanting—to indulge to the uttermost in all the absurdities of Burschenism, as a
college life was then called.

The main object of a thorough-paced Bursche's
ambition was to assume a behaviour and appearance which should be the wonder of all decent
people. To accomplish this object, there was
no extravagance or foolery that he would not
readily commit. Leopold had distinguished himself by the pertinacity with which he kept up

all the nonsensical customs that had from time to time been introduced by the raw madmen who abounded, and by the ingenuity he had displayed in inventing new absurdities.

He had fought more duels than any other man in college ; and was so fond of this method of displaying what he thought his valour, that he would even take up the quarrels of other men, and fight them out. He wore his beard and mustachios of an unbecoming and even filthy length. His hair was suffered to hang in loose curls upon his shoulders. His boots were large and heavy ; and his spurs were of such a size, and made so sonorous, that they might be heard from one end of a street to the other. A studied negligence was apparent in his dress ; and he even rubbed holes in the elbows of his new coats, that he might, in no respect, forfeit the character of a fierce academical sloven. It was acknowledged universally that he could smoke more tobacco and drink more beer than any of his companions; and he performed both of these feats, not because he liked either of them, but because they made him notorious. In short, there was no vagary, which the young and too hot brain of a youth exposed to all the evils of bad example could suggest, that Leopold did not shine foremost in. He fancied that, in doing these things, he gave so many unquestionable proofs of manhood, and that he kept up the dignity of the academy in a manner worthy of it and of himself.

Notwithstanding all these follies, he was a young man of excellent talents, and of a kind and generous heart. His imprudences were the mistaken excesses of a haughty, but noble, temper, from which experience and a more extended knowledge of mankind could not fail to produce far more worthy results. He was the very soul of honour, the stanch opposer of every attempt at oppression on the part of the superiors, and the firm and liberal friend of all those students whose courage and parts made them respectable, while their limited means prevented them from carrying things with so high a hand as he was enabled to do. He was universally respected by the Burschen, and loved by such of them as knew him more intimately.

Captain Schwartzwald was a soldier: he had upon many occasions shown a great inclination for the company of the students, and was one of the very few persons who, without being of their fraternity, were allowed to join their revels.

He was a profligate daring person, with a most forbidding countenance. His conversation was as odious as his manners were disagreeable. A professed free-thinker in matters of religion—by turns a bully and a sycophant, but always ready to back his opinions and his insolence with his sword—he was feared and hated by most of the Burschen, to whom, however, he contrived, upon many occasions, to make himself useful. His example was infinitely pernicious among young men already too apt to be seduced into wrong: and he was so well known to be a corrupter, that every new-comer to the university was cautioned by the rectors not to associate with him.

Leopold neither feared the captain nor any other person; but he hated him cordially, and to this feeling he added an utter scorn of him. In the first hour of their acquaintance they had quarrelled, and had fought in consequence. Leopold was wounded in the duel by an unfair blow, as he thought. The seconds, however, decided that the blow, if not quite fair, was purely accidental and unavoidable; and the captain made a very handsome acknowledgment of his antagonist's courage, and of his own error in the cause of quarrel. Leopold had shaken hands with him on the ground, and he made it a point of honour not to renew the disagreement. He, however, hated the captain not a jot the less than before; and, although he did not care for his society, he resolved never to shun it, and always treated him with a familiarity and carelessness which had a good effect in subduing Schwartzwald's domineering temper. Leopold was the only man in the university with whom he dared not to trifle.

The soldier and the student now sat smoking their large pipes, and puffing the dense clouds into each other's faces with a very laudable diligence: the bottle was stationary, and one of those deep pauses prevailed which sometimes ensue after very noisy revels. At length Leopold broke the silence.

"Captain," he said, "you and I are the only honest men in Göttingen. You see the whole pack of those noisy curs, who but now were barking so loudly, have drawn off; and, spite of good wine and good company—for the wine is excellent, and such company as yours and mine is almost as good—the drowsy sots have sneaked into their beds. May the devil rouse them for it!"

"Amen," said the captain, as he set down his empty glass; "but I wish little Reichard had staid. When he gets sufficiently drunk he grows devout, and tells stories about saints and miracles, that are more comical, and not less true, than the 'Fairy Tales.'"

"You, captain," said Leopold, "are little better than an atheist. You have been trying to convert little Reichard from the faith of his fathers to your own no-belief: but you can't succeed; he is a worthy pillar of the church, and defies the foul fiend. What is the matter with the dog, that he howls so?" he asked, as a large black hound that always accompanied the captain whined.

"He doesn't like cant," replied the captain.

"Then I wonder he remains your dog so long; for you have been pouring the cant of infidelity (which is no less hypocritical than Reichard's) into the ears of all the striplings that would listen to you, until there is not as much piety amongst us as would serve a monk."

"Piety!—*You* talk of piety!" said the captain with a sneer.

"Under your favour, noble captain," said Leopold, "I do not talk of piety in my own person; I only mean to say that you are one of the most impious and mischievous incendiaries that ever got within the walls of a college, to the ruin of foolish young fellows: not that you ever did me any harm; for, although I am not vain, I do think myself a match even for you in almost all shapes of wickedness. I mean, however, to take up, and mend; and as the first step towards it, since my pipe is out, I'll empty the bottle, and away to my truckle-bed."

"What, thou turned sneaker too!" said the captain; "thou flinch from thy liquor, like a shoemaker's 'prentice, who fears a drubbing from his master!—Nay, then, if thou goest, all good fellowship is gone."

"Why, look ye, soldier," said Leopold, "I

like drinking as well as another man; and I
have been trying for the last five hours to see
you under the table, without being able to make
the least impression on you. By all the gods of
antiquity, I think that every hair in those black
mustachios of yours acts as a conduit-pipe to
carry off the fumes of the wine you drink, or you
could never stand it! Now, I am as decently
drunk as any gentleman could wish to be; while
you sit there with your imperturbable ugly black
face, and, saving that you look more stupid, you
are, for aught I can see, as sober as when you
begun."

"You do me honour, most learned flower of
college wit," replied Schwartzwald; "but, if I'm
not so drunk as you would have me, I am no
less a good fellow : I'll join you in any plan of
rational amusement you like to propose. Shall
we take a walk ? Shall we storm the governor's
house, and run away with his nieces ? Shall we
break into St. Ursula's convent, where the blue-
eyed girl is going to take the veil, and prevent
her locking up so much beauty from the world?
Any thing that is mad and wicked, and I'm your
comrade."

"'Tis All-hallows Eve," said Leopold. "Hark
how the wind blows ! the devil and all his imps
are riding on the night-blast! Would you walk
on such a night ? Do let the dog be turned

"... you never witness ..."

"... admit ... again whined ..."

"I ... to hear the wind," said Schwartzwald; "... if ... the devils, surely you, who defy ... every thing in this world as well as in the other, don't pretend to care two straws for all the ... that ever plagued the earth."

Schwartzwald knew very well that the only thing that Leopold feared—if he feared at all— was the agency of supernatural beings; but he knew also that he would rather die than confess so much. The soldier had discovered this point in his companion's character, and he was resolved ... in his attack upon it.

"Come," he continued, "if you really don't fear the evil, and would like to run the chance of ... a pretty wench, take a stroll with me to the hut of the old witch, Alice, and let us have adventures again."

Leopold had two reasons for not refusing this ..., which he, nevertheless, shuddered at the thought of accepting. He would not have had Schwartzwald fancy that he was really ... by superstitious fears; and he ... that ... in which ... Alice ...
... resorted ... your ... who be ... the ... their fare ... more ...

them on the present evening; and lateness of the hour was in favour of this supposition, because, for Alice's sake, as well as their own, these consultations must be kept profoundly secret. Fathers are in general very great enemies to such practices: there is no persuading them that fortune-tellers are not thieves and impostors, and that all kinds of danger may not ensue to young girls who visit these evil prophets. A zealous constable, who, besides his own hatred and horror of witchcraft, his reason to deplore his only daughter having thrown herself away upon an idle ruffian, whom old Alice had pointed out as the girl's future husband, once went so far as to get a stake and a tar-barrel ready for the sorceress; and, but for Schwartzwald, and some of his Jägers, who rescued her, she would have enjoyed a foretaste of that punishment to which all the charitable people of Göttingen, who thought about the matter, believed she was inevitably destined. Her house was well known to be a place of resort for inquisitive young girls, whose curiosity will sometimes lead them to affront dangers, the mere mention of which, under a less powerful excitement, would frighten them into fits.

"Come," said the captain again, "will you come and have a peep in the old hag's magic ——?"

"—— with you then willingly," said Leo-

out," he added, as the animal again whined loudly.

" I like to hear the wind," said Schwartzwald; " and, as for the devils, surely you, who defy almost every thing in this world as well as in the other, don't pretend to care two straws for all the fiends that ever plagued the earth."

Schwartzwald knew very well that the only thing that Leopold feared—if he feared at all— was the agency of supernatural beings; but he knew also that he would rather die than confess so much. The soldier had discovered this point in his companion's character, and he was resolved to persist in his attack upon it.

" Come," he continued, " if you really don't fear the devil, and would like to run the chance of meeting a pretty wench, take a stroll with me to the house of the old witch, Alice, and let us have our fortunes spelt."

Leopold had two reasons for not refusing this invitation, which he, nevertheless, shuddered at the thought of accepting. He would not have had Schwartzwald fancy that he was really influenced by superstitious fears; and he knew that the hovel in which old Alice resided was constantly resorted to by the young girls of Göttingen, who believed that she could tell them their future fortunes. Nothing, he thought, was more probable than that he should find some of

them on the present evening; and the lateness
of the hour was in favour of this supposition,
because, for Alice's sake, as well as their own,
these consultations must be kept profoundly
secret. Fathers are in general very great enemies to such practices: there is no persuading
them that fortune-tellers are not thieves and impostors, and that all kinds of danger may not
ensue to young girls who visit these illicit prophets. A zealous constable, who, besides his
own hatred and horror of witchcraft, had reason
to deplore his only daughter having thrown herself away upon an idle ruffian, whom old Alice
had pointed out as the girl's future husband, once
went so far as to get a stake and a tar-barrel
ready for the sorceress; and, but for Schwartzwald, and some of his Jägers, who rescued her,
she would have enjoyed a foretaste of that punishment to which all the charitable people of
Göttingen, who thought about the matter, believed she was inevitably destined. Her house was
well known to be a place of resort for inquisitive
young girls, whose curiosity will sometimes lead
them to affront dangers, the mere mention of
which, under a less powerful excitement, would
frighten them into fits.

"Come," said the captain again, "will you
go and have a peep in the old hag's magic
mirror?"

"Have with you then willingly," cried Leo-

added, as the animal agai

to bear the wind," said Schw
for the devils, surely you,
very thing in this world as
, don't pretend to care two
nds that ever plagued the ea
rtswald knew very well tha
t Leopold feared—if he fear
agency of supernatural being
o that he would rather die th

The soldier had discovered
mpanion's character, and he w
t in his attack upon it.

e," he continued, " if you
devil, and would like to ru
g a pretty wench, take a w
use of the old witch, Alic
fortunes spelt."

d had two reasons for no
, which he, neverthel
ght of acceptin
wartswald fanc
by superstit
hovel
ly

pold; and, quitting the tavern, they sallied forth into the street.

It was now twelve o'clock. The night was totally dark; not a star was visible through the thick black clouds which palled the heavens. The wind blew in fierce gusts; and, as it rushed through the ample sky, shrill sounds, which seemed horrible and unnatural, were mingled with its fitful blasts. The old houses shook, the signs creaked in the wind, chimneys were heard to fall into the silent streets, window-shutters flapped, and watch-dogs howled. The hoarse cry of the sentinels placed in different parts of the city were the only human voices to be heard; and these, as they mingled at certain intervals with the other noises of the night, seemed like the shouts of roving demons. Nothing could be more gloomy, nor oppressive to the spirits, than this weather; and Leopold, more than once, wished that he had never begun the adventure.

"We shall be sure to find company at the old crone's," said Schwartzwald: "the girls will be afraid to return home while the wind blows thus."

"A man need have some inducement to go out on such a night," replied Leopold; "I mean something beyond that old woman's juggling. —I look for some pretty wenches; and, if I nd them, they shall pay for it. I won't take all this trouble for nothing; nay, if I should even find some of those fiends, which, as, folks say, visit the old sorceress, provided they come in the shape of young and pretty women, I will boldly make love to them." Leopold said this merely for the sake of saying something, and for keeping up the character of a dare-devil, which he had got. He knew Schwartzwald was a man, who, if he gained the slightest advantage over him in the way of ridicule, would not fail to bring upon him the quizzing of all their companions.

" Well said, Orlando Innamorato !" replied the soldier; " even such a cold wind as this, I see, cannot cool hot young blood ;—but here we are at the gate." He gave the word, which, as an officer of the guard, he was acquainted with ; and being, moreover, well known, he and his companion were permitted to pass.

They quitted the town, and struck into a path diverging away from the road, which led them on to a barren heath. A quarter of an hour's rough walking brought them to a low hovel, the lights in which they had seen some time before they reached it. A loud sound of laughter, mingled with screams, was heard, but ceased as the soldier and the student approached. The lights, too, were extinguished ; and, by the time the visitors were at the door, all was dark and silent.

"This is odd," said Leopold: "it seems we are just too late; the revelling is finished."

"We shall make them begin again," replied Schwartzwald. "After coming so far, and in such a night, we must enforce old Alice's hospitality."

. He knocked sharply at the door with his sabre-hilt, and his dog set up a loud and disagreeable bark.

Immediately afterwards the door was opened, and the withered face of the wretched beldame, who called herself the mistress of the hovel, was seen by the light of a small lamp which she bore.

"How now, mother?" cried Schwartzwald; "are they robbers or goblins that you fear, since you are so cautious in opening your doors?"

"You are not alone," mumbled the old woman, without replying to the soldier's observations, as she saw the figure of Leopold beyond.

"I am not," replied the captain; "I bring a gentleman to visit you on this auspicious night; he wishes to see some of your—— But, zounds! why do you keep us standing in the cold here?" he said abruptly, as he pushed into the cottage, and was followed by Leopold.

The place exhibited the most desolate appearance. On the hearth were some scanty embers; on a table near it stood the homely food on which it seemed that the old woman had been regaling when her visitors interrupted her supper. This consisted of some of the coarsest bread of the country, and a raw onion. A starved black cat was lying near the fire, and was not disturbed either by the entrance of the student and the soldier, or by the black dog of the latter, with whom she seemed to be on very good terms.

Leopold looked about in astonishment : he was sure that he had seen lights and heard sounds of rude merriment a few moments before ; and he was sure too that they could proceed from no other place than the room he was in, which now was as dull and gloomy as a midnight tomb.

"Come, mother," said Schwartzwald, " we thought to have found some of the lasses of Göttingen here, who had come to see their future husbands in your famous mirror."

"What ! on this night ?" cried the old woman.

" Aye ! why not ?" said Schwartzwald : " when were mad-cap girls to be frightened by bad weather from what they had set their hearts on ?"

" There is not a girl in all Göttingen," said Alice, " that would come out to-night, even if she were sure of getting a husband to-morrow by doing so."

"Come, come, my good old dame," said Leopold, " tell us where you have hidden these young ladies. I am sure that I heard sounds as I came

along the heath, which could be no other than
female voices. Beseech them to come forth now,
my gentle Sybil; for, if you don't, I must begin to
court you. I am pledged to make love to some
one this night."

The old hag grinned, and shook her palsied
head, swearing over and over again that there
was no female in the house but herself.

"You have some wine hidden, if you have no
women," said Schwartzwald: "come, produce
that, mother, and then we'll talk about the other
affairs; but the wine in the first place, for my
walk and the night-blast have made me as cold
as a corpse."

The old woman removed one of the tiles with
which the floor of her hut was paved, and produced, from a hole which it covered, a large old-
fashioned flask. She placed it on the table with
glasses.

"Come, Alice," said Schwartzwald, "let us
have a peep into thy mirror."

"What would'st *thou* see?" asked the old
woman emphatically.

"Nay, *I* care not for thy tricks," he replied;
"but Meinherr there will like to view some of
thy juggling; and I can tell thee also, by way of
putting thee on thy mettle, that he has no faith
in it—he thinks thee an arrant cheat."

The old woman looked angrily at each of her
visitors; and Leopold, who thought that in his

character of guest, and an uninvited one too, it would be the extreme of ill breeding to affront the lady of this noble mansion, disclaimed his friend's imputation, and assured the old woman that he had the highest opinion of her skill.

The hag muttered some unintelligible words between her teeth, but in such a manner that Leopold did not know whether his compliment had appeased her, or whether she was still indignant at his want of faith in her practices. He therefore repeated his request that she would permit him to see the mirror.

Schwartzwald, in the mean time, seemed to enjoy mightily the old woman's anger, and Leopold's endeavours to propitiate her. "Come," he said at length, "produce thy charmed mirror, and let us see what is to be our destiny."

"The mirror is destroyed," said the old woman; "and, if it were not, you know it is against the laws to make use of it."

"Thou dost mistake, gentle Alice," said Schwartzwald, "it is not destroyed; and, when thou talkest of laws, for whom dost thou take us? Are we Philistines?* are we meek and hypocritical tradesmen? are we like the quaking citizens who come to consult thy art about stolen spoons; and who, if they cannot find them, would denounce thee, or doom thee to that

* In college slang it is common to call the citizens and trades-people *Philistines*.

singeing from which I once had the honour and
the happiness to rescue thee? Come, come,
my good lady, away with thy scruples; Meinherr
is a gentleman—the main-spring and life-blood,
as it were, of college youths—true as steel, and
secret as a father confessor. Produce, then—
bring forward thy wonders, and without delay."

Leopold repeated his request that she would
do so; for his curiosity was now highly excited,
as well by the speech of Schwartzwald as by the
old woman's evident reluctance to comply with
their request.

The hag yielded to their united importunities;
and, still muttering, while her aged frame shook
with an increased agitation, she arose, and
began to make her preparations for exhibiting
the mirror. She first carefully raked up all the embers of the fire into a heap, and covered them
with a close vessel, so that the faint light which
before streamed from them was now wholly obscured. She next went to a recess in one corner of
the room, and, removing a quantity of rags and
lumber which stood against the wall, she opened
a door, within which was seen a black curtain.
She then took Leopold by the arm, and, placing
him directly opposite this curtain, she extinguished the lamp, and the room was left in utter
darkness.

"Now," mumbled the old crone, "what is it
you would see?"

Leopold had, in spite of himself, been in some degree overawed by the hag's manner, and the caution of her preparations. He hesitated as to what he should choose.

"I should like," said Schwartzwald, "to see the place of my burial, as, in all probability, when I visit it for the last time, I shall not be able to recognise it."

"Thank you for the hint," said Leopold; "it shall be so;—show me my grave."

The curtain was heard to be slowly withdrawn, and Leopold saw a small square mirror before him, which was perfectly distinct, and in which light seemed to be reflected, although there was none in the chamber. He looked again, and the surface appeared to be dulled, as if by some vapour passing before it. This soon cleared away, and he saw within the mirror a sight which rivetted his attention. A small square enclosure, surrounded by high walls, and thinly planted with cypress-trees, seemed to lie before him. The walls were like those of a cloister, and were covered with a climbing shrub: the branches of some acacia-trees, loaded with blossoms, hung over; and in that part which was opposite to him, and beyond them, he saw the spires of a building, which seemed to be either a church or a monastical establishment. Looking down, he perceived that the small enclosure was thickly covered with graves, on each of which a small

wooden cross had been placed, and flowers thickly planted. One grave was open, as if it had been
just dug: he looked upon the wall against
which this open grave was made, and he saw
upon it a marble tablet, with an inscription. He
gazed upon the tablet, and read his own name,
" Leopold Von Desterreich," in large and distinct letters. An emotion, for which he could not
account, held him fixed to the spot: he rubbed
his eyes, to be sure that he was under no delusion; still the silent burial-ground lay before
him—still his own name seemed to be uttered
from the marble on which it was written, and to
ring in his ears as well as to pain his eyes.
A cold sweat settled upon his brow—his head
turned round—and he would have fallen but for
Schwartzwald.

The hag, who knew well enough, although she
could not see, what was going on, called out, in
an almost unearthly voice, " You have looked
upon it once—of the third time beware !"

A hollow and discordant voice, which he believed to be hers, then groaned, rather than
sung—

> " Hither, hither, shall you come ;
> This your last and lowly home.
> Wheresoe'er your way you bend,
> Hither must your travel tend :
> Roam the earth, or swim the deep,
> Hither, hither, still you creep,
> In this dull cold bed to sleep."

While this melancholy strain still lingered in his ears the curtain was again drawn, and the lamp lighted. Leopold felt sick at heart, and could not rally his strength so as to reply to Schwartzwald.

" Why, zounds!" said the soldier, " the old woman has frightened you indeed."

Leopold heard the taunt, but he could not reply to it.

" Here," said Schwartzwald, pouring him out a large glass of wine, " try this never-failing specific against the blue and every other sort of devils."

Leopold swallowed the wine, which was at once delicious and powerful : his spirits returned, his heart glowed, and even more than his wonted animation pervaded his frame. He felt a powerful excitement, and laughed aloud, all the fears which the sight of the grave had occasioned being forgotten.

" Why, what matters it," said Schwartzwald, " where a man is buried ? We shall all be in our graves some day, perhaps ; and the knowledge where they are situated cannot bring them one step nearer to us. Drink, then ; and, let Death come when he will, he shall find us properly prepared for the journey, as far as good liquor can prepare us."

Leopold filled his glass again, and, as he drained it, a noise like that of suppressed

laughter was heard at the door. Old Alice opened it, and began to talk to some persons who were standing on the outside. It was soon apparent that the new-comers were females ; and Leopold, who was now in very high spirits, leaped from his chair, and, rushing to the door, swore that, whoever they were, they should enter. Schwartzwald followed him, and they dragged in two girls, whom they found talking to Alice.

The wenches struggled a good deal, and seemed very averse to entering the cottage : but the two gallants were men not to be denied ; by main force the fair ones were seated near the fire, and their cloaks taken off.

Leopold pressed his suit very vigorously ; he was going through the forms usual on such occasions, swearing all those oaths which he had found to prevail often before, and which your accomplished lover always swears, and never means to observe, when Schwartzwald slapped him on the shoulder.

" Bravo !" he said, " you redeem your pledge bravely : you said that you would make love even to fiends if they should come in your way ; and who do you think our friends here are ?"

" I think they are very true flesh and blood, and no fiends, but the daughters of some good Philistines of Göttingen."

" To see how a man may be imposed on, now ! and a learned man too—a student—a sage that is to be! But I must undeceive you. Know, then, most renowned *Bursche*, that you have been gulled, and that you have fallen into a trap I have long laid for you. I thought that your daring impudence and rashness must at some time or other yield you into my hands, and that all the pains I have taken with you could not be thrown away. Once I was as you are ; now it is my business to make such as you are what I am. Your profligacy and your audacity have made you an easy prey to me ; and you have this night, by dabbling in forbidden, and, as you would call them, unholy things, sealed my power over you. Still I would rather be your friend than your foe ; and, if you will give yourself up to me voluntarily, I will secure to you all the happiness that, in your wildest moments, you ever dreamed of. Refuse this, and it shall be my business to poison every moment of your life—to drive you to despair and to death by torments at which you now cannot even guess. How say you?"

Leopold was stupified. The hellish potion he had drunk had bewildered his senses ; the events of the night—the horror of the open avowal of Schwartzwald, or the demon, as he now seemed to be—had shaken his reason to its very centre. He looked around, and saw that the two supposed girls were as old and as ugly as Alice ; and they all three now stood together

in a group, with their sunken glazed eyes
fixed upon him, waiting to know whether they
should hail him as a brother or not. He gasped
for breath, and, putting his hand to his neck, he
opened his collar. As he did this he felt a small
cross, which his mother, who was a very pious, but
superstitious woman, had caused to be made
from an unquestionable relic of St. Anthony's
staff, and which she believed was a never-failing
preservative against witchcraft and evil spirits.
Upon this occasion it brought back to Leopold's
recollection subjects which he had but too long
neglected. He thought of his mother—of the
care she had taken in training his infancy to
pious habits: he remembered the satisfaction he
had once taken in the practices of devotion, and
a ray broke in at once upon the dark despair
that had begun to overspread his heart. He
grasped the cross; his courage revived; and with
a great effort he said to Schwartzwald, " In the
name of Heaven, and of the God of Heaven, I
defy thee !"

A loud scream burst from the hags, and
Schwartzwald advanced to him with a threatening gesture. Leopold drew his sword, and made
a fierce lunge at him. The sword glanced off his
breast; and the captain, or, as he should now be
more properly called, the demon, seized Leopold
by the throat. The youth felt his strength was
unavailing : he struggled, but it was in vain ; he

fell, and saw the eyes of the demon glare exultingly over him. The power of sensation forsook
him; he believed he was dying, and uttered a
groan, with which, as he imagined, his spirit
departed from him.

On the following morning some peasants,
going to their work, found what they took at
first to be the corpse of a man, lying near the
town-wall. They carried it into the city, and,
medical aid being procured, the body was found
still to possess animation. Proper remedies
were applied, and the sufferer recovered. He
was soon recognised to be Leopold; and, some of
his companions hearing of the affair, he was
carried by their direction to his rooms, where
he was placed under the care of the persons who
usually attended him.

He gradually recovered, and, when he was well
enough to reply to questions, he was eagerly im-
portuned by his friends to tell them the particulars of the adventure which had brought him into
the situation in which he had been found. Before
he attempted any explanation he inquired after
Schwartzwald. He was told that the captain
had disappeared ever since All-hallows Night;
and that, from the time they had quitted the town
together, no tidings had been heard respecting him.

Leopold could not make up his mind to detail
all the circumstances of the horrible night he
had spent in Alice's hovel; but, as his com-

panions were entitled to some portion, at least, of his confidence, he told them that he had accompanied Schwartzwald thither, where he had seen sights of the most dreadful kind, and which it would be so painful to him to describe, that he must be excused from attempting to do so.

His friends were, of course, not satisfied with this account; but they saw from his manner that they had no more to expect from him, and they ceased their importunities. As, however, might have been expected, they did not keep their suspicions secret; and, their ignorance of the real facts exaggerating the wrong notions they had formed, they whispered about that Leopold had been dealing with the devil, and that he had fared the worst in the business. It soon got wind, and the young gentleman's reputation was torn to pieces amongst the malignant and curious people with whom the university abounded.

By slow degrees Leopold recovered his health, but the tranquillity and self-possession, which even his excesses had not before been able to disturb, seemed now to have fled for ever. He was not ill; but a heavy weight hung upon his mind, and prevented him from enjoying any of the amusements which had formerly given him so much delight. His courage, and the fiery temper of his mind, were still unsubdued: he looked back upon the events of the dreadful All-hallows Night with horror, but not with fear. He despised the dark powers which had assailed him; but mingled with his scorn was a feeling that their spells had power over him, and that a clankless and invisible chain fettered his very heart.

Among the follies into which he had plunged was that of affecting a scepticism—even of expressing exulting doubts as to the veracity and efficacy of the principles of religion. This he had been rather induced to do by the contagious effect of example, and by that braggart spirit which is common to very young men, than because he was sincere in the opinions he gave utterance to.

In the sickness of heart that now oppressed him he became convinced of his error, and in the religious impressions of his infancy he alone found consolation. Still he was too proud, and too much afraid of the ridicule of his late companions, to avow openly his belief, or to attend the regular offices of the church, but performed in secrecy and in solitude these devotional exercises, which afforded him some relief, and which increased his hatred and contempt of the demoniacal influence under which he suffered.

At length he resolved to seek his late friends, in the hope that their society would dispel some of that heavy melancholy which weighed upon his heart. Here, however, he found himself doomed to experience another disappointment: instead of being received as usual with open arms, and hailed as the flower and chief ornament of the academical youth, he found that he was treated with a cold and formal politeness, which was as far removed from a friendly feeling towards him as it was from affording him an opportunity of resenting the altered behaviour of his friends. This was the unkindest cut of all : he requested an explanation from some of his most intimate acquaintances, all of whom declared that their affection for him was unabated, and insisted that the change of which he accused them existed only in his own fancy. He soon found, too, that he was an object of curiosity to many men of the university, and that he was pointed out to new-comers as a sort of wonder. This was more than he could endure ; and, one day, when he passed through the cloisters, he overheard a young man, whose ill manners and vulgarity had made him universally disagreeable to the better class of students, mention his name ; and, turning round his head, he saw him pointing his finger at him, while his countenance expressed at once scorn and derision. His fury instantly became ungovernable. He asked the man who had given him this offence what he meant by having done so ; and, the fellow stammering some insolent and unsatisfactory apology, Leopold wholly abandoned himself to his passion, and, after heating him unmercifully with his walking-cane, he left him.

He went home, expecting, of course, to receive a message from this person, appointing the time and place at which he would be required to give him satisfaction; for duelling was then of daily occurrence in the university. To his astonishment, however, instead of a challenge, he received a visit from a captain of the city guard, who summoned him to repair, under the escort of himself and a file of his men, to the council-room of the university. Leopold immediately obeyed; and, on his way to the council, he learnt from the captain that he was called upon to answer for having beaten one of the collegians. This was so unheard-of a way of settling such a dispute among the students, that he was still more surprised at it.

When he arrived at the council-room he found the president and fellows of the college sitting in judgment, and his antagonist ready to prefer his complaint, which he did with no small exaggeration in his own favour.

Leopold was called upon to reply. He disdained even to allude to the misrepresentations which his adversary had resorted to, but at once admitted that feeling himself wantonly, and without provocation, insulted by the student, he had chastised him on the spot; and he added that he was willing to abide the consequences there or elsewhere.

" Yes," vociferated the poltroon who had been

beaten, " it is likely, indeed, that I am to meet in open fight a man who deals with the devil, and who, for aught I know, may bring a fiend for his second."

This taunt furnished Leopold at once with the explanation of the coldness he had experienced from his friends.   He saw, in a moment, the reason why his company had been shunned, and his person become a mark for the

> " slow and moving hand of Scorn
> To point the finger at."—

He was so much overcome by anger and shame, that he could not reply but by a look of haughty indignation.

After whispering for a few moments with the fellows, the president began a long harangue to Leopold, in which, without noticing the allusion of the other student, he enlarged upon the necessity of preserving public peace in a place devoted to study ; and then, reading one of the edicts of the college, in which the penalty for striking a blow within the walls was declared to be the expulsion of the offender, he pronounced that sentence upon Leopold, and ordered him forthwith to quit the university.

Leopold, in a short and angry reply, declared that he heard the sentence with indifference, and that he would not condescend to avail himself of the opportunity he had of appealing from the impartiality and injustice with which an obsolete law was thus put invidiously in force; but he denied and threw back the infamous slander which had been uttered against him, and which, he said, had only been used for the purpose of sheltering the cowardice of the person who had resorted to it.

The president replied that this imputation, heavy and horrible as it was, formed no part of the grounds upon which the sentence had been passed; but, as he said this, Leopold saw, or thought he saw, that the old man believed the calumny in its fullest extent.

Disgusted and enraged, Leopold left the chamber and retired to his own, where a short time sufficed to complete the preparations necessary for his departure. The next morning saw him on his way to Switzerland, where he resided for a time. Here he received the news of his mother's death, by which event he became the possessor of a large patrimony. He was, however, not inclined to return to Germany; but, committing the care of his estates to the steward who had managed them for a considerable number of years, he resolved to travel he cared not whither, and solely in the hope of distracting his mind from the contemplation of the thoughts which burdened him. In pursuance of this resolution he crossed the Alps, and entered Italy.

In the hotel at Milan, where he took up his abode, he found some of the officers of a French regiment then quartered in that city. The inward oppression which almost consumed his life had become still more burdensome while be was alone, and he gladly made acquaintance with these gentlemen, in whose society he found great relief. The manner of their existence was much to his taste, for they mingled with the serious and active business of war the elegant accomplishments and amusements of polite life. Some occupation, he felt, was absolutely necessary for him, and he yielded very readily to their persuasions that he would join them. The commanding officer, who saw that Leopold's high spirit and acquirements would make him a valuable acquisition to the service, offered him a commission, which the student, however, declined, proposing to join the army as a gentleman and volunteer.

In this character he served throughout the Italian campaign, and had, in a great degree, overcome the impressions which the fatal All-hallows Night had made upon his mind, although he had not forgotten them, when a circumstance happened which recalled them with all their original force.

It was on a beautiful summer's evening that the party to which he was attached drew near the place appointed for their quarters. The fatigue of a long march had not rendered him insensible to the beauty of the country he was traversing. He was in a remote and unfrequented road among the hills beyond Bergamo; and the eminence which he had attained commanded an extensive view of the fertile country. The setting of an autumnal sun shed a blaze of liquid radiance over the plain, which lay laughing and rioting, as it were, with plenty; while the rich and varied colours of the foliage and the fields glittered under its beams with indescribable splendour. As the march led him through the hills, which sometimes hid the landscape from his sight, and sometimes presented it suddenly and strikingly, Leopold thought he had never seen the beauties of nature in a more fascinating point of view. The day rapidly closed in; and the sounds, which denote the activity of a country life, one by one ceased: the lowing of the homeward-driven cattle, the song of the husbandman, the horn of the shepherd, and the deep-mouthed baying of his dogs, died away gradually; and now nothing was heard but the melancholy notes of the vesper-bell—fit music for such an hour.

Leopold thought of the beautiful verses of Dante; and, although he had no friends to whom his heart turned as the time and place softened and saddened it, yet there was a yearning after some such object, on which its affections might rest, which made him feel his utter desolateness still more. Tears, such as he had not shed for many a day, started to his eyes as he repeated—

> Era già l'hora che volge 'l desio
>   Ai naviganti, e'ntenerisce 'l core
> Lo dì, c'han detto a i dolci amici, A dio;
>   E che lo novo peregrin d'Amore
> Punge, se ode squilla di lontano,
>   Che paia 'l giorno pianger che si more.*

Before the day had quite closed the detachment had reached the place at which they were to halt for the night: it was called the Convent of Santa Croce, and was situated upon a gentle eminence, commanding the whole of the view which had so much delighted Leopold.

The appearance of the French soldiers threw the fair recluses into no small embarrassment. A party had been dispatched to announce the arrival of their companions; and the abbess had made such good use of the time which this afforded her, that all her flock were safely locked up in the higher chambers of the building, and

---

* The late lamented Lord Byron's translation of this exquisite passage—to all but to him untranslateable—is so beautiful, that I reckon upon being thanked for inserting it.—*Ed.*

> Soft hour, which wakes the wish and melts the heart
>   Of those who sail the seas on the first day
> When they from their sweet friends are torn apart—
>   Or fills with love the pilgrim on his way,
> As the far bell of vesper makes him start,
>   Seeming to weep the dying day's decay !
>
>   Don Juan, Cant. iii. St. cviii.

beyond the profane touch of the French soldiery. Experience had taught the necessity of this precaution; for, notwithstanding the devoted sanctity of the gentle nuns, there had been instances of their not being able to withstand the persuasions of *les braves;* and, during the campaign, many of the fair sisters had renounced their rash vows of celibacy, and had become the wives of the soldiers. The abbess of St. Ursula was of such incorruptible piety, and the strictness of her discipline was so famous, that she had no reason to fear the backsliding of any of her holy sisterhood; but, although she was fully convinced of this, yet, like a very prudent old lady, who had been once young, she thought there was great virtue in a lock and key, and she therefore had every one of her flock, with the exception of the lame porteress, whose ugliness was a sufficient protection to her virtue, fairly fastened up until the troops should have departed.

She, however, had provided for the reception of the soldiers, who found a repast prepared for them in a large out-building, and where also they were to take up their abode. The officers and Leopold were her own guests, and were received by her in her parlour, where a simple, but elegant, supper was laid out. The abbess was a lady whom the misfortunes of her noble family, and the changes of affairs in the country, had driven to a cloister. She was a well-informed and agreeable woman, and engaged unreservedly in the conversation with which the evening was consumed. It was nearly time to retire, when one of the officers, attracted by the beauty of the evening, proposed a walk in the garden of the convent, which was seen through the windows of the room where they were sitting.

This suggestion met with universal approbation, and, Leopold offering his arm to the abbess, the whole party quitted the parlour. The garden was disposed with great taste, and was well filled with flowers and fruit-trees, exhibiting—as, indeed, every thing about the convent did—the good taste of the person who presided over it. The soldiers complimented the old lady upon the beauty of her garden; and, as this was one of those innocent enjoyments in which she indulged, and of which she was rather proud, their praises were highly gratifying to her.

" There is another part of my domain," said she, " which, although it is somewhat melancholy, looks so very beautiful by moon-light, that I will show it you, if you will permit me."

" By all means" was uttered simultaneously by the whole party.

" It is the cemetery," she said; and, calling to the gardener, she bade him unlock a door in the garden-wall.

They entered the burial-ground, which was one of the most striking that, perhaps, was 'ever beheld. The moon was now declining, and threw its strong broad light against one side of the square, while the other was in deep shade. Cypresses were thickly planted within the square, and the white marble pillars of the cloisters which surrounded it shone in the clear moonlight between their black trunks and their sorrowful motionless foliage.

"This cemetery," said the abbess, "is one to which I have almost become attached ; and, weak as you may believe it, I should feel great pain if I thought that my bones were destined to rest in any other. The perfect tranquillity which prevails here—the beauty of the situation—those eternal mourners, the cypresses—the soft broad gleams of the moon's light—all combine to make it, in my opinion, most fit for the calm restingplace of mortal bodies, until that change which is to transfer them to another sphere shall take place. This is, I know, a weakness, and you must think I am wrong to indulge in it; but, when you consider how much our lives are swayed by fancies, you will find some excuse for me."

Leopold assured the abbess that he thought her selection so good a one that it needed no apology.

They had now walked down one side of the quadrangle, and had passed under that cloister which was in shade. On turning out of it a

sight met Leopold's eyes, which fixed him to the
spot with astonishment.

The moon, which was now at his back, shone
full upon the wall of the opposite cloister;—
behind it arose the acacia-trees, loaded with
their white streaming blossoms, and waving like
plumes in the soft night-air. In the distance
were seen the slender white spires of the convent, against which the moon-beams fell, and
showed distinctly the richly-carved crochets
which decorated them. In short, he saw the
very scene which he had beheld in the mirror
at old Alice's hovel!—He looked again at the
wall nearest to him. The stone upon which, in
the mirror, he had seen his name inscribed, was
not there; but the branches of a clematis that had
been trained against the wall had left a square
space of exactly the size of the tablet of his
vision. Nothing was wanting but the name. He
gazed at it with horror; a cold sweat stood upon
his brow, and a groan burst from his overcharged
bosom.

" You are unwell, I fear," said the abbess, who
saw the paleness of his face, and felt the trembling of the arm she held.

Her voice recalled Leopold to himself. " I
find the night-air chill," he said; "and the length
of the march has fatigued me more than usual.
With your permission we will return."

The company proceeded back to the convent, and Leopold was able to master his emotion so well that his momentary indisposition was universally believed to have arisen wholly from the cause to which he had attributed it. Having taken some wine, at the entreaty of the abbess, he retired to his chamber.

In vain he attempted to sleep : when he closed his eyes the scene in the cemetery was as vividly before his sight as it had been when he gazed on the real substance. At length, feverish, and worn out with tossing in his bed, he arose, and went to the window. Upon opening it he found that it commanded a view of that part of the garden which adjoined the burial-ground, where it had been foretold his own grave should be dug. The moon was now nearly sunk, the night-breeze had freshened a little, and, blowing against the tall cypresses, they seemed to beckon him towards the narrow spot which at some period he believed must be his own. He gazed at them until, his fancy aiding the impressions he had before received, he became convinced that this was the place destined for his dissolution—perhaps this was the very time when that event was to happen.

As he pondered over the events of his life, and reflected on the bitterness with which they had been tinged since the fatal All-hallows Night, he felt little occasion to regret even if this should be his fate. At this moment the notes of the organ in the chapel of the convent fell upon his ear; and, soon after, the voices of the nuns were heard in celebration of the funeral office for one of the sisters who had lately died. Leopold listened: the coincidence was so striking, that for a moment he could have fancied that his apprehensions had been realized, that he had in truth ceased to exist, and that it was for him that these midnight orisons were sung.

It was not long, however, that he remained under this delusion. Shaking off, by a violent effort, the thick-coming fancies which crowded upon his brain, he recommended himself to the protection of Heaven; and, resolving that he would no longer vex himself with speculating upon an accident, which, however frightful it had been rendered by circumstances, he could neither prevent nor hasten, he closed the window, and retired again to his bed, where his attempts to sleep were more successful.

He rose in the morning refreshed by his rest, but he could not entirely get rid of the seriousness which the sight of the burial-place had occasioned. After breakfasting with the abbess the order for marching was given; and, having bidden the old lady farewell, the whole party set off from Santa Croce.

Leopold felt relieved when he had quitted the convent; and, as he pursued his journey, the conversation of his companions, and, still more, the increasing distance which every step put between him and that place of terror, contributed to restore his cheerfulness. When they had passed the Alps orders were received for the return of the troops into France, where they were to go into quarters; and Leopold, not choosing to accompany them in the dull country life they were about to lead, went to reside at Berne with some others of the officers, who had obtained leave of absence, intending to rejoin the army at the commencement of the next campaign.

In the festivities of Berne, which has the invidious reputation of being the most gay of all the towns of Switzerland, Leopold thought he should find the means of passing the winter very agreeably. Society had become necessary to him, as the only means of dissipating the disquiet which often assailed, and sometimes depressed him.

He had been living here for some weeks, when one day, as he entered the church on a religious festival, he saw a procession of young girls passing along the aisles, and collecting the contributions of the devout people who filled the church. His attention was particularly attracted by the sight of so much loveliness engaged in so pious an office.

The cunning directors of the Romish church, who have always been deeply versed in the

feelings of the human heart, and the means by
which they may be profitably assailed, have
been continually in the habit of resorting to the
agency of youth and beauty, among other expedients, for the' purpose of exciting charity.
On the present occasion they had been extremely
happy in their selection, for every one of the
girls who formed the procession was distinguished for personal charms, and none of them
had yet reached the age of eighteen years.

One among them attracted the attention of
Leopold by her remarkable beauty, which even
the neighbourhood of so many other lovely faces
only rendered still more striking. She appeared to
be about seventeen years old, and the bloom of
youth was just ripening into the mature graces
of womanhood. Her figure was of perfect symme-
try, and such as even the most exalted imagination, and the best efforts of painters and sculptors,
could not surpass. In all her movements there
was an eloquent dignity, and her every gesture
seemed to be under the influence of that instinctive
loveliness which pervaded her whole frame. Her
walk, bounding and elastic, bespoke all the firm-
ness and vigour of youth, but was repressed by
a grave modesty, suited to the place and the
occasion. Her face was more fascinating and
lovely than her form, because it seemed even
to pass mortal beauty : it was like one of the
sublime creations of Guido, which are, as it were,

improvements upon humanity, and which, while
they seem to defy comparison with any known
models, deserve all the praises which have been
bestowed upon them : like them, it possessed that characteristic *sovrumana bellezza* which
commands universal admiration. It would be
impossible to describe accurately such a face ;
and, if the imaginations of the hearers cannot
supply them with an adequate notion of it, it
must even go undescribed, so totally is it beyond
the feeble power of words to do justice to it. An
expression of perfect goodness and simplicity
added to it the only charm which it could have
received.

Leopold gazed with a rapturous admiration
that engrossed his whole faculties. The ceremony he had been witnessing had already excited
his feelings to a pitch of exaltation and enthu-
siasm : the solemn music—the loud choir—the
fervent responses of the devout congregation—
had prepared a mind like his to be easily wrought
upon. As he looked now upon the enchanting
being, who moved at the head of her companions
through the crowded aisle, soliciting the charity
of the people, he fancied that she was one of the
inhabitants of heaven, who had visited the earth
only for the pious purpose in which he saw her
engaged.

While he looked at her this notion gathered
strength, and, at the same time, a feeling of pure

and holy love mingled with it. He thought that it was through the intercession of such an angel that he could alone hope to gain pardon for his sins, and to shake off the hellish influence which he at once hated and obeyed.

So much was his mind occupied with this idea, that, when the maiden approached him, he knelt down, and, casting his purse into the little flower-woven basket which she carried, he murmured "Pray for me, heavenly Virgin!"

These words were uttered in so low a tone of voice that they could scarcely be heard by any of the persons near him; and, if they had been, their import would, probably, have been misunderstood. The lovely object of them, however, seized at once their meaning, and a deep blush suffused her beautiful features as she passed on.

Leopold remained gazing upon her as she retired; and it was not until the bustle of the persons near him, in leaving the chapel, reminded him of the singularity of his posture, that he quitted it. He arose and went to his hotel, filled with melancholy, but not disagreeable, reflections upon the vision he had beheld.

He could still scarcely persuade himself that it was merely a human being; and when, by dint of reasoning, he had succeeded in doing so, his desire to know more of her became still more powerful.

" In her, perhaps," he said to himself, " I may

find that which I have hitherto sought in vain—
one being, beautiful and good, who may furnish
me with a motive to live on, and whose virtue
and innocence may counteract the dark spell
which seems to bind me still. The prayers of
such an angel must be efficacious, and will
prevail against the banded powers of hell."

His first business was to inquire the name and
family of the young lady whose charms had made
so sudden and so powerful an impression on him.
He learnt that she was the daughter of an Italian
gentleman of respectability, whom the changes
which had taken place in his native country had
driven into exile, and who had now resided in
Berne for some years upon the remnant of his
fortune. He was a widower; and his daughter,
whom he had very carefully educated, was his
only child.

Signor Baldini was a man of retired habits,
and of austere devotion. He was known to
practise the most severe rules of the Catholic
church, and he had openly announced his intention of placing his daughter in a convent as soon
as she should be of such an age that her own
consent might ratify his wishes in this respect.
It was believed, too, that the young lady was
perfectly willing to comply with her father's
desires.

The latter part of the information Leopold
heard with some anxiety, and he resolved that
no effort should be wanting, on his part, to effect

a change in the destiny of the lovely Laura at least, if not in that of her parent.

He immediately set about finding out some person among his acquaintance, which was numerous, and of the first respectability, who would introduce him to the Signor Baldini. He soon learnt, however, that the retired habits of the old gentleman rendered this almost hopeless; and in the mean time he was obliged to content himself with haunting daily the neighbourhood in which he lived, in the hope of seeing the beautiful Laura, as she might by accident quit or return to her abode.

This, it must be confessed, was as convincing a proof as any man in his senses could well give of being irretrievably in love. Leopold was too little a novice in affairs of the passion not to be aware of this; and he willingly encouraged the growth of an affection which seemed at once to meliorate and to tranquillize his heart.

At length chance afforded him an opportunity of disclosing to Signora Baldini the secret of his soul. He had watched her one day going from her own house to vespers, at the church where he had first seen her. She was accompanied only by a female servant, and when the service was finished she returned to her father's house. On her way she was met by a party of riotous young men, who appeared to have been drinking freely, and who addressed her with some rude and familiar expressions.

The shrinking girl was excessively terrified, and endeavored to avoid these vulgar boys, but in vain. One of them had thrown his arms round her waist, and she had just uttered a faint shriek for help, when Leopold was in an instant at her side, and had dashed her assailant to the earth so roughly, that all his amorous ardour was dispelled in a moment.

The rascal rose as well as he could, and joined his companions, who drew themselves up in a threatening position, and appeared resolved to avenge their companion. They, however, changed their minds as soon as they saw Leopold's sabre drawn, and retired with precipitation, confining the display of their valour to the mere utterance of some unmeaning and disregarded threats.

Leopold assured the trembling girl that she had now no cause for alarm, and begged that he might be permitted to accompany her to her own house, in order to protect her against any further accident.

She thanked him in the most graceful manner, and every word she uttered served to confirm the passion of the enraptured German.

Her fears had magnified the danger in which she had found herself when Leopold's prompt assistance rescued her ; and, her gratitude being in proportion to that imaginary peril, she expressed it with all the energy of her character.

She begged that Leopold would permit her

father to thank him for the services he had rendered her ; and he, who desired nothing so much
as an introduction to the old gentleman, did not
say a word in objection to this proposal.

When they arrived at the house, the gentle
girl, who was still somewhat agitated, rushed into
her father's arms, and told him that she had been
assailed by a band of ruffians on her return from
church ; and added that, but for the assistance of
the gentleman who accompanied her, she should
perhaps have been killed.

This was not quite true, but she thought it
was ; and her manner of relating it at once alarm-
ed the old Italian, and called forth his thanks
to Leopold, who now felt obliged to disclaim
some of the praises which were bestowed upon
his courage.

He told Signor Baldini that these redoubtable
assailants were probably only artisans, who had
been at a short distance from the city to spend
the holiday, and whose weak brains the festivities
of the occasion had somewhat inflamed. For his
own share in the affair he renounced all praise
and thanks, because he had merely interfered, as
every gentleman must have done, to protect a
lady from the annoyance of such persons.

After some further compliments on each side
an agreeable conversation ensued, in the course
of which Leopold found the signor to be a man
of information and polish, although there was a

gravity in his manner—occasioned by the settled
sorrow which he had labored under ever since his
wife's death—which might, to persons less interested than Leopold, have seemed in some measure repulsive.

The lovely Laura, although she was no longer
surrounded by the *prestige* which the place and
the occasion on which her lover first beheld her
had enveloped her with, was not less charming.
The artless innocence and gaiety of her conversation, her pious attention to her father, and the
vigilance with which she seemed to anticipate his
every wish, not less than her rare beauty, which
Leopold now gazed at with still greater admiration than before, confirmed him in the opinion
that she was the most amiable and fascinating of
created beings.

He staid as long as decency allowed him, and,
before he retired, he had obtained permission to
wait upon the signor again.

He did not fail to avail himself of this permission at the earliest opportunity; but, to his
great disappointment, the real object of his visit,
the Signora Laura, was not visible. He, however, passed some time in conversation with her
father, in whose good opinion he thought—and
he thought justly—he had made some progress.
After a few more visits he told the old gentleman
that he entertained the most fervent passion for

his daughter, and made a formal demand of her hand in marriage.

" I regret very much the disappointment I must occasion to you by declining the honour you propose to me," said Signor Baldini ; " but my daughter is already engaged."

" Is it possible ?" cried Leopold in despair ; " and does she love another ?"

" I speak not of human engagements," replied the signor ; " Laura is the devoted bride of heaven."

Leopold breathed again, and, since he knew it was no mortal rival that he had to fear, he returned to the charge.

" But will you not permit me, sir," he said, " to endeavour to engage her affections ? Surely beauty and virtue such as hers will be more properly and more serviceably employed in the world, which has need of such examples, than in a cloister."

" But in a cloister," replied the signor, " the possessor of such beauty and virtue as hers— and which even the partiality of a doting father does not, I think, make me overrate—will be protected from the thousand perils and snares with which the paths of the world are strewed."

" And yet, sir," continued Leopold, " the protection of a fond and faithful husband, who would seek his whole happiness in her, and who, in return, would make her felicity his dearest care, might be a sufficient safeguard even against such perils."

" I know," replied the signor, " that to a young and impassioned lover (such as you say, and as I believe, you are) arguments will not be wanting to induce me to change the resolution I have formed. I do not hesitate to tell you, also, that, if I had to decide upon this matter alone, all your arguments would be in vain, so maturely have I considered the subject, and so firm is my resolve : but, while I am a father, and feel called upon to exercise a father's caution, I have no disposition to exert any authority beyond that. Laura shall judge for herself ; she is entitled to make her own choice in so important an affair, and she has discretion enough to make a wise one. I feel obliged to say that my objections to her marrying are not personal as regards you ; your family, your fortune, and your character— for, as I have foreseen this event, I have inquired into all these circumstances—are unexceptionable ; and, if my daughter resolves not to take the veil, I should prefer you to any other man I know for her husband."

Leopold thanked him for his good opinion.

" You owe me no thanks," replied the old man ; " I speak to you quite plainly ; and I tell you, besides, as I will not tell Laura, that my wish to see her enter a convent is founded upon the dying request of her mother. She, who was, perhaps, too much given to superstitious forebodings, told me on her death-bed that she was convinced our child's happiness and existence depended upon her never forming any other attachment than for spiritual objects."

" But, my dear sir," interrupted Leopold, " can you wish that your child's destiny should be entirely influenced by the anxious forebodings of her mother, whose fondness for her child, and whose own ill state of health, may have led her to imagine—— ?"

" We will discuss this subject no further," said the signor : " I repeat to you, that, if I felt myself at liberty to persuade my daughter, she should become a nun without delay, because I am convinced that her happiness must depend upon it."

Signor Baldini here put an end to the conversation by rising ; and, telling Leopold that he should hear from him, they parted.

Soon after this interview Leopold received a letter from the signor, authorizing him to address his daughter. The young man did not suffer the slightest delay to elapse before he exercised this permission, which he knew he should not have obtained if Laura had not decided against the veil and her father's wishes.

The blushing girl heard the avowal of the passion she had excited, and which her own heart experienced no less ardently, with a timid hesi-

tation, which was caused by her doubting whether the pleasure that filled her bosom was not
too intense to be real. She felt as if it was all
a gay, brilliant, happy dream, from which she
must awake, and the enjoyment of which was
diminished by this fear. At length, when she
grew more satisfied and assured of the truth, her
rapture partook of the enthusiastic nature of her
mind. She loved infinitely and entirely ; the
passion became a part of her existence ; and she
loved as persons of sensibility love for the first
time in their lives, and as none can ever love
twice.

She did not hesitate to avow her feelings to
Leopold ; and the simplicity and innocence of
her character added a thousand charms to the
confession.

The earlier part of Leopold's life had been
one of professed gallantry. He had sworn, over
and over again, that he was in love ; and, when he
swore thus, he had been perfectly sincere ; but now,
for the first time in the course of his existence,
he found that he had mistaken his feelings, and
that the light attachments which he had formerly
dignified by the name of love bore a very faint
resemblance to that dominant passion. Now,
indeed, he loved ; for every thing in the world,
compared with his passion and its object, was
suddenly lowered in the scale of his estimation.
His affection, like a pure flame, seemed to have

expelled every dark and unworthy feeling from
his bosom, while it filled the space with its own
splendour and warmth.

The gloomy cloud which had lowered over
him for so many years was dispersed; the weight
upon his heart was removed; " his bosom's lord
sate lightly on his throne;" and all was laughing
joy and sunshine around him.

The Signor Baldini, after the conversation in
which his daughter had expressed her affection
for Leopold, never reverted to the objections he
had so frankly expressed to his future son-in-
law; and, although the old gentleman's cheerfulness was in no degree improved, he neither said
nor did aught that could induce the lovers to
believe that they had diminished it in the slightest degree.

" Now," said Leopold, as he held the beautiful
Laura in his arms in her father's garden, and
gazed upon the moon, which seemed to shed a
favoring light upon the lover's embraces—" now,
indeed, for the first time in my life, am I happy;—
now can I gaze upon yon bright moon without
feeling upon my heart the thick interposing
shadow of my dark griefs;—now I can drink in
its beams, and defy Fate and forebodings."

Alas, how utterly vain are all the attempts
of men to elude the decrees of Fate!

A few weeks had now only to elapse before
the day on which it had been fixed that the holy

rites of the church should unite Leopold and his Laura, who were already bound together by a fond and firm passion, which nothing could disunite. At Leopold's request the retired habits of the Signor Baldini and his daughter had been changed, and they had joined some of the festive parties of the city.

On one night they were together at a ball given by the Prussian Chargé d'Affaires in Berne, whither all the most important persons, as well natives as foreigners, who then happened to be in the city, were invited. The assemblage was, of course, very numerous. Among all the beauties of the saloon (and they were many) Laura Baldini shone the most conspicuous, and excited universal attention. Her approaching marriage was quite notorious, and added, perhaps, to the interest which was felt for her. Leopold, too, was now well known in Berne ; and the elegance and suavity of his manners, his talents, and his military reputation, had gained him universal regard. His person, too, was hardly less remarkable for manly beauty, than was Laura's eminent among the loveliest of women. They shone in this brilliant assembly, enjoying the admiration and envy of both sexes.

Leopold had so completely got over the gloomy notions which had once entirely poisoned his happiness, that, although he knew this night was the anniversary of that fatal one on which

he had been present at the infernal revels which
were held in old Alice's hovel, he never once
allowed the circumstance to master him.

.Once, indeed, recollection came across him,
but the impression which it made was momentary ;—it was as he entered the saloon with
his lovely Laura on his arm. He heard some person near him say, in German, " This is the famous
All-hallows Night." A tremor ran through his
limbs as he looked round to see whence the voice
had proceeded. A crowd of gentlemen, among
whom he recognised no person of his acquaintance, were talking together. He turned, and
his glance met the eyes of Laura, sparkling
with the anticipated pleasure of the dance : her
lovely joyous look restored him to himself, and
chased away the thoughts which this accidental
expression had begun to conjure up.

The evening passed away rapidly and delight-
fully. The music—the exhilarating effect of the
dance—the lively and agreeable conversation of
his companions—and the society of his beautiful
bride, who seemed to drink joy from his eyes—
contributed to exalt Leopold's spirits to a height
they had seldom reached of late years. The
days of his youth and innocence seemed to
return, and his spirit had thrown off the load
which former mispent time, and the sins of hot
blood and a restless temper, had burdened it
with.

" Now," he said to himself, as he looked on
the gay group around—" now, once more, my
heart seems to be my own, and all my past
sorrows are like an imperfectly remembered
dream."

This thought had scarcely passed through his
mind, when a voice sounded in his ear, which
was at once familiar and horrible. He knew he
had heard it before; but he could not recollect
in what place, and under what circumstances.
He looked about, and yet he could not discover
whence it proceeded. Still it sounded in his
ear audibly, though he could not distinguish the
words it uttered, owing to the suppressed tone in
which they were delivered. He turned entirely
round ; and directly behind him, leaning against
one of the pillars of the saloon, he saw the
Signor Baldini engaged in deep conversation
with a tall man, whose back was turned to him.

" Are you sure it is he?" asked the signor.

" As sure as I am of my own existence," replied
the stranger ; and as he spoke he turned slowly
round.

His eyes fell upon those of Leopold, who, to
his horror and surprise, saw in the stranger the
same tall student who had been the occasion of
his leaving Göttingen.

" This wretch," he said, " pursues me every
where. Is it not enough that the pusillanimous
slanderer has once made me miserable, but he

must endeavour also to poison my happiness here? He shall pay dearly for his temerity," he added; but, recollecting suddenly that this was not the place nor the time to seek redress for any affront that might have been offered to him, he curbed his resentment, and advanced towards the student and the signor.

The latter was evidently embarrassed at the sight of Leopold and the manner of his approach. The same usual insolent look beamed in the eyes and pierced through the dull and inanimate features of the student, who now wore a military habit, not unlike that of the captain of the guard who had been his companion at Göttingen on the All-hallows Night.

Leopold's agreeable fancies were in a moment dispelled: his mortification increased when he saw, by the manner of Signor Baldini, that his presence was unwelcome as well as unexpected.

" Are you ready to depart?" said the signor: " it grows late." Leopold thought this was uttered with evident embarrassment.

He could not doubt that the altered manner of the signor was caused by something that had been said to his disadvantage by the quondam student of Göttingen. He saw that this was an inconvenience to which he might be exposed as often as the chattering coxcomb who thus harassed him should happen to fall in his way : he resolved, therefore, at once to put an end to such an annoyance, and turned to seek Laura, whom he intended to have seen to the carriage with her father, and then to return and demand an explanation of his conduct from the insolent person who presumed to interfere with his character.

He looked through the ball-room for Laura, but in vain : he hastened into all the adjoining rooms, but she was not to be found ; nor did he meet with the signor in his search. He then inquired of the servants, and learnt that the Signor Baldini and his daughter had gone home.

He was astonished beyond measure that they should have quitted the party without him, and still more that they should have done so without bidding him good night. Some reasons must have induced them to so singular a step, and he could think of none unless they had been furnished by the slanders of his accursed fellow-collegian.

His resentment against this person was heightened as he thought of this ; and, viewing his conduct as a direct and premeditated attempt to insult and to injure him, he hastened in search of him, to chastise his impertinence, and to prevent all future annoyance from him.

He caught a glimpse of the object of his search at the further end of the room, and saw that he was taking his departure. He darted towards him, and reached the hall-door almost as soon as he. He paused here a moment, for he thought it would be better to let his enemy gain the street than to accost him in the hearing of the servants and the guests, who might, in repeating the scene, have given it an injurious colouring.

Waldenburg (for this was the student's name) took his cloak from a servant, and, folding it about him, went down the steps, and turned to walk towards his own hotel. Leopold was in a moment at his side.

"A word with you, sir," he said, grasping his arm at the same moment, and with not the most courteous pressure.

Waldenburg stopped, and gazed at Leopold with that malicious but stupid grin which his features always wore.

"You know me," said Leopold.

"I do," replied the other.

"You have been speaking of me this evening?"

"I have done, then, no more than all the world does."

"I cannot make war with all the world, even if they did as you say; but I can check your insolence, and I will."

"Insolence!—I only said that this time two years you went out to old Alice's hovel, near the city of Göttingen, and mingled in certain hellish ceremonies, which rendered you unfit for the company of good Christians."

"Liar and villain, draw!"

"I have no sword;" and Waldenburg opened his cloak as he spoke, to prove the truth of his assertion.

Leopold was never better disposed to kill a man than he felt at this moment; but the knowledge that his foe was unarmed checked his rage.

"I am in your debt," he said, "for a civility somewhat of the same nature, and, depend upon it, you shall not go unpaid now. You can procure a sword."

"By day-break to-morrow I can, and will meet you at whatever place you think fit to appoint," replied Waldenburg, with the most provoking coolness.

"Upon the east rampart, then, at five o'clock," said Leopold.

"Agreed, upon one condition, that you bring no second with you: you know that I objected to this on a former occasion."

"I do not condescend to reply to your insolence, since the hour is so near at which your best blood shall pay for it."

"If you beat me only with words I shall not be much harmed. Adieu till five o'clock!" and Waldenburg wrapped his cloak about him and continued his walk, which had been interrupted by this angry colloquy.

Leopold returned home, where he employed the short time which remained before day-break in writing a farewell to Laura, to be transmitted to her if the result of his encounter should be fatal. This finished, he prepared to meet his adversary, whose coolness had exasperated him nearly as much as his insolence in spreading reports to his disadvantage.

The time having arrived, he buckled on his sword, and left the hotel, as he believed, unperceived. He repaired instantly to the ramparts, where he found Waldenburg waiting.

He approached, and, without a moment's delay, loosening his cloak, he threw it from him; then, drawing his sword, he called to his antagonist to do the same.

"But one moment," said Waldenburg.

Leopold lowered the point of his sword, but did not quit his position.

"I have said nothing," continued the other, "that you need be so much enraged at. There may surely be some less hostile mode of arranging any slight differences between us."

"You should have thought of that before," said Leopold.

"But surely you cannot be so very angry at my having told what you know to be truth."

"If you would not have me attack you at a disadvantage, prepare yourself!" said Leópold, who saw that his adversary's object was to excite his rage. By a great effort he restrained his passion, and displayed so earnest an intention to begin the attack that Waldenburg was compelled to draw in all haste.

"Since you will provoke your own destruction, then," he said, "you will only have yourself to blame if I should kill you here, and old Alice's magic looking-glass be proved false."

Leopold was utterly astonished when he heard this allusion to a circumstance which could only be known to Schwartzwald (of whom nothing had been seen since the fatal night) and to himself. He looked again at Waldenburg, and saw, to his horror and astonishment, instead of the stupid pedant, the demoniac features of Schwartzwald!

"You know me, then, at last!" said the latter with a hellish grin.

"I know and defy thee!" cried Leopold; and he pressed on him with deadly thrusts.

The supposed Waldenburg and the real fiend, as Leopold could now no longerndoubt him to be, parried every blow with as much coolness as if he had been practising in a fencing-school instead of being engaged in a mortal combat. He continued at the same time to address Leopold.

"And did you think to escape me after giving

mé so much trouble ?" he said : " could you suppose I would permit you to marry the beautiful
Laura, after you had been false to another fair ?
Fickle boy !—You have improved in your fence,
though. And you would fain turn pious too—you
who have so often outraged heaven and earth
with your blasphemies !"

These taunts enraged Leopold to such a
degree, that he totally lost possession of himself.
If his antagonist had chosen to quit his defensive
system, and to attack in his turn, he might have
soon put an end to the conflict: he, however,
continued to parry with imperturbable *sang froid.*
At length the desperate impetuosity of Leopold
broke through his guard—the sword of the supposed Waldenburg flew several yards from him—
and his adversary's weapon must have been
through his heart, but that at the same moment
he drew a pistol and discharged it at Leopold,
who fell instantly.

The fiend stood over him, laughing exultingly.
" With my last breath," said the fainting Leopold,
" I defy thee !"

A loud noise was at this moment heard, and
the voices of persons approaching. The fiend
looked over his shoulder, and, without pausing
a moment, rushed to the edge of the rampart,
from whence he leaped into the fosse. Some of
the people who saw him retreating ran towards
the spot, but to follow him appeared impracti-

cable. He had, however, succeeded in his attempt to escape, and was nowhere to be seen.

The persons who had arrived at this moment
consisted of some of the guard and some peasants, with Leopold's servant. The latter had
been aroused by his master's going out at so
early an hour; and, suspecting that it was occasioned by some affair of honour, his attachment
to Leopold induced him to follow his steps to
the ramparts. He saw the adversaries engage,
and watched the course of the combat with the
utmost anxiety, not daring to discover himself,
lest he should encounter his master's anger. He
had seen the assassin fire, and then instantly
gave the alarm, which brought up the guard and
the peasants to his assistance.

When they reached Leopold he was insensible,
and they carried him in this state to his own
lodgings. His wound was immediately attended,
and was found to be highly dangerous. His
surgeons ordered that the strictest silence should
be observed, and that nothing tending to produce
the least irritation should be allowed to approach
their patient. After remaining for many days
in a weak and almost insensible condition he
was pronounced to be out of danger.

His first inquiry was respecting his Laura;
and his servant gave him, by the advice of the
surgeons, such evasive answers as might put a
stop to his questions, without exciting his anx-

iety or his suspicions. It was soon, however, found impossible to deceive him on this subject, and he was informed that, on the morning of his duel, Signor Baldini had departed from Berne, accompanied by his daughter, in a carriage hastily hired for the purpose; but that the cause of their abrupt departure, and the place whither they had retreated, were equally unknown.

Leopold was thunder-stricken at this news: he saw that they had been brought to believe some horrible calumny against him, and he could not doubt that the signor had used or would use this as a further inducement for his daughter's embracing a monastic life. Great as was his affliction at this circumstance, it did not bring with it so profound a despair as had preyed upon his mind before. His passion for Laura had ameliorated and strengthened his heart; and he, moreover, cherished the hope that he should still be able to find her, and to prove thus that he was worthy of her love.

This reflection supported him through his painful convalescence, and, perhaps, mainly contributed to his ultimate recovery.

When he was able to walk he employed himself in making inquiries as to the means of conveyance which the signor and his daughter had availed themselves of to leave the city; and, after much time had been spent in vain, he learnt at last that the signor had hired an Italian vetturino, who had brought a family from Venice in his carriage, and who was about to return thither when the signor engaged him.

Leopold was little benefitted in his search by this intelligence, for he could learn no more of the vetturino than that his name was Paulo. His ordinary residence no one could tell—for this simple reason, that he had none. As he was without wife or family he had no need of a home; his business always kept him on the road; and it was an even chance whether he was now at Naples or at Paris, or indeed in any other part of the Continent.

Weeks passed away, during which Leopold remained in a state of most painful suspense, which was more hard to be endured than any thing else in the world, excepting the certainty that he had lost Laura for ever. This belief his heart would never admit; and he consoled himself with the hope that she would—that she must—still be his: so powerful are the delusions of one's own creation, and so easy is it to believe that on which our warmest wishes depend!

One morning Leopold's faithful servant, Baptiste, came to his bedside, his eyes beaming with pleasure.

" At length, sir," he said, " I have found the vetturino who carried away the young lady and old Signor Baldini."

Leopold was out of bed in an instant. " Let

me see him directly," he said : "lose not a moment in bringing him."

"He waits below for your rising," replied Baptiste; "but I fear that you will not be able to
make much of him : he is as uncommunicative
and as sly a fellow as I ever met with."

"Bring him to me without delay," cried Leopold. Baptiste retired, and, in a few moments,
returned with the vetturino.

Paulo was a good specimen of the lower order
of the people of the duchy of Milan, whence he
came. He, was about five-and-thirty years of
age : his face was handsome, regular, and prepossessing; his black eyes rolled with an expression of archness and fire which betokened
his character ; a profusion of black curling hair
grew under the small travelling cap which he
always wore. His figure was tall, and well pro-
portioned; his dress that of most of the brethren of the whip in his country—that is to say,
loose blue linen trowsers, a red waistcoat, with a
profuse number of buttons covering its front, and
a velveteen jacket, on which were as many more
buttons. A thick horsewhip—his inseparable
companion—graced his right hand.

"You are the vetturino ?" said Leopold.

Paulo bowed.

"You carried the Signor Baldini and his
daughter from this city—did you not?"

Paulo shook his head. "I never knew any

persons of that name," he said, with a knowing look.

Leopold saw the fellow was a sort of humorist, and he knew that your humorists are always assailable on one point. He produced his purse. " Come, my good fellow," he said, " you and I must understand each other better. Here are five louis d'or : now, 'perhaps, you will see that I don't wish to make you useful to me without rewarding you for your communications, and you will disclose to me what you know of the Signor and Signora Baldini."

Paulo pocketed the gold with a still more intelligent grin, while his lively eyes showed plainly that this was a method of dealing infinitely to his taste.

" It is impossible," he said, " not to understand the signor, when he takes such a straightforward way of explaining himself. As I told the signor before, I do not know any such persons as those whose names he has mentioned ; but the reason of that is, that they cautiously concealed their real titles, and travelled under others, which they thought fit to assume for the purposes of the journey."

" But they lived in the small house beyond the city gates, on the banks of the Aar ?"

" They did," replied Paulo, " and the young lady is as lovely as an angel."

" You say she is," said Leopold eagerly : " then

you have seen her lately ; tell me where is she—
let me fly to her."

" Signor, I cannot tell you where she is."

" Why not ? I will give you all I possess in
the world. Let me only once more see her—let
me call her mine ; and my fortune—all that I can
command in the world—shall be yours."

" See, now, how hard it is to be an honest man
in a world so full of temptations!" cried Paulo
with a mock solemn air. " One gentleman gives
me fifteen scudi, and makes me swear not to
tell whither I carry him ; another gives me five
louis in hard cash, and a promise of all his fortune, to make me break my oath. What can a
poor fellow like me do ?"

Leopold repeated his persuasions and his offers ;
and at length Paulo, who, although he had a
proper sense of his own interest, was at the
bottom a very honest kind-hearted fellow, began
to be moved by Leopold's passionate entreaties.

" Look ye, signor," he said, " there is nothing
I would not do for the service of a generous fair-
spoken gentleman like yourself,—save breaking
my oath. The old Signor Bal—— (you know
who I mean) made me swear by the Holy Virgin
(here Paulo devoutly crossed himself) that I
would never tell any living soul the name of the
place to which I carried his daughter. I did
swear, but it was before your honour gave me
the five louis ; and I am very sorry I did."

" But," said Leopold, " are there no means without breaking your oath—which I will not urge
you to do—by which you can enable me to find
out the place of the Signora Laura's imprisonment ? for nothing short of imprisonment would
keep her from me."

" There is one way," said Paulo, and, as the
thought crossed his mind, his black eyes were
lighted up with an unusual lustre—" there is
one way, signor ; and I think I can meet your
wishes, at the same time that I shall save my
own faith."

" For the love of Heaven, then, tell it me,"
cried Leopold.

" I swore, you know," replied the vetturino,
" that I would never tell mortal man where the
Signora Laura was gone to—and as the blessed
Virgin may help me in time of need," he ejaculated, again earnestly crossing himself, " I never
will—but I did not swear never to pass the
place. If the signor chooses to engage me to
carry him to Venice or to Florence, or to Rome,
who can tell but that some lucky accident may
render it necessary for him to stop exactly at the
very place where the Signora Laura may now be
living ?"

Leopold was delighted with this suggestion ;
he could have hugged the vetturino for having
made it ; and, immediately closing with him, he

engaged to give him double the usual sum to take him to Venice.

Paulo quitted him to make the arrangements for setting off on the same evening, for Leopold's impatience to be on the road would allow of no delay. He congratulated himself upon the dexterity with which he had managed to keep his oath inviolate, and yet to make so excellent a bargain with his intended passenger; and perhaps, of the two, although so good a Catholic, he was better satisfied with the latter than with the former achievement.

With the close of the evening the preparations for their departure were completed; Leopold, accompanied by the faithful Baptiste, had taken his seat in Paulo's *calêche*; and the vetturino was in the saddle, ready to begin his journey.

They proceeded immediately towards the Alps, and travelled with as great rapidity as was possible, but still far more slowly than the desires of Leopold would have had them go.

Paulo had stipulated that he should be asked no questions; and this being agreed to by Leopold, the vetturino promised to use the utmost dispatch, and to take the shortest road to Venice, as he persisted in calling the place to which they were journeying, although his manner convinced Leopold that it was at some less distant point that he proposed to stop.

Paulo drove his own horses, which obliged the travellers to rest every night on the road. This was sufficiently trying to a person of Leopold's impatient temperament ; but so much depended upon the vetturino's information, that he resolved to do nothing which should interfere with the desire which the fellow had to oblige him ; and he therefore endured, as well as he could, this tedious mode of travelling.

He asked a thousand questions, and each of them was repeated over and over again, as to what Paulo had been able to observe of the manners of the young lady.

" Poor signora !" said Paulo, " she used to weep almost all day long, until I was sometimes obliged to weep with her, for company. The old signor never wept : he used to talk all about the saints and our holy religion, and then the poor young lady used to weep the more."

" At least, then," said Leopold to himself, " she did not quit me willingly ; and it must have been the recollection of me that caused her tears. Dearest Laura," he cried, " the time approaches rapidly when those tears shall be dried, and when not even the power of fate itself shall again separate us."

Baptiste exerted himself indefatigably to draw his master from the melancholy thoughts in which he was too much inclined to indulge. He cracked jokes with Paulo, who was not behindhand in this " keen encounter of their wits," and who seldom failed to have an answer for the Frenchman.

They passed the Alps, and were descending upon the road towards Como, when Paulo turned out of the main way into a sort of cross road, which he pursued during a whole day. It was so bad that it called forth frequent complaints from Baptiste, who said it was the worst he had ever travelled.

" Never mind, Monsieur Baptiste," replied Paulo ; " you would find the road to an enemy's fortress much worse."

" I am not sure of that," replied Baptiste ; " for, whether a man has his head shot off or his neck broken, ought, as it seems to me, to be a matter of perfect indifference to him ; and, for any thing I can see, the latter is like enough to be our case."

" Then, Monsieur Baptiste, you would have the honour of being the very first gentleman whose neck I had been so happy as to break since I had the good fortune to become a vetturino. That must be now nearly twenty-five years ago, for I assumed this distinguished calling in the eleventh year of my age."

" Just at the time when you ought to have been made to feel, instead of being permitted to exercise, a horsewhip."

" Monsieur Baptiste, you are as quarrelsome with my horsewhip as if you had ever felt it."

" I feel it! *Sacre bleu!* I wish you would use it to your tumble-down horses, who are lagging down this accursed hill as if they were drawing a waggon."

" Patience, monsieur, for a minute; you see yonder sign of the ' Three Kings?' There I intend to stop for a few minutes; and, after having presented your mightiness with a cup of as good drink as our host can afford to sell under the name of wine, I shall drink one myself, and then you shall see how my horses will go, notwithstanding they seem a little tired; for, as they say in your country, ' *Quand le chevalier a la tête salpêtrée le cheval est toujours bon.*'"

" That is the wisest thing I have heard you say since day-break," said Baptiste, " and the sun is now rapidly sinking."

" To say one wise thing in a summer's day is much more than many men can boast of, M. Baptiste, and I feel much obliged to you for the compliment."

After a short stay at the little inn of the " Three Kings" the travellers resumed their journey. The moon soon arose, and displayed the surrounding scenery, as well as the vineyards and orchards between which the road lay, in the most beautiful and picturesque light.

Leopold endeavored to recollect exactly in

what part of the country they were: but his
attempts were in vain ; the turn which Paulo
had made from the road wholly baffled him. He
saw that they were rapidly descending an eminence, but he could not form any distinct notion
of the direction in which it led. To ask Paulo
would have been a violation of their compact;
and he knew, moreover, that it would be fruitless,
for the vetturino was quite in earnest about
keeping to the strict letter of his promise.

At about eight o'clock in the evening Paulo
drew up the carriage at the door of a very small
and unpromising inn, and, approaching the *calêche*,
he informed Leopold that the day's journey was
finished, and that there they were to pass the
evening.

" These seem but sorry quarters, Signor Paulo,"
said Leopold, looking out.

" The signor will be satisfied, I think," replied
Paulo significantly.

Leopold alighted and entered the inn, where
every thing he saw convinced him that it was
one of the most wretched description. He was
half inclined to be angry with Paulo for bringing
him to such a place, when the vetturino, drawing
him aside, said—

" Signor, there is a house near this where you
would, perhaps, find a better lodging than in
this inn."

" Let us go thither, by all means, then."

"The signor may go if he pleases," said Paulo, "and I will show him the road to it, which lies across yonder vineyards; but, for myself and Monsieur Baptiste, this *bettola* will do as well as the duke's palace."

"Come, then," said Leopold, who had acquired a habit of obeying Paulo, and who thought there was something more than usually knowing in his air and looks, "lead on, if you please, to this other house of reception."

"It is a religious house, signor," said Paulo, loading himself with a small bag which contained Leopold's dressing apparatus.

They set out across the vineyard which Paulo had pointed out. Leopold endeavored to get from him an explanation of his intention in taking him thither.

"I conjure you, Paulo," he said, "to tell me if it is true that I shall meet my Laura here, as I more than guess. For Heaven's sake do not add to my misery by keeping me thus in suspense."

"God knows," said Paulo, "I would not willingly do so; but remember my oath, signor; a poor man has a soul to be saved as well as another; and as we enjoy little happiness in this world, we must not, if we can help it, run the risk of being tormented in the next. You know, signor, you are to seek the Signora Laura every where; and, as this house to which we are going is filled with religious ladies, surely no place can be so proper to make inquiries in."

Leopold saw at once the drift of the vetturino, and had no longer any doubt that he had brought him by a circuitous route to the place in which Laura was residing, that he might make what he thought a very ingenious compromise with his conscience.

" The signor will remember," said Paulo, "that if any accident should happen to keep him here, and prevent his going on to Venice, that will be no fault of mine."

" I shall remember," said the delighted Leopold, " that you are a very honest fellow, and that I have every reason to be satisfied with the way in which you have performed your engagement."

" *Grazie,* signor," cried Paulo, as he skipped on before Leopold, and knocked at the gate of the building, at which they had now arrived. It was a lofty edifice; but as the night had now entirely closed in, and the moon was on the other side of the building, the deep shadow prevented Leopold from discerning its form more particularly.

The door was opened by a sour-looking thin-visaged old man, to whom Paulo told a voluble lie, about the signor being overtaken by night in the road, unable to proceed to the next town, and in such a state of health (having lately recovered from a bad illness) as rendered it impos-

sible for him to pass the night in the only inn
which the neighbourhood contained.

The old man retired, and, in a short time, returned. " The lady abbess," he said, " had
given permission for the signor's lodging in
that part of the building which was set apart for
the reception of strangers."

Leopold dismissed Paulo, who bade him good
night with an affectionate cordiality, and hinted
his wishes in an enigmatical manner that the
signor might succeed in his search. " But I fear
very much," he added with a knowing grin,
" that you will not be able to go on to Venice
to-morrow."

Leopold then requested the old man to return
to the abbess, and to say that he begged permission to wait upon her.

This was unhesitatingly granted, and he followed the old porter through the narrow passage
which led to the parlour of the principal.

The abbess was a prim, but kind-looking, old
lady. She received Leopold with an air of
stately politeness. He looked about the room,
and could have fancied that this was not the
first time he had been in it. He thought of the
nunnery of Santa Croce, but this abbess was not
like the principal of that house ; besides, he was
convinced of this being situated in a different
part of the country ; and, upon looking again, he
saw that, although the general plan of the rooms

might be the same, that in which he was now sitting was deficient in the severe elegance which characterized the parlour of Santa Croce.

The religious emblems, which are common to all such establishments, were there—the bad painting of the Madonna, and the crucifix, hung against the walls; but the fresh-filled flower-vases were absent, and every description of even allowable ornament was rigorously banished.

Leopold, mastering his agitation as well as he could, approached the abbess, and, telling her his name, said he had come in search of the Signora Laura, who he had reason to believe was now within these walls.

" I assure you," replied the abbess with a cold and formal manner, " that she is not."

" I beseech you, madam," said Leopold—while his features expressed the anxiety and pain of his mind—" I beseech you not to trifle with the feelings of one who is already on the very edge of despair. I implore you, by all that you hold most sacred, not to make two persons utterly wretched. This cannot be the end of true religion; and this, perhaps worse than this, must be the consequence of your separating me from Laura. Our passion is mutual; our happiness—our lives—nay, the salvation of one of us—depends upon our being permitted to meet once more."

" My son," replied the abbess, who, apathetic as she was, could not avoid feeling moved by the vehemence of Leopold's manner, " it is not any more in my power to unite you than to increase the space which separates you. Pray calm your emotion, and arm yourself with Christian patience to endure those evils which must be the lot of all of us in this world."

" Is she here ?" cried Leopold impatiently.

" My son, she is not," replied the abbess.

" But she has been here ?"

" It is very true that she has been here, but she has departed hence."

" When did she go, and whither ? Tell me, and the speed of the winds of Heaven shall not equal mine in pursuit of her."

" Again I say to you, be patient ! Remember that sorrow and suffering are the lot of mortals, and that it is by them alone we can hope to enjoy that true happiness which is in Heaven."

Leopold would have rushed from the room without listening to any more of the old lady's exhortations, but the desire of learning whither Laura had gone restrained him.

" If you will moderate that transport, which even now shakes your every limb, and will promise to bear like a man that which man is born to suffer, I will tell you whither our dear sister is departed."

Leopold bowed. There was a solemnity in the manner of the old lady's last address to him which shocked him. He had thought that to find the place of Laura's abode was to be happy. Now, for the first time, he began to think that some sinister accident might have happened, more fatal to his hopes than even her flight.

" I do promise," he said, and the blood receded from his cheeks as he gazed almost breathless on the abbess.

" The track of many years had obliterated, I thought, the very scars of former sorrows from my heart," said the abbess, as her eyes streamed with tears; " but the sight of your sufferings makes me feel the old wounds again. My son, the sister Laura has gone to her home—she is dead !"

Leopold gasped, and looked in stupid astonishment for a moment—then fell at the old lady's feet, as if a thunderbolt had struck him.

She immediately rang for assistance; the porter, a priest who performed the religious services of the cloister, and some of the elder nuns, entered. At first it was thought that Leopold was dead : no pulse could be felt in his veins, no respiration on his lips, and his face was pale and rigid, as if death had already inflicted the last blow of suffering on him. At length, however, the cares of the surrounding persons were successful; he slowly opened his eyes, and, as the recollection of the fatal information he had received recurred to him, a cold shuddering convulsed his frame.

"Tell me, when did she die?" he asked, in a scarcely audible tone.

"Five days ago," replied the abbess; "and yesterday she was buried."

Leopold groaned deeply.

"I know," said the abbess, (who thought that if she could get him to listen she might be able to relieve him by diverting his thoughts,) "the whole history of your ill-fated attachment, and I pity you most heartily. But you are not yet aware that we believed you were dead."

Leopold made no answer, but by his gestures showed that he was attending to the abbess's discourse.

"Sister Laura," she continued, "loved you too well to be moved by the absurd reports which her father so readily believed; and she lived in the hope of being united to you, until the receipt of that fatal letter, by which she understood you were dead."

"What letter do you speak of?" asked Leopold.

"The letter which you wrote, and in which you said you should be no more at the time it would reach her hands. This it was that killed her; this destroyed the hope that sustained her; and she died, because, without you, the world had no joys for her."

"Show me that letter," cried Leopold with a faint effort.

The abbess did so immediately; and he recognised the letter which he had written on the morning of his duel, and which he had since sought in vain. He sunk back in despair. "The fiend triumphs!" he said; "it is in vain to contend further. The last blow is now struck."

After a few minutes he recovered again, and, fixing his lustreless eyes upon the abbess, he said, " Lead me, I implore you, to her grave."

The abbess, hoping that the sight of this melancholy spot might, by exciting his tears, assuage that mortal agony which racked his heart, complied with his request. She added some words of consolation, which fell as much unheeded upon the ear of Leopold as if he had already been laid in the grave he sought to visit.

The old priest and the porter supported him, for his own limbs almost refused their office; and, followed by the abbess and the nuns, all of whom wept at the piteous spectacle which Leopold exhibited, they proceeded towards the convent cemetery. Leopold never raised his head from the shoulder of the kind priest until they stopped.

" Here," said the father, " is the low grave in which lies she whom you loved, and who was the personification of beauty and virtue."

Leopold looked up. One glance was enough— the well-known spot, which nothing could have erased from his memory, was before him. The ivy-covered wall—the tall cypresses—the white tablet, on which the moonbeams fell with a silvery lustre—the sparkling marble spires of the convent in the back ground—all convinced him at once that this was the cemetery of Santa Croce—that the spot on which he stood was that predestined to be his grave.

Once he looked round, as if to assure himself— once he gazed on the grave of his Laura, where the flowers strewed by her weeping companions lay yet unwithered—then turned his eyes to the dark blue sky, and, sinking again upon the shoulder of the priest without speaking a word, and uttering but one long sigh, his spirit fled for ever!

In that spot he was buried, and on that space in the wall was a tablet placed by his affectionate servant, Baptiste, with no other inscription than his master's name. So much of this story as relates to the woful termination of the lovers' lives is well remembered in the cloister to this day; and the younger devotees indulge that feeling of sympathy, which even their religious mortifications cannot entirely stifle, by strewing fresh flowers on the graves of Laura and Leopold.

"Well, now, Harry," said the captain, when the story was finished, "let me ask you whether you believe all that rigmarole which you have been telling us?"

"Believe it, sir!" replied Harry, affecting great surprise; "certainly I do; the gentleman who related it to me was a man of veracity."

"Why, as to that, you know, Harry," said my uncle, "one can never be sure of the companions one travels with. Fair outsides often cover foul intentions. I have been taken in myself in the course of my life, and so no wonder that you should be."

"Then, sir," asked Harry, "you do not, perhaps, think that the original relater of this tale was an honest man?"

"I don't say that, Harry," replied the captain; "it is wrong to take away a man's character upon mere suspicions; though I must say appearances are confoundedly against your friend. He might, however, have been imposed upon himself, and have thought it was all true."

"But still, sir, you don't believe the story itself," said Harry.

"Not a syllable, lad," replied the captain: "pretty work we should have of it if Davy Jones, or any of his crew, had power to come ashore like a press-gang, and carry fellows off just as they liked."

"Well, sir," replied Harry, "I am sorry that you criticise so severely a story which, I must say, seems to me at least as probable as that of your friend, Charley Russell."

"Egad you're right, Harry," replied the captain; "just as true, and not a bit more so."

"At least," said Mr. Evelyn, "if the question were to be decided by numbers, the majority would be in favour of the truth of such calls; for, among the various superstitions which have abounded at all times in the northern parts of Europe, none seems to have been more familiar and general than that which is the foundation of Mr. Beville's story—I mean the foreknowledge of the time and place at which death is to await certain individuals. In the highlands of Scotland this belief, which is prevalent, has been beautifully alluded to by Collins in his ode on the popular superstitions of that remote country:

'They, whose sight such dreary dreams engross,
With their own vision oft astonished droop,
When, o'er the watery strath or quaggy moss,
They see the gliding ghosts embodied troop;

, Or if, in sports, or on the festive green,
    Their destined glance some fated youth descry,
Who now, perhaps, in lusty vigour seen,
    And rosy health, shall soon lamented die !'

" Not, however, to go so far for an illustration
of this fact, I may add that I know the belief
continues in England at this day."

" But," asked Elizabeth, " did you ever know
any one who pretended to have the power of
foretelling the death of others ?"

" Yes," replied Mr. Evelyn, " an instance of
it came under my own immediate observation."

" I should be much obliged to you, sir," said
Elizabeth, " if you would tell me the particulars
of that extraordinary circumstance ; for it seems
to me so unenviable a faculty, that its possessor
would gladly be silent about it."

" If he had been wise or honest, he would,"
replied Mr. Evelyn ; " but the man I allude to
was neither the one nor the other. You know,
of course, the common superstition relative to
St. Mark's Eve."

" Yes," said Elizabeth ; " it is that, immediately after midnight, the disembodied spirits of
all the inhabitants of a parish, who are fated to
die in the course of the ensuing year, will enter
the churchyard gate, and walk into the church."

" Exactly so," replied Mr. Evelyn : " such is
the belief in England ; elsewhere it is supposed

that not only the ghosts of those fated to die
are allowed to roam, but that all other unsubstantial beings are let loose on the earth;—to use
again the words of Collins, that, in that thrice-
hallowed Eve,

‘ Ghosts, as cottage maids believe,
Their pebbled beds permitted leave ;
And goblins haunt, from fire or fen,
Or mine or flood, the walks of men.’ ”

" But," said Elizabeth, " although I have heard
of the belief, and know that it is entertained by
cottage maids, who ‘ hold such strange tales devoutly true’ only through fear and ignorance, I
never yet met with any person who had actually
undergone the ceremony of watching in the
church porch during the midnight hours, when
the grisly troop is said to roam."

" Then you see one now, for the first time,"
said Mr. Evelyn ; " I have passed through that
perilous adventure."

" Pray tell us, then, what you saw, and what it
was that induced you to undergo such a frightful
watch," said Elizabeth eagerly.

" Which question shall I answer you first ?"
asked Mr. Evelyn.

" Oh, just which you please," she replied ;
" but pray do tell me, for I wish of all things to
know somebody who has really seen a ghost ;
and I am sure, Mr. Evelyn, that you will not in-
vent any fables, as Harry would, only for the
purpose of quizzing me."

" Indeed," said Harry, " you do me great wrong, Elizabeth; it is upon the veracity of my stories alone that I pique myself. Attack them in any other point if you will, but at least do me the justice to believe them."

. " It is not worth while to dispute the veracity of your stories, Harry," said Elizabeth; " but let us listen to Mr. Evelyn's account of his adventures on St. Mark's Eve."

" They happened," said the clergyman, " many years ago. When I first took orders I went to serve a curacy belonging to a friend of mine, in a parish situated on a remote part of the coast of Norfolk. The village was about a mile from the sea, and the church stood half-way between them, in a bleak spot, which even in summer was dismal enough; but in winter it was so dreary that it might be deemed, with some reason, the haunt of beings that shun the cheerful and busy parts of the creation. The whole of the village, and a great portion of the surrounding lands, were the property of a gentleman, whose seat was immediately adjoining. This gentleman, as may be imagined, was interested in all the affairs of his tenants, and he endeavored to promote their comfort and happiness as far as he was able. He was a plain unaffected man, and a good sample of that class of the community to which he belonged—the English country gentlemen. I was treated by him with great cordiality and kindness during my stay in his neighbourhood, and we had already begun to be very intimate, when he came to me one day for the purpose of consulting me, he said, on a subject which had given him some trouble.

"There was in the village a blacksmith, who, besides setting a very pernicious example of habitual drunkenness, pretended to possess the faculty of foretelling the deaths of his neighbours. This fellow was a great knave, and he had, in many instances, exercised his divinatory powers for the purposes of wantonness and revenge. He, however, carried on his practices with so much cunning, that the simple villagers feared him at least as much as they hated him. Some of his predictions had happened to be true, but they were always such as might have been very safely made without the possession of any supernatural skill. When young people had the visible marks of consumption, and when old ones were rapidly decaying, it was safe enough for the blacksmith to foretell that in the space of a year they would be no more. The rogue, who had wit enough to see that his neighbours were fit subjects for imposition, thought it would be as well to add a superstitious *eclat* to his predictions; and for this purpose he used to pass St. Mark's Eve alone, in the church porch, where, as he said, he beheld the unsubstantial forms of those who were doomed to die passing in

order along the churchyard path. Among
others, for some offence which he had taken
against the aged mother of a young man who
was then serving in the navy on a distant station, he gave out that the youth would die in
the course of the year. Of all his mischievous
predictions this was most likely to have had
a fatal effect. The young man was to be married
on his return to a girl who lived in the village, and who was one of the best as well as
the prettiest 'low-born lasses' that ever dignified
an humble station by her eminent virtues. The
year was drawing near a close, and no news had
been received from her lover, although the
period at which they were expected had long
since passed. Poor Mary had borne up for a
long time against the apprehensions and anxieties
which the blacksmith's predictions had occasioned, but now they became too heavy and
terrible to bear. Her health declined, her spirits
were gone, and it appeared too likely that she
would form one of the grim troop, who, on the
approaching St. Mark's Eve, were to make their
appointed journey through the churchyard. The
cause of her illness was well known, for, in a
village like that of which I am speaking, every
body is acquainted with his neighbour's affairs at
least as well as his own. The matter was talked
of every where, and had spread a panic throughout the place, which greatly vexed the squire.

"The object of his visit to me was to consult as to what should be done for the purpose of restoring tranquillity. To drive away the blacksmith was an easy matter, but this would not have been a sufficient remedy for the evil. · It was the squire's wish that the people should be convinced of the rogue's impostures in the first place : he proposed to me, therefore, that I should pass the fatal eve in the church porch, and that I should publicly announce the result of my observations during the terrible hour to my parishioners.

"I had no objection to this—I did not believe in the superstition, and I was in hopes that my visit would have the effect of convincing the good folks of the village of the folly of their fears, and of the falsehood of the blacksmith's prophecies. The only precaution that I thought it necessary to take was that the author of the mischief might be watched, lest he should be induced to play me some trick which could have defeated the object of my vigil.

"St. Mark's Eve arrived : I supped with the squire, and remained chatting with him and his family until within half an hour of midnight, when I quitted them, and, wrapped up in a warm and capacious cloak, walked towards the church.

"The weather was mild for the season ; the wind and rain had prevailed for several weeks, but the sun had occasionally, and for short inter-

vals, given promise of the approach of the tardy
spring. The moon was up, and, sometimes
shining in unobscured brilliancy—sometimes
only shedding a dim and doubtful gleam through
the fleecy clouds which coursed rapidly across
the sky—gave a thousand different tones to the
landscape. My road to the church lay, for the
greatest part, through the squire's plantations,
which were thickly grown; and, although now
only at the end of April, the leaves of most of
the trees were out. I have seen a more serene
night, but I never saw any more beautiful. The
plantation abounded with nightingales, some of
which poured out the rich liquid melody of their
songs, as if they would never end. I paused
more than once upon my walk to listen to the
profuse deluge of vocal sounds uttered by
these birds upon the midnight air, which
seemed charmed into stillness by the spell of
their eloquent music. The quaint, but powerful
and beautiful description, in a little poem called
' Music's Duel,' by an almost forgotten English
poet,* came into my mind. This author has versi-
fied a story told by the Jesuit, Strada, of a musi-
cian, who, playing in a wood, found that a nightin-
gale in a tree near him endeavored to imitate the
modulations of the air he was performing. He
increased the power of his song, and the bird its
exertions to keep up with him, until its heart

* Crashaw.

broke with the effort, and this 'music's enthu-
siast' fell dead upon the artist's lute.

> ' Oh fit to have,
> That liv'd so sweetly!—dead, so sweet a grave !'

"The passage to which I particularly allude is
this :—

> ' Her supple breast thrills out
> Sharp airs, and staggers in the warbling doubt
> Of dallying sweetness, hovers o'er her skill,
> And folds in waved notes with a trembling bill
> The pliant series of her slippery song;
> Then starts she suddenly into a throng
> Of short thick sobs, whose thundering volleys float
> In panting murmurs, 'stilled out of her breast,
> That ever-bubbling spring, the sugared nest
> Of her delicious soul, that there does lie,
> Bathing in streams of liquid melody;
> Music's best seed-plot, when, in ripened airs,
> A golden-headed harvest fairly rears
> His honey-dropping tops, ploughed by her breath,
> Which there reciprocally laboureth.
> In that sweet soil it seems a holy quire
> Founded to th' name of great Apollo's lyre;
> Whose silver roof rings with the sprightly notes
> Of sweet-lipp'd angel-imps, that swill their throats
> In cream of morning Helicon, and then
> Prefer soft anthems to the ears of men,
> To woo them from their beds, still murmuring
> That men can sleep while they their matins sing.'

"But, to return to my adventures, from which
the nightingales and Crashaw have diverted me—
I went on to the churchyard, and took my seat in
the porch of the ancient building, the appearance of which was at least as rude as the times

in which it was erected. The wind had freshened a little, and blew with a mourning noise from the sea across the flat high lands which lay between. It sung through the old church tower a wild and fitful song. The moon still remained high in the heavens; its beams fell on the silent graves, which were thickly strewed in the slanting churchyard at my feet; and the thin shadowy clouds flitting over the white grave-rails, which told the names of the lowly dead beneath, gave to them an appearance of animation.

" I could not help thinking that, with a very slight exertion, a person of imagination might people the whole of the silent scene before him with active beings, and create fictions out of his own mind, which he might dwell upon until he believed them to be realities. I felt, however, that it would be better for my present purpose not to indulge in such speculations, and I chased them as well as I could from my mind. Still, however, an oppressive feeling hung upon me, for which I could account in no other manner than by the stillness and solemnity of the scene; for, as I have said before, I disbelieved the whole story of the spectres.

"The moments crept on with a painful slowness. I thought that the lapse of time had never before seemed so tardy. The silence was wholly unbroken, save by the harsh ticking of an old

clock which stood in the church tower, and by
the alternate wailing and sobbing of the keen
night-wind. I began to wish that the hour of
my watch had expired. The coldness of the air
had chilled me, and I could not repress a slight
shivering which occasionally ran through my
nerves. I had now about ten minutes to stay,
and began to pace quickly across the small porch,
for the purpose of warming myself a little, when
I heard the creaking of the churchyard gate. I
turned immediately towards the place whence
the sound proceeded, and, looking down, I saw in
the clear moonlight a figure advancing up the
churchyard path. At this moment I must confess that my fears got the better of my reason
and of my resolution. The shivering increased
with uncontrollable violence as I continued to
gaze on the approaching object. By no natural
accident which I could imagine was it possible
that any person could be traversing that path at
such an hour. It led only from the wild sea-
shore to the village, and was so difficult of
access from the cliffs, that even the smugglers,
who sometimes frequented this neighbourhood,
would have shunned it. These reflections
flocked through my mind, and aided the impression which my fears had already made. I wrapped my cloak more closely about me, and with
some effort stepped out of the porch, that I might
see more distinctly the figure which had so

strongly excited my apprehensions. It was now much nearer, when it suddenly stopped, and turned round. This pause enabled me to look more narrowly, and you may imagine that my fears were not lessened when I saw that it was dressed in a naval uniform. I rubbed my eyes, to ascertain exactly that I labored under no visual delusion. Still the figure stood with its back towards me; the white trowsers shone under the moonlight; the glittering buttons, the sword hanging from the belt, the single epaulette —all convinced me that the figure wore the dress of a lieutenant in the navy. The prediction of the blacksmith came upon my mind, and, in the confusion which this sight occasioned, I was almost inclined to admit its truth. I had never seen the young sailor who had been the subject of it, but the coincidence was so strong as to stagger me. The figure turned round, and, as I saw its features, they exactly answered the description I had so often heard repeated. The moonlight has the effect of making pale the human face, and this, together perhaps with my own imagination, gave to that of the figure before me a deathlike appearance. The recollection of the duty which I had undertaken to perform now forcibly occurred to me, and subdued, in a great measure, the panic which had seized me. I stepped forward, and called out 'Who goes there?'

"'A friend!' replied the figure, in a hoarse, but perfectly natural, voice.

"'What do you seek here, at this hour of the night?' I asked.

"'Before I answer you,' replied the unknown, 'let me know what right you have to question me?'

"'I am,' I said, 'the curate of this place.'

"'Then, sir, I must say you have chosen a cool night for the performance of your devotions; but, since you are the curate, I have no objection to answer your question :—My name, sir, is Benson; I am a lieutenant on board his Majesty's sloop, the Greyhound. My mother, whom you probably know, lives in the village yonder, and I am now on my way to surprise her with a visit, which, though it may break her night's rest, she will not complain of. My ship is making for the Downs; but the captain, knowing that my mother lived hereabouts, permitted me to be landed from one of the boats; and, as this wind has compelled us to keep pretty close to the shore all day, this was not so difficult to effect as it is sometimes.'

" For a few moments I could not answer, I was so wholly overcome with surprise. This was the very person for whom his mother was sorrowing in all the terrors of anxiety, and the fear of whose death was weighing his destined bride down to the grave. I was, however, soon able to explain to the young officer the reasons of my watch, and the situation of his mother and his betrothed. With some difficulty I prevailed upon him not to present himself before them on that night; but I had still greater difficulty to restrain him from rushing to the blacksmith's cottage, and taking a summary revenge upon him.

"We proceeded to the house of the squire, whom we found still sitting up: his persuasions, added to mine, induced the young man to take a bed there; and to permit me to disclose the news of his arrival to his mother and his bride on the following morning. I will not attempt to describe the joy which this news occasioned. The lovely Mary, when her anxiety and terror were dissipated, soon recovered, and, in a few weeks after her lover's return, I had the pleasure of uniting them for life. The blacksmith's predictions were proved false, and he was banished from the village, to the great comfort of the inhabitants, many of whom, however, still believe the story of St. Mark's Eve and the spectres, although they are glad there is nobody, like the blacksmith, to bring home to them a direct application of their terrors."

"And is this all?" said Elizabeth.

"Yes," replied the curate.

"And you saw no real ghost?" she continued.

"None at all," he answered.

"Then, I must say, it is very provoking of you," said she : "twice have I been disappointed in my expectations of a ghost; I shall now, therefore, give up the hope, and look for nothing but plain matters of fact in future. Whose turn is it to go on, grandmamma?" she asked.

"Mr. Evelyn," said the old lady, "the turn falls upon you."

"I shall obey you with great readiness, madam," replied the clergyman; but, after the horrors of Mr. Beville's tale, I fear so homely a narration as that which I have to offer you may hardly be palatable."

"On the contrary," said Elizabeth, "it will be quite a relief to us to hear some sober true history after the *diablerie* with which Harry has regaled us, and the fright which you occasioned us with your adventure on St. Mark's Eve."

"I am glad, then, that, whatever may be the faults of my tale, I shall be able at last to comply with the terms which you impose upon me. Although it is a 'traveller's story,' it is, I am convinced, entirely authentic. The character of the person from whom I immediately received it would, if you knew as well as I do his worth and piety, satisfy you of its veracity. I have, besides, seen and conversed with the chief actors in it, and have received from their lips the confirmation of all the incidents I shall relate. I do not know that this may add to the value of the tale;

but, after so many fictions, I think it at least necessary to make this preliminary announcement, that my relation may lose nothing of the little interest which it possesses by being supposed to be a fiction, and that the partiality of my friends may not give me credit for an invention to which I have really no title. I will now, if you please, begin, premising only that it is a story which I picked up during an excursion I made through the valley of Chamounix, about three years ago."

LE MORT A TUÉ LES VIVANS.

The Curate's Tale.

———·— "This shows you are above,
You Justicers, that these our nether crimes
So speedily can venge!

LEAR.

LE MORT A TUÉ LES VIVANS.

—

THE small valley of Magland lies between Cluse and St. Martin, on the road from Geneva to Chamounix. It is usually passed too rapidly to be well recollected, although, to my thinking, it is one of the most beautiful parts of the road. In the course of the delightful little tour, of which it forms a part, there are many things to be met with more striking, more sublime, and more wonderful ; but there is no spot which so completely occupies the mind with a placid delight—a tranquil enjoyment—that charms rather by lulling than by exciting it. The valley is completely shut in ; and, after having entered it by a very abrupt turn, it appears to the traveller that there is no possible egress. The roaring Arve pursues its turbulent course at the bottom of the vale, making a hoarse music among the granite rocks which lie in its

bed ; meadows of most luxuriant pasture rear up
their gentle slopes to the foot of the high moun-
tains which rise on the opposite side of the river,
and, with their robes of firs and larches, curtain,
as it were, one side of the valley. On the other
side, and at a considerable elevation above the
bed of the river, is the road, thickly planted on
one side with fruit-trees, which form a sort of
natural *garde-fou.* A green esplanade, of only a
few paces, lies on the left, between it and a pile
of perpendicular rocks, which rear their heads to
an elevation of from eight hundred to one thousand feet, and look like the giant bulwarks of
a world beyond that which we inhabit. In some
places the surfaces of these rocks are so accurately smoothed, that, but for their immense size,
it would be difficult to believe they were not the
work of human hands. In others, where small
crevices and irregularities in the cliff have made
spaces for the deposition of earth, self-sown seeds
have sprung up into luxuriant forests, and lofty
trees flourish in all the pride of their inaccessi-
bility, lending, as it were, the decoration of their
foliage to the bare rock, in return for the protection which it affords to them. At intervals,
also, patches of a few roods of smiling green lie
in the midst of the desolation which has given
them birth, and look like the recollection of long
past moments of joy in a life of sorrow and disappointment. In every such place little *chalets,*

or wooden cottages, have been built, and, seemingly suspended on the steep, they look like small rude bird-cages; for, at the distance from which they are usually regarded, it is impossible to suppose that any other means than wings would enable the inhabitants to reach their dwellings, and it is no less difficult to understand how they can descend. The rock seems to be perpendicular; and, although trees are seen to grow upon it, the spectator thinks that, unless one had the faculty of extending roots like a tree, it would be impossible to traverse the unpromising ascent: this, however, arises only from the distance at which they are beheld.

It does not usually fall within the purpose of the numerous travellers who journey through this valley to make *detours*, the object of which would be merely to see a rude *chalet*, or to converse with a people whose information is as bounded as the realm in which they vegetate. They are, perhaps, right; they are in search of wonders which would not be obtained by the contemplation of beings so simple as the Savoyard peasants of the valley of Magland. But there are others who journey no less for the purpose of seeing the people than the scenery of a country; and to them it is the source of a pure and delightful sensation to observe the manner in which those passions and conditions of sentiment which are common to humanity are moulded by climate, education, national prejudice, and other circumstances purely local. Amongst this number do I rank myself. To me the contemplation of a family of hardy peasants, whose wishes have never been taught to stray beyond the confined limits of the spot of earth on which their destiny has placed them, but whose piety and purity of morals prove that they have found a road to heaven no less direct than those of a more presuming people, is a high delight.

The character of the inhabitants of this part of Savoy, and particularly of those who live remote from the public road, is of the most simple description. They are generally loyal, virtuous, and pious; and, although they are not exempt from the failings of humanity, yet their sins are commonly of a venial description, and the commission of atrocious crimes is almost unknown among them. I was, luckily, so fortunate as to procure frequent opportunities of observing their manners, and the result fully justifies my assertion.

I happened to sprain one of my ancles in crossing the river upon the granite stepping-stones which form the only bridge there; and this accident, for which I have to blame nothing but my own carelessness, obliged me to remain in a small cottage in the village of Magland for several days.

The Curé of the place very obligingly offered

me all the assistance in his power, and, what was
more useful, as well as more agreeable, his good
company. He was a man of little learning, but
of a warm heart, and loved the remote valley in
which he dwelt better than all the world beside.
He had numerous anecdotes of the place and its
inhabitants to relate to me ; and, when I had recovered so far as to be able to walk out, he obligingly accompanied me, and made all the objects
of the neighbourhood infinitely more interesting by the little tales he had to tell connected
with them. He one day proposed that we should
take a walk up a path, from the summit of which
we could view Mont Blanc, and the surrounding
country, to great advantage : " It is called," said
he, " *Le Mort a tué les Vivans* ; but, as the exertion
of climbing the mountain and telling a story are
hardly compatible, I will reserve, until we reach
the top, the relation of the circumstance which
gave it so remarkable a name."

We accordingly set out on a path which led
us from the road to the foot of the mountain, and
thence tended upwards in a zig-zag direction.
For a short distance it was tolerably smooth, but
after a few turns it entered a thick plantation of
firs ; and now the only means of ascending was
by climbing the fragments of the rock which lay
between the trunks of the trees. After nearly an
hour's walk the way enlarged again, and we
found a piece of level road before us formed by

a break in the rock, the effect of some mighty convulsion, which had left a small shelf of less than three feet in width on the very face of the cliff.   On one side was the mountain towering high above, and seeming to frown upon the presumptuous traveller ; while on the other side was a flat precipitous descent, so deep that the eye aches, and the brain turns, but to glance upon it ; while

> ' The crows and choughs that wing the midway air
> Show scare so gross as beetles.'

The inhabitants, however, pass along rapidly, fearlessly, and safely.   If any foreigner should essay the pass, I recommend him to take breath for five minutes, and a glass of *Kirschenwasser,* the brandy of the country, which he will find to be an admirable help to the nerves.   This perilous pass, however, soon ends, and the ascent is again commenced.   Here the path becomes little better than a rude ladder.   In some places steps are cut in the cliff, but at unequal distances ; at others broken pieces of the rock are the only footing, and instant death would be the cousequence of one false step—a death so horrid that its mere contemplation is painful.

Arrived at the top, we saw a small meadow of about four acres, part of which was planted as an orchard.   A small, but extremely neat, wooden chalet rose at the end, the rock forming one side of the building.   As we approached, a matronly looking woman, of a countenance which had once been beautiful, approached us, bearing a child in her arms. The Curé introduced me as a stranger who was travelling to see the country. She welcomed me with a warmth and frankness common to this people ; and, inviting us into her house, the table was immediately spread with bread, cheese, grapes, cream, and wine of a most excellent kind and delicious flavour. After praying us to partake of this repast, for which our walk up the mountain had admirably prepared us, she retired to attend to her domestic employments.

When we had satisfied our thirst and hunger I claimed M. Le Curé's promise to tell me the origin of the name of the path which had led us to this singular place ; and he complied thus :—

" The chalet, under the roof of which we are now sitting, was built by Pierre Boisset, a peasant of the neighbouring valley. He was at that period about forty years of age, and bore the character of one of the most honest and good-tempered men of his district. He had been married early ; but his wife had died, leaving him one son, who, after vexing his father with all the wickedness of a wayward boy, had quitted his home ; and, no tidings having been heard of him for some years, it was supposed he was dead. Pierre, after living unmarried for a considerable time, was captivated by the charms of the youth-

ful, daughter of a peasant of Balme ; and, although
his age was no recommendation to his suit, yet
his reputation for a kind and manly disposition
gave his pretensions the advantage over wooers of
greater personal attractions.; and, notwithstanding the disparity between eighteen and forty, he
made the blooming Catharine his wife.

" Immediately before his marriage, having obtained a grant of the land upon which this dwelling
is situated, he built it for the reception of his bride.
After the performance of the nuptial ceremony he
conveyed her hither ; and here he dwelt in a state
of tranquil happiness which is equally beyond
the reach and the comprehension of the rich and
proud. One daughter was the only fruit of this
marriage ; and the beauty of her person and the
amiability of her temper-rendered her the pride
of her parents, and more than counterbalanced
the pain which the misconduct of his son had
occasioned to Pierre.

" Time rolled on unmarked by any other oc-
currences than the change of the seasons, and
the progression of the lovely Marie to blooming
womanhood. She was now nearly eighteen years
old ; and, although the place of her abode was so
remote, she was celebrated for beauty and goodness throughout the valley. Those bad passions, which flourish so luxuriantly in the rank
soil of cities, find no place, or at least no en-
couragement, in these simple regions. In the

little church, which I pointed out at the foot of
the mountain, Marie was the most beautiful of
the young peasants ; and I believe that, notwithstanding all the common-place sayings about
female envy, not one of them could have been
found to dispute her title to that distinction.

" Her hand had been sought by Jacques, the son
of the richest man in the commune : you may smile
when I tell you that he was the Crœsus of the
neighbourhood, because he possessed a comfortable chalet and half a score of cows. In point
of wealth, Marie, too, was by no means a con-
temptible match : the heiress of old Pierre, who,
although he had no cows, had an extensive stock
of goats—and whose chalet, though not remarkable for the facility of its access, was sheltered
and substantial—might, without any great advantages of person, have looked among the best
of her neighbours for a husband. The attachment of the lovers was approved of by their
parents, and they waited only for the arrival of
the spring to consummate their happiness.

" During the winter, however, Pierre, who had
enjoyed that uninterrupted health which is ever
the consequence of temperance, happened, in
descending the mountain, to slip and fracture
one of his legs. This accident, though by no
means so serious in itself as to have endangered
his life, yet, owing to the difficulty of obtaining
surgical assistance, soon put on alarming appear-

ances ; and upon the arrival of the medical prac-
titioner, three days afterwards, he pronounced
his patient to be in considerable danger.

"My services," continued the good priest,
" were then required ; and I was summoned to
administer those consolations which are most
eagerly sought when human remedies appear to
fail. Previous to my setting out I was surprised
by a visit from a soldier in the uniform of the
Austrian service. He was in a state of considerable intoxication ; but he informed me, as
intelligibly as he could, that he was the son of
Pierre Boisset, and that, having obtained leave
of absence from his regiment, he had come hither
to see his father. I was grieved for the afflicting intelligence I had to impart, and still more
to see the condition into which this young man's
excess had reduced him. He received the news
of his father's danger with the most perfect
apathy, proposing, however, to accompany me
on my visit. On our way I found, from his narrative, that, since he had quitted the valley, his
life had been passed in riot and bloodshed, and
all those vices which, though not necessarily the
consequences of the military profession, are too
often its accompaniments.* Those irregularities,
which in a boy might have been amended, I saw
had now ripened into serious and irreclaimable
vices.

* The good Curé spoke of the *Continental* soldiery.

" Upon my arrival at the chalet I had become tired and disgusted with my companion, and could not help entertaining a suspicion that his visit to his father had some interested motive. I found old Pierre in such a state as convinced me he had a very short time to live ; and, having discharged the duties of my sacred calling by administering the last ceremonies of religion, I informed him of his son's arrival.

" The good old man, who was perfectly aware that his dissolution was about to take place, signified a wish that he should approach. He reached out his hands to give him his blessing, which the son received with an air of stupid insensibility.

" ' In a sad hour are you returned, my son,' said the expiring parent ; ' and yet it is a consolation to me to see you once more before I die. I trust that time and experience have eradicated those faults which were the cause of your misery and of mine ; and while my last prayer is, that your death-bed, though far distant, may be as tranquil as mine, remember that integrity and piety alone can make you happy in this world, and in that to which I am hastening.'

" He sank upon his pillow as he finished speaking, and, his strength gradually declining, his eyes at length closed, and he died without the precise moment of his dissolution being perceived. His wife and daughter were overcome with their emotions, and remained kneeling by the bedside.

The soldier alone stood unmoved, and, muttering

time, he coolly lighted his pipe at a lamp which hung in the room, and sat down amongst us.

" When the females were in some degree recovered, I intimated to the son that it would be better for him to retire. He grumbled, and seemed reluctant ; but at length arose, and, without taking the slightest notice of his mother and sister in law, he walked out.

" After offering such consolation as was in my power to the widow and her daughter, and leaving them in the care of some humane neighbours, I prepared to return home. I soon overtook the son of the deceased Pierre, whom I found complaining of the difficulty of the descent, interlarding his speech with the most vulgar imprecations. With the exception of this occasional blasphemy he preserved a sullen silence, and, on arriving at the turning which led to my dwelling, he quitted me abruptly.

" It is the custom in this country to bury the dead very shortly after their decease, and I learned that the next day but one was fixed for the interment of the remains of old Pierre. I attended, as was my duty, to accompany the corpse, and found the little chalet filled with the neighbours and friends of the family. The coffin lay in the midst, and the mourners were seated round it. The disconsolate widow sat overwhelmed

with grief; and her daughter beside her, endea-
voring to comfort her, looked like an angel.
The saddened tone of her features, and the tears,
which dimmed the brightness without diminish-
ing the beauty of her eyes, rendered her still
more engaging. They waited, as I understood,
for the son, who had intimated his intention
of bearing his father's coffin to the grave.

"At length he arrived, bringing with him a
companion. This was a man who lived in the
neighbouring town of Cluse, of notoriously bad
character : every one shunned him, and, although
their dealings sometimes led them into contact
with him, it was with reluctance they spake
together. He was a cheat and a liar ; and generally believed to have some indirect methods of
acquiring money. He had long previously proposed himself as a suitor to the fair Marie, but
had been indignantly rejected.

"The son soon manifested symptons of drunkenness ; and, looking round him with a rude
stare, he at length went up to the widow, and, accosting her, said ' I am come to bury my father ;
but, before we set out, you must know that you
cannot return to this chalet. It is mine ; that
is to say, it was ; and I have sold it to my honest
friend here,' pointing to his companion.

"The widow looked up, but seemed incapable
of speaking. At length she said ' You will not,

surely, have the cruelty to turn me out of my house.'

"' *Your* house !' he replied with a sneer; 'I tell you it's *mine!* It was my father's : he died, and I am his heir. As to turning you out, that is not my affair ; if you can persuade this gentleman,' pointing again to the man who stood beside him, 'to let you stay, I'm sure I have no objection.'

" At this moment I thought proper to interfere. 'Young man,' I said, 'I charge you, by the respect which you owe to the memory of him whose mortal remains lie before you, and whose spirit is at this moment witnessing your deeds, to forbear your wicked purpose. If you are entitled, as you say, and as I fear is true, to this house, at least postpone your claim until your father's widow and his daughter have some other dwelling. Would you at this season turn them upon the desolate mountain, homeless, and without the means of sustenance ?—At this season, when the very beasts of the field cannot bide the inclemency of the weather ?'

"' I tell you again,' said the apathetic ruffian, whom drunkenness had made still more brutal, ' that I have no voice in the business : the house was mine, and I have sold it, with all that belongs to it. You had better try to persuade the man who has bought them.'

" The person to whom he alluded stepped forward as he spoke. He was about fifty years old; thin, with à hook nose and small eyes; and of a most forbidding aspect. The people in the neighbourhood said he was a Jew, and I believe they were right in their conjecture. He approached the distressed widow.

" 'Madam,' said he, ' there is a very ready method by which you may retain possession of your dwelling : if the offer which I made to Marie, your fair daughter, and which I now repeat, shall be received with less scorn'——

" The gentle Marie, who, upon ordinary occasions, had seemed of so mild a temper that the slightest exertion was foreign to her nature, started from her seat, her eyes glancing with indignation.

" ' Monster!' she cried, ' you shall find that the base and cruel plan you have laid shall be defeated. Not for worlds would I marry you; begging and starvation would be happiness compared to the disgrace of being united to a shameless and unmanly wretch, who has thus sought to increase the load of a widow's affliction in her most trying agony.' She flung her arms around her mother's neck. ' We may be poor and desolate, my dear mother; but we shall, at least, have the satisfaction of not deserving our misfortunes.'

" The hardened villain shrank back abashed at

the rebuke of the young mountaineer. The by-
standers murmured, and proposed to put him, out
by force; but I checked them. ' My friends,'
said I, ' do not let any violence on your part add
to the outrage which has this day been offered
to the dead. It is only for a time that the wicked
appear to prosper; their own guilt shall one day
bear them down, and bitterly shall they repent
the daring impiety which they have now committed. In the mean time remember that they
carry with them the contempt of every honest
man; and, successful as they appear to be
in their wicked designs, which of you would not
rather be this houseless and bereaved widow and
orphan than the men who stand before you ?'

" They were calmed :—some of the elder villagers who had known the son had now gathered
round him, and were endeavouring to persuade
him to undo the disgraceful contract he had made.
It was in vain; he listened at first indifferently,
and at length impatiently, to their representa-
tions, till, with a volley of imprecations, he
asked why they did not proceed with the funeral.

" Finding that all remonstrance was useless,
they at length set out. The only road to the
churchyard lay down that path by which we arrived here to-day. The alleged purchaser of the
chalet went off some yards before; and the son
and three of the deceased's relatives bore the
coffin. The widow, leaning on her daughter's

arm, and accompanied by those friends and
neighbours who had assembled on the occasion,
followed at some distance. It was in the middle
of winter, and the difficulties of the road had
increased by the lodgments of ice in various
parts of the rocky path. The son, who was in
the front, according to that practice which even
the solemnity of the occasion could not make
him lay aside, swore loudly and often as he descended. The worst part of the road had now
been passed, and the procession had reached a
turn in the rock, when the son, with a movement
of levity, and because he thought all danger was
over, took a long step : his foot slipped, and,
falling upon his face, the coffin was loosened from
the hold of the other bearers by the violence of
the shock :—it fell upon his head, and the blow
produced instant death !

" The impulse thus given to the coffin was so
great that it turned over on one side, and continued to roll towards the intruder, who had preceded the company, and who had now gained a
lower portion of the rock. He saw it coming,
and earnestly, but vainly, tried to escape ; the
coffin struck him on the legs, and he was hurled
over into the deep abyss ! when the trunk of a
pine-tree prevented the further descent of the
corpse. A cry of surprise and horror burst from
the following mourners. The body of the son
was picked up totally lifeless ; but that of the

other man was not found until the next day—so mutilated and disfigured that it would have been impossible to have recognised it but by his dress.

" When the consternation caused by this event had in some measure subsided the coffin was recovered, and was borne without further accident to the churchyard, where it was quietly interred. There being now no persons to dispute the right of the widow and Marie to their chalet, they returned thither ; and, having addressed the assembled villagers upon the fearfully mysterious event which had just happened, I retired to my own home to meditate upon the awful and righteous dispensations of Providence. The female whom you have just seen is the Marie of the tale I have related to you, and from this circumstance the mountain path is still called by the peasants ' *Le Mort a tué les Vivans.*' "

" I KNOW the spot to which your story relates," said Harry to the curate, as the latter finished his tale : " it is in a most romantic neighbourhood, and would, I dare say, well repay the trouble of any one who should go tale-hunting there; I would be sworn there is not a crag that has not its history. You remember the echo at the foot of the rocks which lead to the footpath?"

" Perfectly," replied the curate ; " I passed a whole morning there once in trying the various sounds which that echo gives back. It is one of the most distinct I ever heard."

" Then you must know the one-legged soldier who lives in a little hut there, and gains his subsistence by the bounty of the travellers who stop to listen to the echo," said Harry.

" He was my most intimate acquaintance," replied Mr. Evelyn, " during my stay there, and assisted me in the various experiments I made upon the reverberating powers of the rocks. He had lived for some years in the hovel you mention. With three small cannon placed on the green sward by the side of the road, he used to exhibit, if I may venture to say so, the echo, and thus drew from the travellers, during the summer, enough to support himself in the winter. He had a great many stories to tell, of which his own was not the least remarkable."

"I am afraid," said Elizabeth, "it is too much to ask you to tell it us now; and you have made no slip by which we can insist upon a second story from you."

"I hope not," said Mr. Evelyn; "but at some future opportunity, perhaps, you shall hear the story of Blaise, the old soldier of the echo of Magland."

"And now, perhaps, Elizabeth," said Harry, "as you have failed in your attempt on Mr. Evelyn for a second story, you will favour us with that which, in the course of the lots, we have a right to expect from you."

"Well," said Elizabeth, "since it is my destiny I must comply;" and as she spoke she produced a manuscript.

"As you are so great a lover of the supernatural," said Harry, "we look for rare ghosts from you."

"Then you will be disappointed," replied Elizabeth, "for I mean to tell you a story as true as Mr. Evelyn's; and now, therefore, listen."

LADY ARABELLA STUART.

Elizabeth's Tale.

"To these, whom Death again did wed,
  The grave's a second marriage bed;
  For, though the hand of Fate could force
  'Twixt soul and body a divorce,
  It could not man and wife divide."

                        CRASHAW.

LADY ABABELLA STUART.

In the year 1610 there stood upon the brow of Highgate Hill a noble mansion, belonging to the Countess of Shrewsbury, of which not a vestige now remains. An avenue of tall trees led from the road to a large gate, beyond which were an extensive garden and pleasure-grounds. The house stood in the midst of them; and, although its situation was so high that it commanded a fine view of the city of London over the then thickly-wooded country which lay between, it was so completely sheltered by the plantations round about, that it possessed all the advantages of perfect retirement.

On an afternoon in the month of May, in the year which has been mentioned, two ladies were walking in the gardens of this mansion. One was a staid matronly-looking person, long past the middle age; the other was one in whose face the marks of deep sorrow had not obliterated, and hardly impaired, the beauty which triumphed there, as in a throne. They were engaged in an earnest, and, as it seemed, a painful conversation. From their dress and demeanour it was evident that they were persons of the higher class of society.

A lame old man, who had been long gazing through the gate, and whose appearance indicated that poverty and old age had dealt hardly with him, now approached them. His tattered clothes were, as might be guessed through the numerous and party-coloured patches which covered them, the remnants of an old military uniform. A long and broad rapier hung at his side; and he leant upon an old matchlock, which he used by way of staff. His head was covered with loose grey locks, and exhibited many scars, which told, more plainly than even the black patch which covered the place where one of his eyes should have been, that his life had been spent in danger, and that fighting had been his trade. In his right hand he held a rusty and battered morion, which he extended to the ladies as he implored their charity. A large wallet was strapped on his shoulders.

"For the love of Heaven, sweet ladies," he cried, "bestow some of your pity upon a disabled soldier."

The younger lady, who had ". a hand open as

day for melting charity," instantly produced a purse, and, before her intention was perceived by her companion, had placed a portion of its contents in the beggar's morion.

"Where did you receive your wounds ?" asked the young lady in a tone of kindness and sympathy which enhanced her bounty.

"In almost every place, gentle madam, where during the last thirty years the soldiers of Britain have had to maintain the liberties of their country. I lost my eye at Zutphen, but not before I saw that flower of chivalry, Sir Philip Sidney, lose his life. Afterwards I fell into the hands of the Spaniards, and lay in their prisons seven years : now, God help me ! I am old, and unable to fight; my friends are all dead ; and I have no dependence but on the bounty of Providence, and of such good Christians as you, lady."

"Poor man !" ejaculated the lady, "and have you no home ?"

"The wide world is my home," said the soldier; "I shall never have any other until I creep into my grave."

"Who knows, friend," said the elder lady, "that you are not an arrant impostor ?"

"Your ladyship's late brother, my honored master, would know it if he were alive," said the soldier, with an emphasis which amounted almost to a rebuke.

" Did you know the Lord Mountchensy ?"
asked the old lady, while a slight agitation passed
over her face at the mention of her gallant brother.

" I knew him," replied the veteran, " for as
brave a soul as ever struck hard blows in a
fair cause; and by this token, my lady, he knew
me also. This ring, which neither prison nor
poverty has yet been able to tear from me, was
given to me by the gallant lord after a hard fight
in the Low Countries."

The soldier, as he spoke, gave the countess a
ring; and, as the old lady wiped away the tears
which her brother's memory forced into her eyes,
he slipped, with great dexterity, a letter into the
hands of the younger one, whispering at the same
moment " *Fedeltà*."

She knew that this word must have been communicated to him by a person whom she held
dearer than her life ; and, concealing as well as
she could the agitation which she felt, she put
the letter into her bosom.

" Will you not order the poor man into the
buttery ?" said she to the countess : " he seems
tired, and I dare say has need of rest and
food."

" Be it so, my love," replied the countess ;
and then, turning to the soldier, she said " Friend,
will you part with this ring for twenty times its
value ?"

" Not for the riches of the whole world," said

the beggar, "to any one but your ladyship; and not to you unless you will take it from my hands as free a gift as it came to them."

"Well," said the old lady, "we must seek then for some way of thanking you that will neither hurt your pride nor weaken your remembrance of my poor brother." The countess then called a servant, and, bidding him take charge of the old soldier, she said she would see him again shortly. The old man retired, loading both the ladies with thanks and benedictions.

The younger lady proposed to return to the house; and, this being acceded to by the countess, she flew to her bed-chamber for the purpose of devouring the contents of the letter she had just received.

It is, perhaps, expedient, at this part of the narrative, that I should give my hearers some more particular information respecting this personage, who has no slight claims upon their interest. She was the Lady Arabella Stuart, the cousin of the reigning monarch, and, as some persons deemed, having a better title to the throne than James I. From her earliest years she had been an object of suspicion to the king. Upon her pretensions to the crown of England was founded the plot of Lord Cobham and Sir Walter Raleigh, which had been detected, and the inventors of which were put to death, banished, or ruined. Although she had no share in that

imperfect and ill-conducted attempt at a con-
spiracy, and was known besides to be of too
gentle and amiable a disposition to harbour any
ambitious notions, the narrow-minded monarch
believed that her existence was full of peril to
himself.   With all the inclination to commit
crimes, and to tolerate them in others when it
suited his purpose, he could not yet screw up his
resolution to attempt her life; but, as a middle
course, in which, while he provided for his own
security, he cared not what sacrifice he might
make of the happiness of others, he resolved that
she should never marry, and that her claims,
such as they were, should terminate with her
existence.

There never yet was a king, however absolute
his power, who could control the impulses of
hearts. The sway of the universal and despotic
passion baffles all the attempts which have been
made, since the world began, to control it. The
lovely and sensitive Lady Arabella could not
live long in a court without feeling and inspiring
that passion. The gallant and accomplished
William Seymour, the second son of the Earl of
Beauchamp, and the worthy descendant of a long
line of heroic ancestors, saw and loved her. He
was at an age when manhood had tempered, but
had not in the slightest degree quenched, the
resolute fire of his youthful blood. To know
that Danger lay in his path, while Love stood

beyond as his reward, was to him only an additional incitement to pursue it. He loved the Lady Arabella; he imparted to her his passion, and had the happiness soon to find that he was a successful wooer. She confessed that she returned his love with equal ardour; and, although they were compelled to keep their mutual flame a secret, this scarcely abated the felicity of a sentiment which ever loves the shade, and is never made more delightful by becoming more notorious.

They were privately, and, as they hoped, secretly married; but the numerous spies whom the king kept in his pay soon discovered the union which they had not been able to prevent. The newly-wedded couple were arrested, and carried before the privy council, where, after an angry reprimand from the king, Mr. Seymour was committed to the Tower, there to remain during his majesty's pleasure; and the Lady Arabella was delivered over to the custody of her aunt, the Countess of Shrewsbury, with a strict injunction that she was not to be permitted to leave her ladyship's house at Highgate.

The imprisonment to which Mr. Seymour had been sentenced was at that time little less perilous than a sentence of death. Of many persons, some of high rank, and others, the humility of whose station precluded all inquiry respecting them, who had been committed to the Tower during the king's pleasure, few had ever

quitted it with life.   Attempts at poison were so
frequent, that the prisoners would seldom touch
any food that was prepared within the walls, or,
indeed, any that was not brought to them from
careful and trusty friends.   In short, although
there have been many periods of English history,
at which open and sanguinary outrages have
been committed by the authority of the monarch
upon his subjects, there never occurred one until
the reign of James I. in which the most dark and
treacherous crimes—such as are not usually held
to be of English growth—were practised with the
sanction and countenance of the crown.

Poor Lady Arabella had already passed a fort-
night in all the terrors of uncertainty and suspense respecting the fate of her husband; and
these terrors were increased by her total inability
to help his escape, or to provide for his safety in
prison.   She knew, however, that he had many
and powerful friends; and she trusted that some
good chance might preserve him, and that they
might yet be happy.   Her fears for her husband
were diverted, but not diminished, by those which
she now entertained on her own part; for, at the
period when this history begins, the countess
had just received an order to hold her niece in
readiness to depart for Durham on the following
day, in the company of persons whom the king
would commission for that purpose.   This news
had, as may be imagined, thrown her into great
affliction; for she felt that, once in the power of

the king's creatures, there was no unfair treatment that she might not have to dread ; and the distance between Durham and her husband's prison seemed to her to preclude the possibility of their being again joined. She had been talking on this subject to the old countess, who, although affectionately attached to her kinswoman, was, besides, so loyal, and so fully impressed with the belief that because he was king he could do no wrong, that she gave Lady Arabella no other consolation than an exhortation to patience. The Lady Arabella saw that she had nothing to hope from the countess ; and so fully convinced of this was she, that she abandoned the intention she had formed of beseeching the old lady to aid her escape to France, or elsewhere, where she might remain hidden until the king could be brought to confirm her marriage.

It·was this conversation between the ladies that the old soldier's arrival had interrupted.

The word which he had whispered had been used as a signal between her husband and herself in all their secret interviews, and she therefore knew that the letter which had been put into her hand was from him. When she reached her chamber the force of her emotions almost took from her the power of action. She sunk into a chair, and the letter lay for some moments on the table before her ere she could summon resolution to break the seal. At length, overcoming, by a violent effort, the sensations which almost paralysed her, she broke the seal, and learnt from the epistle intelligence which turned all her fears to joy—the intelligence that her husband had escaped from his imprisonment in the Tower.

She loved with all the intensity of a first passion, and it is the property of that sentiment to neutralize every selfish feeling. All remembrance of herself and of her own fate had been abandoned; but for that of her husband, and for the peril in which she, with too much reason, believed his life to be, she had been sick with apprehension. When she learnt that he was safe she threw down the letter, and, falling upon her knees, poured forth an incoherent rhapsody of thanks to Heaven for having granted the prayer she had hourly repeated. A flood of tears relieved her heart, which was ready to burst with its various emotions, and she soon regained composure enough to finish reading the letter, the sequel of which informed her of the particulars of Mr. Seymour's escape.

Having procured, by the assistance of some kind friends, who had never relaxed in their attempts to provide for his escape, the dress of a countryman, he had walked out of the Tower-gates behind a cart which had come in loaded with billets for fuel. He wrote, besides, that he had since gained the coast, and had procured a

véssel which would carry them to France, where
they might live in obscure, but happy, retirement.
He recommended her to place implicit confidence
in the bearer of the letter, who would furnish the
means for her escape, and who, notwithstanding
the meanness of his disguise, was a gentleman of
good family, and Mr. Seymour's old comrade.
His real appellation was Hugh Markham; and,
although he had so successfully imitated the
weakness of old age and the suffering of poverty,
he was in fact neither old nor poor, but one who,
to serve a friend in time of need, would have
affronted the most terrific dangers.

He was one of those men who seem to be possessed with an innate love of wandering. Like all
such persons, he was fond of enterprise; but it
was only for the sake of the excitement which it
afforded to his mental and physical energies.
This had led him into fights and scrapes innume-
rable, and all those adventures which other men
think misfortunes, but which were to him mere
amusement. He was now about the age of eight-
and-thirty. He had served in several campaigns
- abroad, as well under the English banners as
under the foreign potentates; and, although he
had always distinguished himself by his valour
and conduct, he could never be induced, by offers
of promotion, or by the honours which had been
conferred on him, to attach himself for a length of
time to any particular interest. He had, however,·

never drawn his sword but in the cause of truth
and liberty, so far as they could be discovered in
the wars which then filled Europe ; and, vagabond as he was, he was known to be as firm and
as cautious, where those qualities were necessary
for the success of the cause he had undertaken,
as he was fickle and unsettled in moments of repose or idleness. The alacrity with which he
had flown to Seymour's aid, as soon as he heard
of his danger, had shown the fervour of his friend-
ship, and he was luckily enabled to complete his
good offices by lending him a vessel. This was
a ship which Markham had manned with a few
English sailors, and in which he had been cruis-
ing about the Mediterranean, solely for the
amusement of encountering Turkish and Alge-
rine ships, which he attacked and beat without
mercy whenever he could.

With the ardour of a young and loving girl, the
Lady Arabella thought, upon reading her husband's letter, that all the obstacles which stood
in the way of her happiness were at once removed.
Her busy imagination pictured rapidly and glow-
ingly the bliss she should enjoy with her Seymour
in some remote spot, where, forgetting, and forgotten by, the world, they should live only for themselves. To quit the court and all its splendours
would never have cost her a great sacrifice ; but,
now that she loved, and that the opposition which
she had met with had roused all the energies of her

pure mind, she could, without a moment's pause, have renounced all that the world contained for her love and for her lover. It, however, soon occurred to her that she had overlooked the difficulties which might attend her attempt to escape ; and she then thought of the supposed old soldier, who was to aid and to accompany her. She had no secrets from her own servant, Bridget—a faithful girl, who had attended her from her childhood. The Countess of Salisbury was, luckily, shut up in her oratory ; and Bridget was therefore enabled, with little difficulty, to introduce the soldier to a small ante-chamber adjoining the Lady Arabella's room.

The mendicant—or Markham, as he shall in future be called—advanced to the lady with an upright and quick gait, which little resembled the posture he had assumed in his character of a beggar.

"Fair lady," he said, "we have no time to spend in ceremony ; every thing depends upon the promptness with which we arrange for your escape. To-morrow, as I learn, it will be too late to attempt it."

"Oh, let us go instantly," said Lady Arabella.

"If we could do so with safety, it were well," replied Markham ; "but we must use a little caution. In this packet," he said, loosening his wallet from his shoulders, and throwing it on the ground, "I have a perfect disguise for you :

when you retire for the night, instead of going to
bed, dress yourself, and be in readiness to set off
as soon as the time shall serve."

" But where is my husband ?" asked the lady.

" I do not know exactly the spot, but he 'will
be waiting our arrival : he knows our ship ; and,
although he dare not stay long in any one place,
he will join us in the river : perhaps, even now,
he is on board."

" And you," said the Lady Arabella, " who
are you ? But the question is needless, for my
husband says I may trust you."

" It is, nevertheless, fit that you should know,
lady," said Markham ; " and now I have before
me as happy an opportunity of giving myself a
good character as a man so much in need of one
as I am could desire : but you shall have nothing
save the truth. I am, madam, a very unlucky,
but, as far as I know myself, a tolerably honest
fellow, who have been in scrapes of one sort or
another from the hour in which I was born to
the present time. I have been a wild youngster ;
I have been a hard-fighting soldier ; and, latterly,
I have been a sailor. There is now lying in the
river as pretty a pinnace, manned by a dozen of
as honest fellows, as your ladyship would desire to
look upon; in which I mean to carry you and
your husband into the port of Calais. Will Seymour and I have been friends since we were boys ;
and, when I heard of his being made a prisoner

in the Tower, I hastened to London to rescue him. Happily I have succeeded in that, and, as his letter has told you, he is free. The next concern is to carry you out of the durance in which I find you. Hitherto all has gone on well, thanks to the credulity of the good countess, who believed a story which, if told by my poor father, had been near the truth, for it was to him that the Lord Mountchensy gave the ring. It would be unwise to prolong this conversation, lest any suspicions should arise which might be fatal to our plans. You must secure me a night's lodging, and leave the rest to our good stars and our own industry. Farewell, madam! keep up your courage, and show yourself in spirit, as you are in all womanly beauty, the worthy bride of the gallant Seymour." As he spoke he kissed the lady's hand with a courtly air, and, having made a low bow, he resumed the hobbling gait of the lame soldier, and crawled out of the room.

With the assistance of Bridget the Lady Arabella concealed the packet which Markham had left, and then went down stairs to join the countess.

She had no difficulty in persuading the old lady to order that her brother's ancient follower should be provided with a lodging. When the butler entered, and his lady made known her pleasure on this head, the old servant, with a familiarity which his age and his long services allowed, expressed his satisfaction at her determination.

" It would do your ladyship's heart good," said he, " to hear him tell the story of the battle of Zutphen. He has made all the servants in the hall laugh and cry by turns, ever since he has been there, with the sad and merry tales that he has been telling them."

" I am glad, good Ambrose," said her ladyship, " to hear they are amused."

" Yes, and if it please your ladyship, he is, for a soldier, as sensible a man as ever I saw. He says that your ladyship's ale is better than any in all Flanders ; and I warrant me I was proud to hear one who has travelled say so much."

Ambrose's simplicity was always quite as amusing as his fidelity was praiseworthy ; and the Lady Arabella, whose spirits were wonderfully raised by the news she had lately received, feared she should laugh outright at this description of Mr. Markham, who, it seemed, was playing his part to admiration in the servants' hall. She therefore dismissed Ambrose, who was not sorry to join his agreeable companion.

" I have been thinking, my love," said the countess to Lady Arabella, " of some means by which we may provide for this poor soldier. It is shocking to think that, at his time of life, he has not a place to put his head in."

" I think, my lady," said Bridget, " that he seems fond of a wandering life."

" Yes, child," said her ladyship ; " but his age

and infirmities will prevent his indulging that inclination much longer. I think of giving him
the rooms over the stable : he will be of little
use ; but he may find a corner in the kitchen
where he will be protected from want; and, as
he is already a favorite with the servants, there
will be no difficulty about it."

" Well, my lady," said Bridget, " I think he
is so much of a wanderer, that, if you were to
give him a place to dwell in to-night, he would
leave it before the morning." Bridget, as she
said this, looked archly at her mistress, who sat
on thorns lest the countess's suspicions should
be awakened.

The good old lady, however, dreamt of no imposition, and went on to answer Bridget. " My
good girl," she said, " if we let such doubts as
you express stand in the way, we should never
attempt to do a good office, lest it should be
ungratefully received."

" And really," said Lady Arabella, " I have a
much better opinion of the old soldier than
Bridget seems to have adopted."

The conversation was then turned to another
subject; and, night having arrived, the whole
household retired to bed, the supposed soldier
being lodged, to his great joy, in a sort of loft
over the offices, and away from the house.

When the Lady Arabella got into her chamber,
she put on, with the aid of Bridget, the clothes

which Mr. Markham had brought; and in a short
time her disguise was so completely effected,
that, as far as merely external appearance was
concerned, it would have been impossible to
see through it.

Her long auburn ringlets were gathered up into
a knot, and obscured under a great French peri-
wig, the locks of which hung down upon her
shoulders. She put on a man's doublet, with a
broad lace collar, and a pair of large trunk hose,
made in what was then thought the *ultra* style of
dandyism, but which were admirably adapted for
a lady's disguise, because they could contain the
whole of her ordinary dress. A pair of russet
boots, with red tops, were fastened by a strap to
the hose; and a small rapier, buckled to her side,
gave her the appearance of as arrant a young
coxcomb as ever lounged in St. Paul's church—
then the Bond Street, or perhaps, rather, the
Burlington Arcade, of the metropolis.

The clock had just struck three, when Bridget,
who was on the watch, heard the noise of a small
pebble striking against the casement. She looked
out and saw Markham, who was so much altered
that she could not have known him but by his voice,
and because she was in a great measure prepared
for the alteration. He wore a plain riding-dress,
and looked, as he was, a gentleman. The window
was but a short distance from the ground; and
by means of a garden ladder, which Markham

brought, the Lady Arabella safely descended, having bidden farewell to Bridget, whose cheerfulness was not proof against parting with her beloved mistress.

The day had scarcely dawned, but there was quite light enough for the fugitives to discern the road they had to take. Markham, in silence, and with the greatest caution, led the trembling Lady Arabella across the lawn, and, lifting her upon the garden wall, he leaped over it himself, and helped her down on the other side.

" Now, courage, lady," he said, " and a brisk walk of a quarter of an hour will bring us to the spot where I have horses waiting. I dared not suffer them to be led any nearer, lest they might excite suspicion."

The lady felt weak and ill. She had not been to bed during the night, and the agitation of the preceding day had acted powerfully upon a frame not of the most robust description. She faltered, and, after several ineffectual efforts to proceed, was obliged to request Markham to stop. A few minutes' rest recovered her; and with the help of Markham, who almost carried her, they reached a small public house on the road to London, where he had a servant and horses.

The beasts were brought out immediately, and Lady Arabella's weakness was now so apparent, that it was with difficulty she could mount her.

horse. The hostler, who held the stirrup for her, declared he thought the young gentleman would never be able to reach London; and he was cracking some jokes, rather more coarse than new, about the effeminacy of the young men of the age, when a smart stroke from Markham's riding-whip put a stop to his witticisms. The fellow rubbed his shoulders, but said nothing; for the noble which was tossed to him reconciled him to the disgrace, if there was any, and the pain, of which there was not much.

The travellers proceeded, and the motion of riding soon brought the blood into Lady Arabella's cheeks. Markham was not wanting in endeavours to keep up her spirits, and he succeeded so well that they reached Blackwall without any further delay. Here Markham found his boat's crew waiting for him; and, without staying a moment, they put off for his pinnace, which had sailed down the river. They reached her just below Gravesend, and the Lady Arabella found the solace and reward of all her pain and anxiety in the arms of her adoring husband, who was there waiting for her.

Their happiness at finding each other again, and in freedom, so engrossed their minds, that all apprehension of future danger was forgotten. Markham, whose generous temper made him keenly enjoy the happiness of those who were

dear to him, was perfectly delighted at the success of his plan, and at the joy which he saw
painted in the faces of his friends.

He knew that they had every thing to fear
from a pursuit, and therefore gave orders for
sailing without a moment's delay. The wind,
however, was slack, and not very favorable.
They crept slowly down the river, and on the
following morning only found themselves entering the Channel. It was resolved to sail for
Calais, and Markham had laid his course for that
port, which he hoped to make in a few hours,
when one of the men gave notice that an armed
pinnace was gaining upon them. Markham
knew very well that, if they were taken, they
should all be imprisoned. He feared that his
friend might lose his head ; and that he would be
deprived, in any event, of his wife and his freedom, was quite certain. He therefore resolved to
resist, in the best way he could, the attack ; and
to complete the escape, which he had hitherto
managed so successfully, if it should be possible.
He called Seymour upon deck ; and the Lady
Arabella, who apprehended some danger, came
with him, resolved to brave every peril with her
husband. The vessel in pursuit continued to
gain upon them, and, being now within reach o
their guns, a shot was fired as a signal to Markham to bring-to. He, however, stood on ; and,
having made every preparation for the engage-

ment,.which he saw he could not avoid, he persuaded Lady Arabella to go below. She at
length acceded to his and to her husband's entreaties. Several other shots were now fired from
the pursuers' vessel, and returned by Markham's
crew; who were always more willing to fight (no
matter in what cause) than to fly, and who, under
his command, were almost sure to have their
desires in this respect gratified. Still the ships
neared, and at length they lay almost alongside of
each other. The commander of the other vessel
called out to Markham, and bade him strike, and
deliver up the Lady Arabella Stuart and Mr.
Seymour, if they were in his ship. To this Markham only replied with another broadside. He
soon, however, discovered that there was little
chance of escape, as the other vessel had, at
least, four times the number of men that were on
board his own ship, and a much greater weight
of metal. But it was now too late to retreat;
and, supported by Seymour, who was roused to
desperation by the strait to which he was reduced, they fought with all that fury which the
hopelessness of their situation inspired.

This could not last long; the greater part of
the crew was soon killed, and not a man remained unwounded. The assailants poured in
on all sides, while Markham and Seymour, back
to back, repelled the numbers who attacked them,
and remained bravely at bay. At length a shot

from a pistol struck Seymour in the head, and he fell dead upon the deck. Markham, seeing his friend fall, collected, as it seemed, the whole of his force into one blow, and, rushing at the fellow by whom the pistol had been fired, he cleft him nearly asunder. This was the last act of his life; half a dozen weapons were plunged into his body at the same instant, and he fell beside his friend, their hearts' blood flowing in a mingled stream.

Just at this moment a shriek, so loud and full of woe that it arrested the frightful and maddening strife that was raging around, burst upon the ears of the combatants. It proceeded from the Lady Arabella, whose anxiety for her husband's life had prevented her from remaining below, and who had reached the deck only in time to see him fall. She rushed through the fighting crowd, who, astonished at her sudden appearance, made way for her, and threw herself upon Seymour's dead body, where nature, unable to endure the agony of that moment, sunk under it, and she fainted. All such assistance as the captain of the king's vessel could bestow was given with the utmost promptitude and humanity; for, although he was one of those men who would do whatever was prescribed to him in the shape of a duty, he was a well-disposed person, and felt bitterly for the sorrows of which he had been unwittingly the instrument.

The fall of Markham of course put an end to
the fight. The captain took possession of the
pinnace, and, steering, according to his instruc-
tions, for some obscure place, he landed at the
Reculvers. The encroachments of the sea have
nearly destroyed even the proof that this place
once existed; but, at the time to which our
history relates, it was a village inhabited by fish-
ermen. He had the Lady Arabella, who still
remained insensible, carried on shore; and,
placing her under proper medical care, ordered
her to be conveyed to London. He then fulfilled
the remainder of his directions, in which the probability of Seymour's being killed rather than
his surrender had been anticipated, by causing
the bodies of both the heroes to be buried in
the humble churchyard of the village.

To avoid the odium which must necessarily
attach to so cruel an instance of oppression, a
report was industriously circulated that Mr. Seymour had got away by another ship, and had
reached Calais in safety. This was universally
believed; for the sailors on board the king's pinnace knew nothing of his person, and the few
who remained of Markham's crew were never
suffered to go on shore.

The Lady Arabella was brought by slow
journeys to London, and committed a prisoner to
the Tower. The care of her medical attendants,
and her youth, restored her to existence; but her

reason had fled for ever. She lingered for some time in a state of pitiable distraction, and at length ended her life of woe, not without well-grounded suspicion that it had been shortened by poison.

The care which was taken to conceal all the facts of this sad history will account for the obscurity which has always enveloped it, and which perhaps, up to the present moment, has prevented the proper exposition of

"A tale so tender and so true."

IT was now my turn, in obedience to the order of the lots, to tell a story. Of all difficult things, this was to me the most so. Although there are few people who can beat me at listening to a story, I am, I must needs confess, wholly incapable either of inventing one myself, or of relating those invented by others. I knew that these excuses, powerful and sufficient as they must be to all reasonable persons, would not be received by the company which, upon this occasion, I was bound to obey; and I felt, besides, that there was something unfair, if not ungrateful, in sitting to hear the tales of others, and making no attempt to help on the amusement by some exertions of my own. Necessity, however—that imperious power to which all human affairs bow— would have it so. If I had been to be hanged for lack of a story, I must have entertained my fate as decently as I could; and, even by dying, I should only have furnished a subject for somebody else to tell " the lamentable tale of me." *Ou il n'y a rien le roi perd ses droits ;* and it was inevitable that my good grandmother and her guests were to go without the story which they had a right to claim from me. I wished, however, to make the disappointment as palatable to them, and as little discreditable to myself, as, under the embarrassing circumstances which surrounded me, might be possible. In order to effect this I had but one measure to adopt: it was that of becoming a delator, or informer, against the good old lady, my grandmother, and, by procuring her to be condemned to tell another story, thus consume all the time that remained of the evening. If this could be effected I knew that I was safe, because, on the following day, I was to depart, and should thus evade altogether the conditions, which I regretted I could not fulfil. With a multitude of blushes, and much unfeigned shame, I confess that it was an exceedingly ungracious thing to do; but I beseech the readers who will be ready to censure me to pause for a moment, and that, before they give vent to their angry reproaches, they will fancy themselves in my situation; and then, if they cannot excuse and forgive me, I shall be sorry for them and for myself.

I knew that my grandmother had almost, if not wholly, translated her tale from a little French story of M. Löeve Weimars; and I also knew that her guests would be so glad to have a second story from her, that they would readily agree, without strictly examining the justice of the matter, that she had infringed upon the conditions to which we had all agreed. She had always a store of tales ready, so that it could not be difficult for her to produce one upon the present occasion. My resolution being thus taken, I waited until the remarks which had been made upon Elizabeth's story were at an end.

When I was called upon to begin, I said that I was perfectly ready to obey, but that I felt it my duty first to submit to the company a scruple which existed in my mind, and without the removal of which I could not comfortably or conscientiously proceed.

" Let us hear his scruple, by all means," said Harry Beville with a sneer, by which he implied a doubt of my sincerity ; and, as it is a case of conscience too, we are happy in having Mr. Evelyn present, who is more competent to decide it than some of us.

" You do well to say some of us," replied I; " for to submit a case of conscience to a lawyer would be like asking for a blind man's opinion of colours. And yet, Harry, as your reformado thief makes always your best gaoler, I think you, who have once been condemned in an offence like that which I have now to denounce, will be convinced of the necessity of bringing the offender to justice. I shall look to you for supporting my accusation."

" I postpone my vengeance," said Harry, "until I shall have heard your story. In the mean time let us hear this mysterious secret which burdens your tender conscience."

"It is nothing more than this," I said : " my grandmother's story was unquestionably a very good one ; but—I grieve while I speak this—it was a translation."

" Ha !" said Harry, with great solemnity, " a grave offence indeed ! What says the culprit ?"

" I do confess," replied my grandmother, "it is a translation ; but then it is within the conditions to which we agreed."

" Nay," said Harry, " I have, as Mr. Prate, the special pleader, would say, a case in point. I was myself convicted, and suffered the punishment which my crime was supposed to deserve. You concurred in that sentence ; and you, therefore, of all people, have the least right to object against the laws which you made and enforced. It is true I think the punishment was an unjust one ; but for that very reason it is that I don't like to be the only victim to its severity. With all the veneration which I owe to you, and with all the pity I feel for your fate, I am compelled to say I think you must tell another story ; and I forbear to add to your punishment by reminding you of the severity which you exercised towards me."

" But I will appeal," said my grandmother, " from so unrighteous a decision. Your case and mine were wholly different : you very lazily read

a story out of a book which is in print, and well
known, at least to unprofitable students like
yourself. I, on the contrary, have taken the
pains to transcribe mine fairly—to make such
alterations in the style and language as I thought
expedient. To what extent those alterations have
been improvements it does not become me to
say; but I submit that they do entitle me to an
exception from the severely literal construction
of the law, which you, Harry, would have me
to bow to."

"Then I call for judgment," said Harry; and
he proceeded, with a gravity worthy of the subject, to collect the opinions of the persons present. They were all, as might be guessed, unanimous in their opinion that my grandmother
ought to tell another story. The old lady pro-
tested, argued, endeavored to persuade; but in
vain—her judges were predisposed to sentence
her, and nothing could divert them from their
intention.

"Well," said the old lady at length, "since I
must obey, I will; but still I deny the justice of
the sentence to which I submit. I shall take my
revenge of you by reading you one of the longest
stories I have" (this was most agreeable news
to me); "and I will, at least, try your patience,
if I should not succeed in amusing you. This
tale is, certainly, no translation; and I beg you
distinctly to understand, before I begin, that, with

all its faults and its merits (if merit it possesses), it is mine. Perhaps, however," she said, turning to me, " you will discover that for some of the descriptions I am indebted to the chronicles of the times to which my tale relates; wherefore, in order to take from you, and from critics like you, the merit of so ingenious a discovery, I publicly avow that, in the account of the tournaments and the combat, I have kept in view the narrations of the honest, valiant, and veracious Messire Olivier de la Marche, the faithful servant of the illustrious house of Burgundy."

The old lady then produced from her writing-desk a manuscript, and read the following tale.

THE KNIGHT AND THE DISOUR.

𝔐𝔶 𝔊𝔯𝔞𝔫𝔡𝔪𝔬𝔱𝔥𝔢𝔯'𝔰 𝔰𝔢𝔠𝔬𝔫𝔡 𝔗𝔞𝔩𝔢.

Der verworrene Knäuel unsers Schicksals ist aufgelöst.

SCHILLER.

Erano in corte tutti i paladini,
Perchè la festa fusse più fornita :
Eran venuti i lontani e i vicini ;

*　　*　　*　　*

E già vicino il giorno era nel quale
Si dovea la gran festa cominciare.

ORLANDO INNAMORATO.

THE KNIGHT AND THE DISOUR.

On the road-side, at about three leagues distant from the ancient and splendid city of Ghent, stood a small, but convenient, house of entertainment. A hieroglyphic painting over the door told to such of the beholders as could decipher it that the place was known by the sign of the "Leathern Bottle." Beneath this device were two lines, written in marvellously bad Flemish, to the following effect—

> " I wish in heaven his soul may dwell
> That first invented the leathern bottel ;"

and on each side of the door was also inscribed a notification that travellers might be supplied with wine and beer, and their horses with hay and corn.*

* It was upon this inn that the famous ballad was written, which was afterwards translated, and became so popular in England. Beautiful as this lyrical effusion is, in all its parts, the fol-

The " Leathern Bottel" was the chief, because it was the only, inn in the village to which it belonged. The host, Peter Badelin, was a man whom Nature seemed to have made as a sample for all publicans. He drank eternally; morning, noon, and night, he was at his cups; and he might have used Boniface's speech—" I have fed purely upon ale; I have ate my ale, drank my ale, and I always sleep upon ale ;" only substituting for ale, (which was not drunk in Flanders,) wine, and the beer of the country. Peter was not ashamed

lowing verse deserves most particularly to be rescued from the oblivion to which modern bad taste has consigned this favorite song of our forefathers. The poet, after examining the comparative merits of wooden cans, glasses, and silver flagons—to all of which he prefers the leather bottle, as the masterpiece of drinking-vessels—comes at last to "the handled pot."

> " What say you to the handled pot?
> No praise of mine shall be his lot;
> For, when a man and wife's at strife,
> (As many have been in their life,)
> They lay their hands upon it both,
> And break the same, although they're loth :
> But, woe to them shall bear the guilt !
> Between them both the liquor's spilt,
> For which they shall answer another day
> For casting their liquor so vainly away:
> But, if it had been leather-bottell'd,
> One might have tugged, the other have held ;
> Both might have tugged till their hearts should break,
> No harm the leather bottel could take.
>
> > Then I wish in heaven his soul may dwell
> > That first invented the leather bottel."

of his propensity to drink : he was wont to say, half praising and half apologizing for himself, "I live by the consumption of liquor; and I were an idle knave, indeed, not to set an example to my neighbours and customers, which they may follow to their own benefit and mine."

Next to his love of liquor, Peter insisted that loyalty was the predominant passion in his bosom. He had, he said, a devoted affection for Philip the Good, Duke of Burgundy, his sovereign and liege lord ; and he had been proving this, on the day when my tale begins, by drinking the duke's health, in the best liquor that his house afforded, from morning to night. The extraordinary impulse which his loyalty and his thirst had just now received grew from the near approach of the great festival of the Toison d'Or, which was, on the following morning, and for several succeeding days, to be held in Ghent, with a solemnity and splen- dour never before witnessed. Peter knew that all the world would make holiday on that occasion ; and he knew, too, that your holiday-makers are always a thirsty sort of folks : he therefore cal- culated, wisely enough, that a considerable quan- tity of such drink as he might find it difficult to get rid of at other times would now, under favour of the festival, be swallowed like so much nectar. For this it was that he drank the duke's health ; for this he wished, at the beginning of many a long draught, that the order of the

Golden Fleece might extend its glories to the
furthest corner of the world. He had too great a
reverence for these toasts to drink them in any
but his best wine;—the other, he said, would soon
go off, and be liked quite as well by the rustics
who were doomed to swallow it.

The night had closed in, and Peter, whose
natural dulness even drunkenness could not
much increase, was sitting in a large wooden
chair by the fire-side in his kitchen, the only
room of reception in his inn. He had driven a
roaring trade all day long with the grooms and
serving-men, and waggoners, who were on their
way to Ghent, and who, according to the good
Catholic custom of such people, never passed a
house where there was a sign or a promise of
good liquor without stopping to pay their devotions to the saint within. Peter was half dreaming and half reflecting, as well as his muddy
brain was capable of any mental operation, on
the delights of his occupation, which enabled him
to get money and to get drunk at the same time ;
and he had come to the sound conclusion, that, of
all the trades in the world, there was none like
that of an innkeeper.

He was too much busied in his own contemplations to attend to what was passing around
him. His wife, a fat comely dame, to whose
thrift and good management Peter was mainly
indebted for the means of indulging his favorite

propensity, sate on the opposite side of the fire, and reposed from the labours of the day, while she listened to a tale which was told by one of the two guests who alone remained of all the noisy and numerous company which had thronged the room half an hour before.

One of them was a mendicant friar. The other was a spare man, of the middle height, in whose appearance there was something at once singular and prepossessing. He wore a doublet and hose of dark cloth, which, although its texture was coarse, was carefully fashioned after the reigning mode. A large cloak, with sleeves of the same materials, but lined with crimson serge, and which he wore when he was out of doors, lay on the chair he sat in. A short broad dagger, or, as it was then called, a basilard, the hilt of which was of a more costly description than suited the other parts of his external appointments, was buckled at his waist. His face appeared to have been once handsome; but Time, who had been at work upon it for somewhat more than fifty years, had left several furrows and marks, that told too plainly of his progress. The guest's large black eyes, which sparkled and rolled about as he spoke, gave an expression of wildness to his countenance. His nose was long and pointed; and his chin, which was of the same character, was furnished with a small black curling beard. The fore part of his head was bald, and

the crisp curling hair which remained at the
back of it was slightly grizzled.

Having described his person, it remains to say
who he was. He was, then, by profession, a
Disour, or, Story-teller, in the exercise of which
vocation he wandered about, visiting the halls
and castles of the various noblemen of this and
the adjoining country of France, and was every
where a welcome guest.

Before the revival of letters and the diffusion
of learning such persons were frequently to be
found, and were esteemed in proportion to the
excellence and ingenuity of their stories. In
all ages of the world its inhabitants have been
fond of listening to tales : no one is proof against
the charms of narrative ; and, besides the proof
which we are now giving, in our own persons,
that the taste for them is not lost, it may be
recollected that, in the eastern and in all other
nations where literary acquirements are even now
rare, there are still to be found Disours, or men
who gain their subsistence by telling tales for
the amusement of others. To me, I must confess,
it seems a more legitimate means of earning a
living than twenty others which I could, but
need not, mention ;—but perhaps I am partial.

In England, and in these times, the circulating
libraries have taken the place of the professional
story-tellers, and feed that appetite for novelties
and curious adventures which still exists, and

probably will always continue. At the period
of our history an accomplished Disour was in
himself a circulating library, and supplied his
customers with tales of every description, according either to their own particular choice, or
selected by him with a view to the taste and
capacity of his hearers, of which he was always
the best judge.

He had one advantage, too, which the actual
circulating libraries do not possess ;—his novels
were always to be had. None of his clients were
reduced to exercise their patience or their good
temper while some antiquated spinster, " with
spectacles on nose," spelt slowly over every word
of a story which they wished and waited to
gallop through. His listeners, too, never met
with that scarcely less afflicting trial, which we
must all of us have undergone, on finding that
the most interesting part of a tale had been torn
out, perhaps by some sentimental lady's maid,
who had relentlessly converted it into curl-
papers; perhaps by some literate shoemaker,
who had coolly lighted his pipe with it. They
never were annoyed by the short but pungent
criticisms, the sympathetic aspirations, the eru-
dite annotations, with which the margins of a
well-read circulating library novel are always
filled. If the Disour's hearers did not like his
tale—which, by the way, rarely happened, for

they were not critical—they at least never interrupted him in the middle of it with an exclama-
tion of " Execrable stuff!" or the more cutting
and personal remark of " The author is a fool!"
While he was describing some interesting scene,
in which a lover urged his passion to an obdu-
rate mistress, although, perchance, some gentle
swain, who might be struck with the resemblance
of the fictitious woes to his own, would venture
to sigh eloquently in his neighbouring fair one's
ear, to tread upon her toes, or to practise some
such allowable means for engaging her attention,
he never would think of bawling out, loud enough
to be heard through all the rooms in the house,
(and writing in the margin of a public book is,
in the comparison I have drawn, much the same
thing,) " Thus, Seraphina Sims, do I feel for
you!"—or "When Miss Jenkins reads this, may
she pity the heart-broken Lothario!"   And yet
all these inconveniences do happen through
the medium of circulating libraries; so that I
am brought to conclude, upon summing up the
advantages and disadvantages on the side of the
middle ages and of our own, that, as far as the
amusement derived from story-tellling is concerned, the Disours were much to be preferred to
the libraries.

The Disour of whom my tale is now to tell
was one of the most accomplished of his tribe:

he knew, perhaps, all the stories that had ever been written, said, or sung, in the existing languages of the Continent. From the glorious and veracious histories of King Arthur and the Knights of his Round Table, down to the more recent productions of the great Boccaccio and his imitators, he was as familiar with all of them as a workman with his tools. He knew, too, all the best songs of the most famous Provençal troubadours, and the *Fabliaux*, and *Lais*, and *Contes*, of his own countrymen. He had himself a ready and neat invention, which enabled him occasionally to vary the incidents of his tales and poems, so as to suit the circumstances of his hearers or the place in which he happened to be; and this, with the agreeable manner of his relating them, made him a great and deserved favorite.

It would have been easy for him at any time to quit the wandering life he led, and to establish himself as a regular and welcome inmate of many a noble castle; but he prized his liberty too well to put on the chains of servitude, however brightly they might be gilded. He therefore travelled about, as free as the wind, whithersoever he listed; sometimes taking up his abode in a peasant's hut—sometimes in a prince's hall—sometimes in a little inn, like that in which he was now found—sometimes in a monastery—sometimes in the open air, with the bands of

wandering minstrels and jongleurs who roamed
about the country. In all these places he was
equally welcome, his wit and his good spirits
never failing him ;—freely dispensing, and sharing
with any one who wanted it, the gold he got
easily ; and, when his purse was emptied, never
caring a straw how it should be filled again.

Most people had a notion that he was crazy;
and they were probably right, for his conduct
seemed to be governed by no settled principle
except that of pursuing his own amusement, and,
by the way, contributing, with the full extent of
his power, to that of others. He was, however,
no more mad than all those men to whom their
genius seems to have assigned one place while
their destiny casts them into another ; and
whose lives are passed, between those two influ-
ences, in a kind of shuttlecock game, which is
apt to make the brain giddy. He was not more—
nor perhaps less—mad than Tasso ; but his good
temper and love of mirth had kept him out
of a lunatic hospital.

His talents had procured him the favour and
the society of persons of the highest rank. His
manners had become insensibly polished, and his
taste refined, by the usages of high life ; while his
fortunes remained as low as ever. He was the companion of princes, but—he was the son of a tailor!
He had been introduced to a new world—a paradise in which he knew he could never hope to

dwell; and, although this reflection sometimes gave him pain, and produced a certain waywardness in his conduct, it did not make him wretched. There was still one region, of which he felt not merely a citizen, but in which he might reign a sovereign—the world of his own imagination. In this he sought and found his greatest happiness. For the rest, he flitted through his existence like a summer butterfly, alighting wherever his fancy directed him ; and, whether it happened to be on weed or on flower, carrying his own means of enjoyment along with him.

At the request of the good old lady he had been telling her a story. She stipulated for a tale of chivalry, and he selected for her one— perhaps the only one which even his extensive stories contained—in which, at the same time that it related to one of the chief flowers of knighthood, there was a dash of comicality well suited to what he rightly guessed must be her taste in such matters.

He related the early part of the romance of the valiant Perceval de Galles, one of the Knights of the Round Table, and the achiever of the perilous adventures of the Saint Greal. The whole of the romance would have been far too long for the occasion ; and the latter parts of it, as they relate wholly to affairs of chivalry, would not, perhaps, have been so amusing to the old woman as that which the Disour selected for her.

" The *Roman de Perceval*," said my grandmother, looking up from the manuscript which
she had been reading, " has shared the fate of
almost all its contemporaries, and has fallen into
total oblivion, its very existence being known
only to persons who are a little infected with
the antiquarian mania, of which number I must
confess myself to be one. It is among the most
rare of all the chivalrous romances : I believe
there is not a copy of it extant in England,
although there are some metrical versions of parts
of it in private libraries ; but these, as far as I
know them, are vastly inferior to the quaint prose
original. The copy which I have read is in the
Bibliotheque du Roi, at Paris, with many other
treasures of a similar description. In one respect
this romance is distinguished from all others of
its kind ; it attempts—and, as I think, with
considerable success—to give a humorous description of the entrance of the hero—a raw boy,
wholly unacquainted with the forms of society—
into the world, and to the practice of chivalry.
He is the last and only son of his mother, whose
husband, and other children, have fallen in battle.
After this catastrophe she retired to a remote
part of Wales, where Perceval was bred up in
utter ignorance of every thing which became his
rank and his warlike descent. The accidental
sight of some knights in a forest awakes a passion for arms, which seems to have been innate ;

and he leaves his home to go to the court of King Arthur, where he claims to be knighted. The bluntness and rusticity of his manners are very whimsically described ; and the contrast which they present to the nobility and valour.of his mind, and to the customs of the courtiers, gives a charm to the relation which none of the other romances possess. It gives also a very curious picture of the state of society in the palaces of kings at that day. I might here introduce a translation of some of the extracts which I made from the very rare copy of the romance which, as I have told you, I saw at Paris, but that I am resolved not again to incur the charge of having infringed the supposed conditions of our sport. Begging pardon, then, for this digression, I resume."

When the Disour had finished his tale the old woman thanked him over and over again, and set about expressing her gratitude in a very substantial manner, by preparing a bowl of mortified clary for the purpose of moistening the storyteller's throat after his exertion.

The host, who had slept soundly during the latter part of the tale, waked as soon as the lulling sound of the words had ceased, and, shaking his ears, he swore roundly that it was the best tale he had ever heard.

" A tale !" cried the Disour ; " it was no tale, man—it was a song."

" Nay, by my holidame," said the host, " it was a tale ; and, if I would, I could tell thee all that it was about."

" And I tell thee, Master Peter, 'twas a song," rejoined the Disour ; " and a main good song too, by the mass !   An' thou hadst said 'twas as good a song as thou ever snoredst a bass to, I had believed thee."

" Thou art waggish, my merry master," replied the host ; and, as his dame was at the same moment handing to the Disour the bowl of spiced wine which she had been so carefully brewing, he adroitly intercepted it.   " But, tale or song," he continued, " here's to thee for the best hand at both that ever was born ;" and as he spoke he took a draught, which, if the earnestness of his good wishes might be estimated by the quantity of his potation, proved that he meant nothing less than what he said.

" I do verily think, thou spongy host," said the Disour, " that, if thou hadst been stone dead a whole week, the clinking of a pottle pot in thine ear would restore thee to life : nay, the drawing an old cork would be to thee like the archangel's trump.   Why, thou art not awake now ; thou art drinking in thy sleep, and the claret is thrown away upon thee.   I owe thee no ill will, Peter," he said, as he took the bowl ; " but, if I did, I would drink to thy eternal sobriety ; and I am sure that nothing worse than that could befall thee."

" No matter," said the host, willing enough to change the subject, " I say those days of chivalry were famous ones to live in. Marry, I should like to see the time come round again when a man might ride his horse into a king's banquetting hall, help himself to his dinner without even the trouble of dismounting, and then ride off again in quest of adventures."

" But they must have been parlous bad times for innkeepers like you, Peter," said the Disour, " since, for aught I can learn, the knights'-errant drank little wine, and even that little they never paid for. By St. Paul, if a host claimed his reckoning of them, he was like to get more buffets than besants."

" Do you think, then, Master Disour," said the host, affecting indignation, " that I have so little heart in my belly as to wish to be an innkeeper when all besides were knights ? No, marry; I would ride and fight, and foin, like Sir Perceval himself."

" Thou must starve first, and reduce thyself until thy girdle would go thrice round that tun of thine. But hast thou no fear of death, and of the fate worse than death, which befell some of the knights you so much admire ? Wouldst thou not be horribly afeard of being swallowed alive by a dragon, the inside of whose stomach was full of fire and brimstone, like the flaming mountain at Naples ? How couldst thou endure to be taken by some fell giant, and hung up for four-and-twenty years by the hair of thy head, in a dungeon under ground, with nothing to eat or to drink during all that time ?"

"Oh," said the host, "but your real pious knights fall into no such mischances : they always conquer the dragons, and cut off the giant's head—or heads, if he happens to have more than one."

"Then thou wouldst like only the sunny side of knight-errantry, my good host," replied the Disour. "By my faith thou art in the right, for the other would be all too cold for thee. But wail not, honest Toss-pot ! the days of chivalry are not all gone. There be many good knights now in harness, and neither less willing nor less able to do all such knightly feats as ever they of the Round Table achieved."

"By St. Thomas's bones but I should like to know who they be, and where a man may once see them !" cried the host doubtingly.

"Nay, then, thou hast but to leave thy cellar keys to our good dame—who, by the way, will take far better care of them than thou—and away to Ghent betimes to-morrow. There will be deeds done that shall rouse thy blood, and make thy heart quiver through all that mountain of fat which incases it. To-morrow the good and gallant Duke Philip holds a solemn tourney in honour of the Order of the Golden Fleece, to

which all the chivalry of his dominions, and
many a bold warrior from beyond their bounds,
will hasten. There will be prizes to fight for
which nothing but sheer manhood and knightly
craft can win."

"And the prizes shall be buts of malvoisie or
hogsheads of claret, as I reckon," said the
host.

"Thou addled brain of a tapster!" said the
Disour, with some indignation; "thou dreaming
drunkard, who thinkest of nothing but toping!
the prizes will be no such trash; but favours
from fair ladies, and honour among knights.
Would that one I wot of were here to join in the
press!"

"And who is he?" asked the friar, who had
sate silent during the whole of this conversation.

The monk was of the order of barefooted Carmelites, and had the reputation of keeping his
vows with much greatet strictness than many of
his brethren. The hostess had a great opinion of
his piety ; and it was, in fact, to receive her confession that he had, on this occasion, come to
the Leathern Bottle. He had been sitting by
the fire absorbed in his contemplations, and apparently not listening either to the tale, or to the
dialogue between the Disour and the host which
succeeded it. His cowl was thrown back from
his head, and displayed a set of mild benevolent
features, in which therew ere marks of gravity,

and even sadness, that might be guessed to have proceeded from woes which religion had calmed, but which no other power than death could erase.

The Disour, who knew him from having often met him in places to which the wandering habits of both had led them, turned to him, and answered his question by saying "I mean young Gui de Montaudun, good Father Philip—the Bastard de Montaudun, as he was commonly called."

"You mean the son of Ralph, the Baron of Montaudun, who died on the same day with the father of the present duke, and who gave up his last breath in my arms."

"I do mean the same," replied the Disour—"as gallant a youth as ever wore a weapon, and not less truly the son of the good Baron Ralph, whom he is as much like as one pea is like another; but, unhappily for him, some of the rites of the holy church were wanting to make his father and mother husband and wife."

"There were none of such rites wanting," said the friar earnestly. "His mother was a noble English lady, who had been taken prisoner by the French, and who was rescuèd from their hands by the Baron de Montaudun. They were wed, but the circumstances of the lady's captivity induced her to wish that her union should remain private until she had an opportunity of apprizing her relatives of the step she had táken, as she was not willing that they should first learn it from general rumour."

"How so, then?" asked the Disour : "'if that be true, he is heir to the broad barony of Montaudun."

"He is as truly the heir of his father," said the friar, "as you are of yours."

"Then nothing can be more legitimate than that, for all the world knows that my father was an honest tailor of Alez, and married seven years before I was born to my good mother, who was a damsel of the same town. Heaven rest their souls! But my heirship stood me in little stead ; for, excepting the *green bays* which some of my partial friends have assigned to me, I inherit nothing of my father's.* The late Baron Philip de Montaudun was supposed to die without any legitimate child, and the Bishop of Valenciennes took possession of his fair domain by virtue of his rank, as liege lord of the province, and for lack of heirs to the Baron. How do you reconcile this with what you have just told me?"

"This, my son," said the friar," is not the time, nor is the place fitting, for such explanations."

"By the mass you say wisely!" replied the

* In the early part of the fifteenth century (long before the birth of Mr. Joseph Miller) this was a newer joke than it may now seem to be.—PRINTER's DEVIL.

Disour; "but remember, holy father, if young Gui should ever come home again, I shall think you bound to make good your present assertions."

"What must be shall be," replied the friar gravely; " but, tell me, where is the youth now?"

" I had rather than a hundred nobles that I were able to tell you," replied the Disour. " I fear he is no longer among the living. The poor youth went to the wars against the Saracens, and, if he did not fall on the field at Varna, as is generally supposed, he is rotting in some dungeon. Alas! his fate has indeed been a melancholy one."

" How so?" asked the friar; " I thought that he was the adopted son of the Baron de Montacute. I am sure that but three years ago I saw him in the castle of that nobleman, the master of all around him, and as much beloved by the retainers of his lord as by the old baron himself."

" You say truly, holy father," replied the Disour: " he was then the very child of good luck, as it seemed: but, alas! this world is full of disappointments; and, when a man finds himself at the very topmost height of Fortune's wheel, he should only note it as a sign that his fall is about to commence. The Baron Philip de Montaudun, of whom we have been speaking, was the bosom friend, the brother in arms, and the counsellor, of the Duke John, the father of our pre-

sent sovereign prince. He was with him when
he received the treacherous invitation to meet
the then Dauphin, now the King of France, at
the bridge of Montereau. The pretence of the
meeting was, that all the causes of difference
might be arranged and removed, and that peace
might be restored to both countries, which had
already suffered enough under the evils of war.
The Baron de Montaudun exerted all his influence to persuade Duke John to accept the invitation, because he knew full well that it was just
then highly important for him to gain breathing-
time before he pursued his enterprises any further. The duke was willing enough to meet the
Dauphin ; but he would go, in spite of the advice
of his friends, accompanied only by a few noblemen of his court, his gallant spirit prompting
him to scorn the precautions which prudence
suggested. On this point the Baron de Montaudun found he could not prevail, and he set
out with his sovereign, without any of the troops
which commonly formed his guard. They crossed
the bridge of Montereau, and rode frankly into
the quarters of the Dauphin, who received them
with every demonstration of kindness, and expressed his delight that the duke had shown
himself thus willing to put an end to the existing contest. After a short conversation, the
greater part of which consisted of compliments
on the part of the Dauphin and his courtiers—

for the good duke was not much given to flatteries of any kind—he was reminded that, as the Dauphin represented the King of France, it was the duty of the duke, who held several important places as fiefs of the French crown, to pay his homage to him as his liege lord. Our noble duke, fearing no treachery, and always as willing to do what the laws of honour and the country required of him as he was resolute in maintaining his own and his people's rights, knelt without hesitation at the feet of the Dauphin's chair, and offered him his homage. At this moment, to the eternal disgrace of the Dauphin, now the King of France, a deed was done, the baseness and cruelty of which will for ever stain his scutcheon, even if it were a thousand times fairer than it is. While Duke John was kneeling at his feet, and the barons and knights who had accompanied them were, as their duty prompted them, assuming the same posture, they were set upon from behind by Tanneguy du Chastel, Guillaume Batailler, and a crew of as base, but less noted, caitiffs, who, with their swords and battle-axes, smote them as they knelt, and traitorously and murderously put them to death. None of those who accompanied the duke survived to tell the lamentable story of his fate, excepting one varlet, who stood at the end of the hall, and who, fleeing for his life, was not regarded in the confusion that ensued. Thus fell the flower of chivalry, the great and gallant Duke John of Burgundy! but, if the spirits of the departed can joy in the vengeance which is wreaked after their decease upon their assassins, his ghost, and those of the warriors who fell with him, have been amply regaled.   The present duke, at the time of his father's death, was only three-and-twenty years of age.   He immediately reassembled the troops, who had dispersed on receiving the fatal news; and, having collected a sufficient armament, he began that bloody war, as successful and advantageous on his part as it was fatal and disastrous to the French, which the peace of Arras has just put an end to;—a war in which he forced the murderer of his father to make the most abject submission, and to offer him the most solemn assurances—would they were true!—that he neither authorized nor consented to the late duke's death; but that it was perpetrated against his will, although in his presence, by men who were the sworn foes of the duke, and who were too powerful for the arm of Justice, shackled as it then was in France, to reach."

" You tell the tale truly," observed the friar: " I was present in the fatal hall at Montereau—not at the moment when the foul deed was done, but almost immediately afterwards.   The poor duke died instantly, so numerous and so fatal were the wounds which were showered upon him; but the baron lived for nearly half an hour longer.

By the mercy of some of his murderers a priest was sought for, at the request of the dying man; and, as I happened to be at hand, I hastened to his aid. I shall never forget the lamentable sight which presented itself as I entered the hall. The Dauphin and his treacherous followers had withdrawn, and left the bodies of their victims to such care as the serving men chose to pay them. The duke's corpse had been covered by some charitable hand with a large cloak, and was stretched upon the steps of the dais, where the Dauphin had been sitting to receive him. The others, with the exception of the Baron de Montaudun, lay just as they had been killed, in the very spots where the weapons of their foes had reached them, while the floor of the hall was slippery with their yet warm blood. An old man, a servant of the castle, and the Dauphin's jester, a half-witted fool, who had more pity in his heart than sense in his crazy brain, were holding up the dying warrior's head. I approached him;—he knew me well; and, having received his confession, made in great haste, but with full and pious sincerity, I administered to him the last sacrament of our holy religion, soon after which he gave up the ghost."

" And is it upon this confession, my good father," asked the Disour, " that you found your belief of the young Gui's being the true heir, as he is the true son, of the Baron de Montaudun?"

" Call it not belief, my son," replied the friar;

" I know, and in fitting season I will make known,
the truth of what I have now said. The Bastard,
as he is now called, is the true Baron de Montaudun."

" You read brave riddles, holy father," said
the Disour; " and, but that jesting suits not
your character nor your calling, I should fear
you were putting some trick upon us. If what
you say be sooth, I am glad to hear it, for the
old baron was my best friend and earliest patron,
and the youth I loved as well as if he were my
own child. But, alas! I fear, even if the golden
dream you tell of were to be realized, it would
avail him little, for the common report is that he
died on the bloody plain of Varna."

" I have heard that one of the few knights
who escaped from that slaughter says he saw
him made prisoner; and that the Bastard of
Burgundy, who loves him well, has sent to nego-
tiate his ransom with the Turk."

" God speed him," ejaculated the Disour, "and
send the young knight safely home again! although I hardly dare hope for such good fortune.
But prithee, holy father," he added, after a pause,
" how does it happen that this news which you
now tell me has remained so long locked up
in your breast? You must know full well that,
when the Baron de Montaudun died, the Bishop
of Valenciennes took possession of his lands for
the use of the church, for want of lawful heir,

and that the broad barony remains in his hands, and its rents in his coffers, to this day. The infant Bastard, as he was universally believed to be, was taken by the Baron de Montacute, and educated with as much care as if he had been a king's son. He became skilled in all knightly accomplishments; and at the age of eighteen, now seven years ago, he had won his spurs. He saved the life of the Lord Anthony, under circumstances of the greatest peril, in the field where he was knighted. Even if he should have escaped from the butchering Turks, and come safely home again, he will have dismal news to greet him. The baron has been dead now nearly twelve months: the young Lady Maud, his only daughter, and the heiress of his domain, is under the guardianship of the Bishop of Valenciennes ; and, although the baron intended, as I know, to have united her to Sir Gui on his return from the wars, I fear me the bishop has other views for her, and he is too powerful to be resisted by a friendless youth. But tell me, again, I beseech you, good father, why has your secret remained so long buried ?"

"The time opportune for its disclosure had not come, my son," replied the friar; "nor would you have known it now but that I am convinced of your attachment to the youth. The might of bad men may triumph for a season, but in the end justice will assuredly prevail." As he spoke thus the friar rose, and prepared to continue his journey.

The hostess besought him not to proceed at so late an hour ; but her persuasions were fruitless. The monk bestowed his benedictions on the inmates of the " Leathern Bottle," and, drawing his cowl over his face, he took the road towards Ghent.

As it was now nearly approaching midnight the Disour proposed to retire to rest. He was conducted to his chamber ; and the sleepy host, rousing himself, fastened his doors, and then went to bed to finish the slumbers which this necessary operation had for a short time interrupted.

The Disour found it difficult to get to sleep. The mysterious discourse of the friar still occupied his thoughts ; and, the more he reflected on it, the more he blamed himself for not having pressed him more closely to discover the reasons which induced him to assert that Gui de Montaudun was the lawful heir of the late baron. He felt warmly attached to the youth ; and, although he could not help fearing too much that he had fallen in battle, yet, as it was possible that he might be saved, he carefully encouraged the hope that he should again see him. After pondering upon the means of securing the friar's secret, so as to effect the restoration of Sir Gui to the barony of Montaudun, if it might be pos-

sible, he resolved to hasten betimes in the morning to Ghent, where he knew he should find the
Lord Anthony, a natural son and great favorite
of the Duke of Burgundy, and who was Sir Gui's
friend and patron, and, by the interposition of
his authority, to persuade the friar to impart all
that he knew on the subject. Having come to
this determination he soon fell asleep.

At an early hour on the following morning he
arose, and, quitting the " Leathern Bottle," he
hastened to Ghent as fast as an ambling pad
of the host's could carry him. As soon as he
arrived he went straight to the quarters of the
Bastard, in pursuance of his design. While he
was inquiring of the porter when his master
would be visible, and before he could obtain an
answer, the steward, who was an old acquaintance of his, had seen him, and came forward to
greet him.

" How now, my good gossip !" cried the old
man jestingly, " what dost thou here ? This is no
time for tale-telling. Away, man ! there will be
deeds done a quarter of an hour hence shall serve
thee to relate for a year to come."

" Have I not cautioned thee, many a time and
oft, good Gilbert," said the Disour, with an
affectation of gravity, " not to begin drinking
until after breakfast ? Fie ! fie ! thou art most
filthily debosht."

" Not so drunk," retorted the steward, " as he

who comes to look for Anthony of Burgundy in
his hall when there be warriors in harness," replied Gilbert.

" Leave thy riddles, good Drain-can, and tell
me where is the gallant Bastard, for, in sooth, I
would fain see and speak with him," said the
Disour.

" See him !" replied Gilbert ; " thou shalt, as
indeed every man, woman, and child, who has
eyes in Ghent, shall ; but, for speaking with him,
that is another guess matter : marry, he will bestow more strokes than words on all who shall
come in his way till the tournay is over. Let
thy gallant steed (which pray Heaven thou
didst not steal from some wandering tribe of
Bohemians !) be stabled, and come with me into
the buttery, where thou shalt break thy fast, and
then I will bestow thee in a place where thou
canst see the brave sights of the joust."

The Disour followed Gervase to the buttery,
which he found filled with some of the upper retainers of the Lord Anthony, to all of whom
he was known, and who received him with a
joyful acclamation.

" Save ye, my merry masters !" said he, taking
off his cap, and making a low reverence to the
jocund serving-men ; " still I see you keeping up
the good old custom of beginning the day with
a well-stored stomach. Marry, ye are right wise ;
for the uncertainty of affairs in this world is

such that no man can be sure of his dinner, and
therefore he does well to lay in a breakfast which
shall enable him to defy fate. We are all
born, but we know not when we shall die ; the
breakfast is before us, but our dinner may be
postponed until the day of doom."

" Here's to stop thy mouth, old friend," said
one of the fellows, handing him a plate bending
under the weighty portion of venison pasty which
he had heaped upon it.

" Gramercy !" said the Disour, as he took his
seat, and fell to with an appetite which did
honour to his entertainment. Several flasks of
excellent Rhenish washed down the repast ; and,
the gentlemen of the buttery having finished,
it was proposed that they should repair to the
jousts, which were now soon to begin.

" But, first," said Gervase, " I beseech thee to
tell, for the information of myself and my com-
rades, who, to their shame and mine I speak it, are
wofully ignorant of the matter, what was the first
origin of this order of the Toison d'Or, the festival of which our good duke is now celebrating,
and why it bears that name."

" I marvel that thou dost not know," replied
the Disour ; " but, since it is so, learn that the
order was instituted by our sovereign, out of the
devout zeal he had to undertake the deliver-
ance of the Holy Land from the Pagan swarms
which infest it. He established the order of the

Toison, that all the valorous nobles and knights
whom he should associate to himself in that ex-
pedition might bear an honorable distinction,
and be knit together in a chivalrous fellowship
for the pursuit of their common object. The
holy Saint Andrew was chosen to be the patron
of the order. There can be no knights of
the Toison who are knights of any other order,
excepting only emperors, kings, or sovereign
dukes. You all know that the habit of the
knights is an under garment of crimson velvet,
with a cloak of the same material, lined with
white silk, turned up on the left shoulder, and
richly embroidered round about with a border of
flames, fusils, and fleeces. They wear also on
their heads a hood of crimson velvet instead of a
cap. The collar of the order is wrought of golden
flames or fusils, with the toison hanging thereat.
This toison is a counterfeit resemblance of the
golden fleece of antiquity, which was achieved
by a worthy knight, called Jason, and his companions; or, as some churchmen the rather ex-
pound it, the fleece of Gideon, mentioned in holy
writ, which signifies ' Fidelity, or Justice uncor-
rupted.' This collar, or the toison, every knight
is bound to wear daily, or, failing, shall incur a
penalty; but if, by mishap, the collar do break,
it is permitted, for the mending thereof, that it
may be carried to a goldsmith; or, if any knight
travelling by the way shall fear to be robbed, he

may lay the collar aside. Yet it is not lawful to increase the quantity of the collar, nor add thereunto any stones or workmanship; and most unlawful is it to sell it or change it. Now, these things, my masters, I tell you, because it is fit that you should know them, your lord being a worthy and distinguished companion of the order."

"Many thanks to you, Master Disour," said Gervase; "thou givest all thou hast amongst us; and I dare swear that, if thy riches were in thy purse as they are in thy head, thou wouldst bestow them with as much free will. But, one favour more—tell us, who was that knight, Jason, thou didst mention?"

"He was a stalwart knight of antiquity," replied the Disour, "who went roaming about the world in a ship called Argo. He was a tall fellow, and had fifty companions of the like temper. They overcame enchantments, and did a thousand worthy feats, which it would take a long Christmas night to tell of. Thou must season thy curiosity touching Sir Jason, friend Gervase, till a more convenient time, when thou shalt know all about him. Now let us to the joust."

The company of the buttery then broke up, and the Disour and Gervase took the way to the place appointed for the tournament.

On their way thither Gervase said to his companion, "I know, old friend, that thou art discreet; and that thou canst, if need be, keep a secret."

" Nay, if thou doubtest it," said the Disour, " keep thy secret thyself—I want none of it."

" Marry," replied the serving-man, " there is nothing I hate worse than doing so. I had rather encounter the hardest day's work that ever yet befell me than be compelled to keep a secret. There is a marvellous comfort in sharing it. Dost not think so ?"

" Out with it, then," said the Disour, " and fear not but that it shall be safely deposited with me."

" And yet," said Gervase, " I would not have thee think that it is from any vain desire to chatter or to blab that I impart this to thee, but because I know thou wilt take an interest in it."

" Now thou must tell me," said the Disour, " for thou hast excited my curiosity; and I will have thy secret, or I will dig it from thy breast with thine own cellar-key."

" It shall not need," replied Gervase. " Thou didst know young Gui de Montaudun ?"

" Knew him, and loved him, as well as any breathing," said the Disour. " If thou knowest aught of him," he added earnestly, " whether it be that he is dead or alive, I do beseech thee to impart it; for, truth to tell, it is for his sake that I am now here. Has intelligence been received of his fate ? is he alive or dead ? Speak,

good Gervase, I prithee—speak, and put an end
to my doubts."

"He is alive, and well," replied Gervase;
" nay more, he is in this city."

" Tell me, then, in what part, without a moment's delay," cried the Disour, turning about.
" Let who will go see the joust ; I shall hasten
to seek Sir Gui."

" It is at the joust that you will see him," said
Gervase, " and nowhere else. He is there, but in
disguise. The state in which he has found
matters on his return home have been so contrary to his wishes and his expectations, that
he does not choose to be known, at least until
this day's sport shall be over. You must wait
until after the tournament, when you can
say what you will to him ; but to seek him
sooner would be only to betray the confidence
I have reposed in you ; and it would, besides, be
wholly useless, for none are admitted within the
places set apart for arming the knights but their
own esquires. So content thee, Disour, with
knowing that Sir Gui is well, and at liberty; and
let us go see his deeds in arms."

The Disour was persuaded by Gervase, because he saw that resistance to his suggestions
would be in vain, and he therefore followed him
to the place of the joust.

The large square where the market was usually
held had been appropriated for this purpose.
The lists were very extensive, and raised above

them were seats occupied by the sovereign and
his court. The duke and the Knights of the
Toison wore the superb habits of the order.
The duchess and the ladies of the court glittered
in all the splendour of beauty and the magnificence of decoration. A numerous body of
nobility completed the exalted company who
were met to witness the feats of the champions.
The butler having procured for himself and the
Disour a good place among the retainers of the
knights, they sat there to see the jousts.

The first course was run between twenty
knights, subjects of the duke, against twenty
strangers. Amongst the former the Disour
looked for Sir Gui, but in vain. Many of the
knights he knew by their devices; but as some
of them did not choose, upon this occasion, to
wear their proper cognizances, and as the
armour effectually concealed their faces, it was
nearly impossible to ascertain who they were.

As, however, the Bastard of Burgundy wore
his own arms upon his shield, and as they were
made more conspicuous by the bar of illegitimacy which crossed them, and of which the Lord
Anthony was rather proud, the Disour had no
difficulty in recognising him. Next to the prince
rode a knight whom he suspected to be Sir Gui.
This knight wore a plain suit of polished steel
armour, over which was a white surcoat, with a
large red cross worked on the breast and back.

On his shield was painted a moon nearly covered with clouds, with the motto "Obscured, not extinguished." The bearing of this knight attracted the attention of the Disour, and he believed and wished that he might be Sir Gui.

On the first encounter several of the combatants on either side were unhorsed, and retired from the lists. By degrees the same accident happened to others, until at length there remained only two on either side. On that of the Burgundians these two were the Bastard and the stranger knight. The joust was for ten lances to be broken; and all had now been disposed of, save two. At the first of these courses the Bastard bore his adversary from the saddle; but, his own horse falling at the same time, he and his antagonist were both declared *hors du combat*, without honour lost or won on either side. The stranger knight was now left to encounter the only remaining champion of the opposite party; and upon their meeting he bore him, although a man of considerable size, a spear's length from his saddle.

This feat called forth the loud applause of the spectators, and the stranger was judged unanimously to have won the prize. He dismounted, and was led to the throne of the duchess, who gave him a ring of some value, which was the fixed prize.

As soon as the knight had received it, and had

paid his homage to the duchess, he mounted his
horse, and rode to a balcony, in which there
sate the Bishop of Valenciennes and his fair
ward.   The knight raised himself in his stirrups,
and laid the ring on the cushion before the
Lady Maud.   This gallantry excited again the
plaudits of the crowd ; and the lady, in the confusion which she felt at exciting the universal
attention of the company, dropped her glove.
The stranger knight caught it as it was falling ;
and, after kissing it devoutly, he fastened it into
his crest, and rode out of the lists.   The Disour
had now no doubt that this was Sir Gui, and he
hastened to the gate by which he had seen him
issue.

In the mean time the stranger knight's demeanour had given great offence to Sir Jacques
Lelain, an approved knight of the duke's court,
who thought that, as his pretensions to the hand
of the Lady Maud were favored by the bishop, her
guardian, no other person had a right to profess
love for her.   He therefore hastened to the marshal, to know who this intruder was ; and, not
being able to learn, he sent one of his friends'to
challenge him to run a course on the instant in
honour of the Lady Maud, meaning to chastise
him for his insolence on the spot.

The knight was talking to the Bastard when
this message was delivered to him ; and, although
the latter would have dissuaded him from ac-

cepting the challenge at this moment, fatigued as he was with his recent exertions, Sir Gui resolved to adventure every thing in such a cause, and, only staying to mount a fresh horse, he rode again into the lists.

His antagonist was in his place; and, their arms being delivered to them, they encountered each other with so much vigour, that the lances were shivered from the handle. They were furnished with fresh weapons;—at the second course the lance of Sir Gui snapped in the middle; and, but for the adroitness with which he turned his horse, his adversary's spear would have struck him. Sir Jacques was highly enraged at this escape. In the succeeding course the lances broke; and Sir Jacques, violently spurring his horse at the same moment, threw the whole weight of his body and his right shoulder against the stranger. If the latter had not kept so firm a seat as it was almost impossible to shake he must have sunk under this rude and rather unfair salutation : he, however, bore up against it, although both the horses reeled with the shock, and Sir Jacques's steed, stepping on a fragment of one of the lances, went down. The victory now might in strictness have been claimed by the stranger ; but he waived it, and, resolving to attempt the chastisement of his adversary, he called for another lance. By his consent his adversary mounted a fresh horse: the charge was sounded, and the stranger, who seemed to acquire strength and dexterity every time he ran, struck Sir Jacques so well and so powerfully as to carry him fairly out of his saddle, and deposit him on the sand of the lists, where he lay incapable of motion.

The stranger staid not to look after him, but, kissing his hand to the Lady Maud, and bowing to the duchess, he again quitted the lists.

The Bastard was waiting for him, and warmly congratulated him on his success : they then rode together to the quarters of the prince, where they disarmed. The Disour had followed them, and was admitted to the chamber of the knight, by whom he was instantly recognised.

The greeting between them was warm and affectionate. The young warrior looked upon the Disour in the light of an old and kind friend, and the difference of their rank made none in their esteem for each other. Sir Gui was indebted to the Disour for many kindnesses in his boyhood ; and he believed that the intense feeling for honorable distinction which had always animated him, and which had raised him to the station he held, had been first awakened by the chivalrous tales of the Disour, to which he had so often and so eagerly listened. The Disour's affection, which had been excited for the young orphan when he found him first in the baron's hall, had been increased as time developed the noble and manly qualities of his character. He loved him as if he had been his own son ; and the delight which he felt at again embracing him was now the keener in consequence of the fears he had very recently entertained that he should never again behold him.

Sir Gui shortly told his friend by what accidents he bad found him in Ghent at this critical period. He had gone to the Turkish wars, commanding a troop of German recruits which had been raised by orders of the Cardinal Julian Cesarini. He was in the fatal combat of Varna, where the Sultan Morad gained a complete victory over Ladislaus, King of Poland, and the Pope's army.

This war, it is well known, was commenced by the Christians, in direct violation of a treaty which had been solemnly sworn to, and which the Turks had preserved with such a scrupulous punctuality as ought to have commanded the admiration of their enemies. By the pernicious advice of the Cardinal Julian, and in pursuance of that virtuous maxim of the Romish church, " that no faith is to be kept with heretics," the weak King of Poland had been induced to violate the treaty ; and believing that, as the greater part of the Turkish army was disbanded, he should have an easy victory, he marched a large force, collected in his own country and in Germany, into the Turkish territories. The cruelties and

excesses of his soldiery roused the Turks to
vengeance. The Emperor Morad, whose sagacity and military skill were renowned throughout
the world, had retired from the cares of empire,
and had left his realm to be governed by his son.
He was, however, called upon by the unanimous
voice of the people to assume the command of the
army, and he complied. The Christian and Turkish forces met on the plain of Varna, where the
perfidy of the Christians received its just punishment. Nothing could exceed the valour with
which they fought : the slaughter was immense,
for none thought of flight. The King of Poland
and the cardinal both fell in the engagement;
and with them, as was said, ten thousand
Poles.

The German troops, under the command of
Sir Gui, fared better than any other part of the
army. They had even made so considerable an
impression on that part of the Turkish force
against which they were opposed, that they
might have turned the tide of the fight if they
had been ably seconded. This, however, was
found to be impossible ; and, succours arriving
to the Turks, nothing was now to be done but to
retreat. Sir Gui consented to this with great
reluctance ; and, while he was in the rear of the
retreating forces, with a lingering hope that some
favorable circumstance might enable him to return to the field, he was struck from his horse

by an arrow from a Turkish bowman. A sharp charge at the same moment prevented his own troops from rescuing him ; and, when he recovered his sensation, of which the pain of his wound and his fall had for a time deprived him, he found himself a prisoner.

Being the only person of condition who had been taken alive, he was carried before the sultan. This magnanimous prince, who was not less wise and merciful in peace than he was vigorous and brave in war, had observed Sir Gui's bearing in the battle, and the favorable impression which he had then received of him was strengthened by the interview which now took place between them. He was immediately released from the bonds which had been put upon him, was allowed perfect liberty in the camp upon his parole, and, his wounds being tended by the sultan's surgeon, he soon recovered. Terms for his ransom were then proposed to him, which were extremely moderate, and were in themselves a proof of the good will of Morad, who was too wise and too liberal to visit upon his prisoner the consequences of the perfidy which had been practised by that party of whom he might reasonably be supposed to be an adherent. Sir Gui represented to the sultan that, although he had no revenues of his own, being merely a soldier of fortune, he had no doubt of being able to procure the required sum if he were allowed to return to Europe.

The generous Morad immediately granted him this permission, notwithstanding that the recent invasion of the Christians had taught him that they did not all strictly perform their engagements. He presented Sir Gui also with a valuable horse; and, having furnished him with the pecuniary means of performing his journey from his own purse, he bade him farewell, requiring him only to promise, in return for these favours, that he would not again bear arms against the Turks. They then parted, the sultan to lay down his sovereignty, and to retire to that calm privacy from which the exigencies of the state had called him, and Sir Gui to his native country, to his companions in arms, and to the lady of his love, whose constancy he never doubted, and whose hand he hoped now to obtain.

The disastrous news which awaited him on his arrival at the castle of Montacute fell like a thunderbolt upon him. He had expected to be greeted by a kind friend, who was to him in the light of a parent, and by a mistress whom he loved with the most passionate fervour: he found that the grave had closed over the one, and that the other was in the power of a man for whom he always felt an aversion which he could not account for, but which he looked upon as a sort of instinct to warn him against a determined foe.

After visiting the tomb of the baron, and paying that affectionate tribute to the memory of his

departed friend which grief wrung from him, he
hastened to Ghent, whither he learnt the bishop
had gone, and had carried with him the Lady
Maud. He reached the city only the day before
the tournay; and, upon consulting with his friend
the Bastard, it was thought advisable that he
should not at present discover himself, but enter
the lists on the morrow as a stranger. He was
induced to adopt this step in consequence of the
information which the Bastard gave him as to the
bishop's intention with respect to the Lady Maud.'

The wily churchman, whose rapacity seemed
to have increased with his years, had long wished
to find a husband for his ward, upon whom he
could impose such conditions as should secure
to himself a large portion of her estates. He
had at length discovered a fit subject in Sir
Jacques Lelain. This knight was a person of
undoubted courage; and, with as great a dispo-
sitiou for fighting, he had no more brains than, a
bull-dog. He was distantly connected with a
noble family, but as poor as Lazarus. He had
been raised for his prowess to an important post
in the army of the Duke of Burgundy, under
whom he had long fought and bled, and who
admired him for the soldierly quality of endu-
rance, which filled up in him the place of almost
all other good ones. He was an honest man
enough, and a great lover of fair play; but,
though he would not willingly do any harm of

himself, he could easily be wrought upon to evil purposes by more cunning persons. Having no sense of his own, he willingly surrendered himself to the guidance of others, and was, in short, exactly that sort of

——— tool,
Which knaves do work with, called a fool.

The bishop found him admirably adapted for his end. He contrived, in the first place, to flatter him into a state of perfect intoxication by praising his courage : he then proposed his ward to him as a bride, and did not find it difficult to procure the consent of Sir Jacques that a large portion of the barony should be annexed to the church lands, in honour of his patroness, Saint Genevieve, to whose interposition the bishop attributed all Sir Jacques's good fortune.

The knight was now of the mature age of five-and-forty, and, little as he was fitted for wooing, he suffered himself to believe that he could easily persuade the Lady Maud to marry him. Being introduced by the bishop, he said what he thought very gallant things to the lady ; and, as she feared at once to repel him with the contempt which she felt for his addresses, he mistook her forbearance for a more tender feeling. He therefore announced himself openly as her lover, and wore a scarf at the tournay, which the bishop had presented to him as from the lady herself.

The bishop encouraged his intention of joining the jousts, and of announcing himself as the lady's knight, because this, by increasing Sir Jacques's reputation, would excuse him in giving his ward to a man who had but little fortune, and whose military renown he intended to allege as the reason for his consenting to the union, which he meant to take place immediately after the festival.

All these particulars the Bastard had learnt from Sir Jacques, who had done him the honour to make him his confidant, and had solicited his advice as to the manner in which he should demean himself towards his intended bride.

The events of the tournay we have already seen. Sir Gui, after having told the Disour all that we have related with respect to the Lady Maud and his rival, expressed the most anxious desire to gain an interview with her.

"The difficulties are, however, very numerous," said he : "she is confined by the bishop, with the utmost caution, in a house in which he resides during his stay in Ghent, and which is situated near the town-walls, towards the western gate. An old duenna, and the bishop's steward, Mahuot, whose character you know well, are her guards."

"I know Mahuot to deserve hanging as well as any man in this or the next country," replied the Disour. "It is but a short time since he stabbed an honest burgher of Valenciennes, because the poor old man would not submit to be cheated in perfect silence. The old burgher's son vows vengeance against him, and I think even the bishop's protection will not be strong enough to shield his vassal from the boy's wrath."

" Mahuot is a stout fellow, and has been a soldier," said Sir Gui.

" And the young man of Valenciennes is also a tall lad of his hands," replied the Disour. " But no matter; I'll instantly set about this affair, and try if I cannot procure you a meeting with the young lady. Before, however, I do so," he added, " I must tell you some news that I have lately heard."

He then related to the knight his interview at the " Leathern Bottle" with the friar, and his assertion that Sir Gui was the real heir of the late Baron de Montaudun.

The knight listened to the account with great attention, and, as may be imagined, with no small interest. He was not, however, disposed to trust much to its authenticity.

" Nothing," he said, " can be more improbable than that, if what he said be really true, it should have remained a secret until this moment. I have too good reason to believe that I am no more than what I am commonly supposed to be. The circumstances of my birth are as obscure as even my enemies can wish. To my own achievements alone I shall owe all the honours which I can ever possess; and I will ennoble my name, or I will die in the attempt. Nevertheless I should like to see this same friar : where is he to be found ?"

" Nay," replied the Disour, " that is far more than I can tell. He said he was coming to this city; and, as I knew that I should meet him again—for he is as great a wanderer as I am—I made no inquiries about his particular destination; but, if I had known that I should so soon fall in with you, I had not let him part so easily. I shall light upon him ere long ; and in the mean time I will go and see about the Lady Maud. Farewell, then, for the present."

As he said this the Disour quitted the apartment, and Sir Gui, having laid aside his armour, went to seek his friend the Bastard. Upon repeating to him the tale which he had just heard, Anthony of Burgundy recommended that a strict search should be made for the friar on the morrow in all the religious houses in Ghent; and he insisted upon this so strongly, that Sir Gui, although he believed that, even if the friar could be found, his information would neither be accurate nor serviceable, complied with his friend's wish, and promised to institute the search. They then repaired together to the duke's hall, where a banquet was prepared.

To the surprise, and not less to the mortifica-

tion, of Sir Gui, the Lady Maud was not among
the company, although the bishop was there.
The only comfort which he could derive from
this untoward circumstance was in the hope that
the Disour, on whose dexterity and intelligence
he knew he could rely, would be able to procure
him an introduction to the place in which she was
kept a prisoner.

The Lord Anthony wished to present his friend
to the duke; but Sir Gui, although he was desirous to pay his respects to his sovereign, was now
so anxious for the Disour's return, that he begged
his friend to postpone this ceremony for some
more fitting opportunity. He paced up and
down the hall with so much uneasiness, that it
required all his efforts to prevent it from becoming
apparent.

Notwithstanding the *incognito* which he endeavored to preserve, he was soon known to be the
knight who had been the victor in the sports of
the morning. All eyes were fixed upon him; and
whispers circulated throughout the hall, some
of which were so loud as to reach his ears. Just
as he began to think that he must, in self-defence,
withdraw, he perceived the Disour making his
way towards him through the crowd with which
the hall was filled.

" How now ?" he said; " what news do you
bring ?"

" Quit the hall immediately," replied the Di-

sour, "and as privately as possible : I will be in
waiting at the gate."

Sir Gui complied with this advice ; and almost
as soon as he was in the street he found himself
joined by his friend, who threw a large cloak
about his shoulders, recommending him to keep
it drawn close, so as to conceal the splendour of
his dress, which would, perhaps, have excited
observation. He then told him that he thought
he had found the means of gaining access to the
lady ; and, as they proceeded rapidly along the
streets leading towards the bishop's house, he
explained what he had been doing.

" I went," he said, " to the house, at which,
at first, I found it extremely difficult to gain admittance. I had previously learned that the bishop was in attendance at the duke's court, and
therefore I thought my attempt was the more
likely to succeed. By dint of cajoling the porter
I at length got into the hall ; and there, luckily,
I saw Dame Marguerite, who it seems, is a
sort of gouvernante to the Lady Maud. I persuaded her that I had great skill in palmistry ;
and I brought into play all the mysterious gib-
berish which I had learnt from my good friends,
the gipsies, so effectually, that I soon made an
impression upon the superstitious duenna. She
is old enough to be my mother, at the least ; but
she is, nevertheless, a coquette ; and a hint which
dropped about a line in her palm, betokening

marriage, made her wholly mine. She ushered
me into a small chamber, in which I found the
Lady Maud sitting. The young lady recognised
me at the first glance; but, like a discreet damsel,
as she is, was too prudent to seem to know me.
The old woman, by way of excusing her own
folly, pretended that she had brought me to spell
the fortunes of the young lady. Taking her
hand, I rattled over the ordinary trash which the
gipsies tell to girls; and which, as it is always
about a lover, and as girls always have a wish to
have lovers, either is, or is believed to be, quite
true. I, however, contrived through this non-
sense to make her ladyship understand that I
alluded to you in all my predictions; and that
you were only waiting an opportunity to throw
yourself at her feet. I was now desirous to get
the old woman out of the room, that I might have
a moment's conversation with the Lady Maud;
and in this I at length succeeded. I asked, with
a most solemn air, whether Dame Marguerite had
ever had her nativity cast. She replied in the
affirmative; and I then begged her to let me see
the horoscope. After a little persuasion she
went away to fetch it; and in the opportunity
which her absence afforded I arranged with the
Lady Maud the means of your visiting her, which
must be thus :—

" At the end of the garden-wall, which we are
now approaching, is a small bay window, which

you may see. It opens from a closet adjoining the chamber in which the Lady Maud and the gouvernante usually sit. This window will be just within your reach as you stand on the wall, and with some exertion you can gain admittance by it. You must, however, be cautious, because, if you fall, you are certain to break your neck. I know if it led into an enemy's castle you would not hesitate to attempt it, though half a dozen spikes opposed your entrance; and I don't apprehend you will be more backward on this occasion."

"Prithee leave all this preaching, my trusty friend," interrupted Sir Gui. "I have listened with most praiseworthy moderation to a very long story, which is now, I trust, finished. But, tell me, what is to become of the old dragon? how can I speak to my Lady Maud while she is in the way?"

"She shall be out of the way, most impetuous Sir!" replied the Disour. "I have cared for her. I told her, when she gave me the horoscope, that I must go home for an hour to consult a curious volume, which was given to me by the Wandering Jew; and I promised to return as soon as I should be satisfied of the strange indications of happiness and long life, and numerous progeny, which her stars seemed to have decreed to her. The old woman was almost distracted with delight: I, however, whispered to her that it

would be better that the younger lady should not
be present at our next interview, because the im-
parting such secrets to a third person was always
highly dangerous. She seemed to feel the force of
this, and said she would receive me in a room on
the lower floor. The porter has orders to admit me :
you, therefore, must wait here for a few minutes ;
and, if I do not return, you may be sure that I
have engaged the old lady. You must then
mount the wall, and gain the window. The Lady
Maud will be awaiting you; and I will take care
that you shall have time enough to arrange with
her some plan of flight, or at least of resistance
to the power of the bishop and the proposed
marriage. Away, then ! and now for my character of seer."

The Disour then went towards the door, leaving
Sir Gui standing behind a buttress of the wall,
which effectually concealed him from view.

As soon as he saw the gate opened and shut
upon the Disour Sir Gui prepared to mount the
wall, which, although of some height, was not
very difficult to him, and with a single spring he
gained the window. As soon as he had entered,
he found himself, as the Disour had told him, in
a closet, at the end of which was a door. He
opened it hastily—and the next moment saw the
Lady Maud in his arms.

Although she had been prepared for the reception of her lover, she could not command the

emotions of delight which filled her heart, and almost overwhelmed her senses. She reclined for some moments in his embrace, in a rapturous trance; and it was not until a flood of tears had relieved her that she regained her recollection. She would then have withdrawn herself from her lover's grasp with a shrinking modesty, but that his arms still held her.

" In this moment, dearest !" he murmured, " do I find bliss enough to reward all the pains and perils which I have endured since our last sad parting."

" And I," she replied, " find that your presence, like a charm, dispels all the grief and terror which have of late beset me."

After the first few moments of tenderness had passed, and when the spirits of the lovers had been restored to something like calmness, they recollected that their interview must necessarily be a short one. Sir Gui learnt from the Lady Maud that she was subjected to the most odious tyranny by the bishop, which was rendered still more disgusting by the formal and hypocritical respect he pretended to pay her. " This, however," she said, " she could have suffered, but that his insolent attempt to marry her to Sir Jacques Lelain had made her apprehend that his designs would not be bounded by the dominion which the law for a short time allowed him over her person and her estates. Now, however, that you are returned," she added, " I have no fears: I shall feel myself in perfect security, and shall not hesitate to defy the proud priest."

" Do so, dearest, then," said Sir Gui, " in the most effectual manner, by at once throwing off the domination which he so unjustly exercises over you. Quit this prison immediately ; give me that title to protect you which your noble father intended to confer upon me ; and, were this bishop ten times as powerful as he is, he shall not dare to interfere with your happiness."

" No," replied the lady, " I will never do that clandestinely which ought to be done in the face of the whole world. It befits not the daughter of the Baron de Montacute—it befits not the affianced bride of Sir Gui de Montaudun—to fly meanly from an authority which she despises. You smile, Gui; but I am become marvellously courageous since your arrival. I will appeal to the duke in person ; and, when this and all other honorable means shall have failed—but not until then—I care not if I confess that I shall be ready to run away with you."

Gui repeated his persuasions that she would at least quit the bishop's palace, and bestow herself in the Ursuline convent of the city, the abbess of which was a lady of noble birth and renowned piety. Here, he represented to her, she could, with more certainty and security, make that appeal to the duke which she meditated.

He could not, however, succeed in shaking her resolution—" She was determined," she said, " that her persecutor should not have any pretence for justifying either the insolence he had already practised towards her or any that he might afterwards attempt."

" Let us not forget," she continued, " that we owe it to ourselves to oppose frankly and openly the designs of our enemies. The duke will not suffer injustice like that of the bishop to triumph : you are already in his favour, and I am sure be loves not the churchman. Boldly demand of his highness my hand in marriage, as a bride affianced to you by my late father ; and let us abide the issue of that experiment."

The impetuosity of Sir Gui's feelings would have induced him to prefer the shorter mode of at once freeing his mistress from the control of the bishop : yet he could not but perceive that her advice was good, and that the means she proposed were more consistent with her rank. He therefore acquiesced in this determination. Their conversation then turned upon that subject most interesting to lovers—themselves. Sir Gui was obliged to relate minutely all the adventures he had passed ; and he forgot all the suffering which had accompanied them while he received what he thought their best guerdon in the tears and admiration of his listening mistress.

The lovers had thought of nothing so little as

the flight of time, and hours might have elapsed but for the abrupt termination which was put to their discourse by Sir Gui hearing the voice of the Disour, in loud and threatening tones, mingled with others in high altercation.

" Fly, fly !" said the Lady Maud, " or you will be discovered."

" I cannot leave him—perhaps in danger," he said, proceeding to the opposite door of the apartment. " Farewell, dearest! farewell! Soon we shall meet again, when no restraint shall mar our happiness." As he spoke he embraced her tenderly ; and then rushed out at the door, and down the stairs, towards the place whence he had heard his friend's voice.

He arrived exactly in the right moment, for he found the Disour in the hall, with his back against the wall and his sword drawn, vigorously repelling the attacks of several servants in the bishop's livery. Sir Gui saw some one standing below him on the stairs : it was too dark to distinguish persons accurately, and it was no time to stand upon ceremony ; so at a single spring, in which he overset this person, who was no other than the bishop, he was amongst the assailants. Before he had time to draw his sword he had knocked down two of the four men who were attacking the Disour ; and then, joining his friend, and having bared his weapon, the others thought fit to draw off. The Disour, who knew that a very short time would bring up a reinforcement, bade Sir Gui retreat ; and then, by slow steps gaining the further end of the hall, he opened the gate, and they got safely into the street with no other hurt than some slight bruises which the Disour had received from the bishop's steward.

When they were out the Disour manfully took to his heels; and Sir Gui was obliged to keep near him at the same pace, lest he should lose his guide in a part of the town of which he knew nothing.

At length they arrived at the quarters of the Bastard of Burgundy, where Sir Gui was lodged ; and, having gained his own apartment, he besought the Disour, when he had recovered his breath, to tell him how he had been discovered.

" Simply because you staid so long a time above stairs," replied the Disour. " I had told the old dame so many lies that I absolutely began to be tired. I had given her two husbands, and a large family by each of them ; and was at my wits' end to know what to say further, when that miscreant knave Mahuot, the bishop's steward, broke in upon me. I don't believe he suspected you to be in the house; but as the bishop, it seems, had strictly forbidden the admission of strangers, Mahuot, learning that a fortune-teller was with Dame Marguerite, resolved to give a proof of his vigilance in the presence of his master, with whom he had just returned from the

duke's banquet.   He had the impudence to
threaten me with the discipline of the cudgel;
and, for aught I know, he would have administered it, but that the sight of my sword kept
him back.   I care not who knows that I do not
love fighting : but then I love a drubbing less;
and, if I must either be beaten or fight, I always
choose the latter.   I believe, however, that for
once Mahuot would have kept his promise in my
favour but for your appearance; and, next to
having brought me out of the hands of the
knaves, I am grateful to you for having knocked
down stairs that greater knave, their master."

"Was it the bishop whom I tumbled over on
the stairs?" asked Sir Gui.

"In good faith it was," replied the Disour;
"and I honour you for having done so, wittingly
or by chance."

"The bishop must thank himself for it," said
Sir Gui : "he was very much in my way; and, if
he continues to remain so, it is like I may over-
turn him again."

Sir Gui then proceeded to question the Disour
as to the possibility of finding the friar who had
held so mysterious a discourse respecting his legitimacy.   The Disour thought it would not be
difficult; and when Sir Gui told him that he felt
anxious about it, and that the Bastard of Burgundy had especially recommended him to make
an inquiry on the subject, he promised to go in

search of the monk on the morrow. He then bade
Sir Gui farewell for the night, and retired to
console himself for the fatigues of the day in a
carouse with his friend Gerald.

The following day was the anniversary of that
on which the late Duke John had been basely
murdered in the presence of the now reigning
King of France. The Duke Philip had already
satisfied his vengeance by the long and fatal war
which he had carried into the country of the
traitors; he even fancied that he had forgiven
Charles the share which he had taken in the matter : but he had resolved that the memory of so
cruel and wicked a deed should not be lost ; and,
in the institution of the order of the Toison, he
had appointed the grand day of the festival to
be on that of his father's death. This day he
ordered to be celebrated with all the solemn ceremonies and pomp of religion; thus at once
uniting the prayers of his people for the repose
of the late duke's soul, and perpetuating in their
minds the recollection of his disastrous fate and
of the French king's treachery.

The city of Ghent had never before witnessed
so splendid a procession as that which on the
morning of this day accompanied the Duke of
Burgundy to the cathedral church of St. Bouvon.

The dignitaries of the church, together with all
the members of the various religious fraternities
with which the city abounded, were assembled to

perform the offices of the day.   The abbesses of
the several convents, accompanied by their nuns,
were seated behind an open grating, placed at the
side of the high altar.   The barons and knights
from every part of the duke's dominions, with
many of those whom the fame of the festival had
attracted from foreign countries, joined the train,
decked in all the heavy, but gorgeous, magnificence of the prevailing modes. Ladies of the rarest
beauty and the highest birth graced the ceremony with their presence.   The burghers and the
artisans of Ghent displayed upon this occasion
all their finery ; and even the poorest members of
the community made an effort to improve the
wretchedness of their appearance in honour of
a ceremonial in which they fancied themselves to
be concerned.   The people of the Netherlands
have always been remarkable for their fondness
for religious spectacles ; and the duke, who was
as politic as he was brave and virtuous, had not
forgotten this propensity of theirs among the
motives which had led him to the institution of
the present ceremony.

The presence of this multitude added to the
imposing effect of the cathedral, which is of itself one of the most striking and elegant of the
religious edifices in this part of Europe.   Near
the high altar an elevated throne was placed for
the duke, and on each side lower seats for the
most distinguished of the courtiers; next were

the places allotted to the ladies; and afterwards those for the nobles, who were arranged according to their several ranks. The side-aisles were filled with the other spectators, who, ranged in a line with the white marble pillars which support the roof, left the middle aisle open for the passage of the illustrious persons who came to the church.

The Disour had repaired to the cathedral at an early hour, in the hope of finding, amongst the friars and monks whom their duties would lead thither, the Carmelite whose conversation at the " Leathern Bottle" had made so powerful an impression on him. His search was, however, unsuccessful; the great number of Carmelite monks, the uniformity of their dresses, and the practice which most of them followed of keeping their cowls drawn over their faces as they entered the church, effectually baffled even his keen penetration. He resolved to wait until the ceremonies should be finished, when he hoped for better fortune in his search; and, therefore, giving it up for the present, he placed himself near the great entrance to the cathedral, for the purpose of witnessing the procession.

He possessed the art of making friends with all kinds of persons; and in a few minutes his neighbours in the crowd had forgiven the rudeness with which he elbowed himself into the best place, for the sake of the jokes with which he continued to regale them, and to excuse his impudence.

Close beside him stood a little old man, dressed in dark grey serge, whose quick glances showed that he perfectly appreciated the Disour's jests; but the solemn gravity of his countenance remained undisturbed. He looked as if he had resolved not to laugh. This person usually sate near the door of the cathedral, and distributed the holy water with a sprinkling brush, from a vessel hanging against one of the pillars, to the persons who entered the church. The crowd had thrust him from his place; but he continued to hold the water-pot in his hand, and to furnish all the devout within his reach with the sanctified element.

The Disour was rather nettled at the old man's gravity, for he thought it was uncivil in the last degree not to laugh at his witticisms. At length he addressed him :—" Hast made a vow, Father Greybeard," he asked, " never to let a profane smile disturb any of those wrinkles which hang like a net over thy face ?"

The old man shook his head, but did not reply.

" Nay, answer me, I pray thee," said the Disour again : " thou mayest talk if thou wilt not laugh ; there can be no harm in speaking."

" In speaking idly there may be," replied the old man slowly, and without discomposing a muscle.

" And didst thou never speak idly?" asked the Disour.

." Ay, marry, as idly as thou dost," replied the old man ; "but the sin is repented of, and, I trust, forgiven."

" Piously said, old Mortification!" rejoined the Disour : " and thou dost then really think that thou mayest even be forgiven for the sin of having laughed? But tell me, I beseech thee, when it was that thou didst commit so heinous an offence : it must have been in thy boyhood, and then but once. I can swear, by the look of those cobweb folds, into which thy wrinkles have fallen, that thou hast not for the last sixty years, at least, disturbed them by a profane smile."

" Go to," said the old man ; " thou art an idle jester, and I am little better for listening to thee."

" Nay, but I beseech thee tell me, didst ever laugh since thou wert weaned?" asked the importunate Disour.

" I have laughed, and made others laugh, too," replied the old man, a little roused by this quizzing.

" But prithee when ?"

" When I was as great a fool as thou art," answered the old man.

A laugh was raised at the Disour's expense, and he was prevented from turning it, or replying, by the approach of the duke, which was now loudly announced by the music which preceded him.

The procession then entered the church. First

came the duke, accompanied by the duchess, and followed by their gallant son Charles, and by the not less valiant, though in his birth less fortunate, Anthony the Bastard. The younger members of the duke's family came afterwards, and next the Bishop of Ghent. Then the Bishop of Valenciennes, the duke's chancellor, his marshal, and the other chief officers of his household. The ladies, the noblemen, the knights, and their esquires, followed in their several places.

The Disour was gazing with delight and admiration at the assembly of beauty and worth which this procession presented, when, just as his friend Sir Gui passed before him at the head of the knights, which place he assumed in right of his recent triumph at the tournament, he felt his arm strongly grasped, and, looking round, he saw the old man, with whom he had lately been talking, clinging to him apparently in great terror.

" What ails thee, old friend ?" he asked.

The old man did not reply, but, clinging more closely to his arm with one hand, he pointed with the other to Sir Gui, upon whom his eyes were intently fixed.

The Disour feared that some fit had seized him, and, turning round, he supported the old man, while he again asked what had caused this agitation.

" It is true, then," muttered the old man—who

seemed to recover himself as the procession passed on and he lost sight of Sir Gui—" it is true, then, that the dead return to the earth."

" What dead didst thou fancy thou couldst see ?" asked the Disour, and he led the old man towards the door, as the crowd pressed on in a contrary direction, closing up the rear of the procession.

" Fancy !" repeated the old man, gasping with emotion ; " it was no fancy. I saw him in all the lustiness of youth, bearing the same bannerol, clad in the same armour, and looking as gallant and gay as he did when he entered that fatal hall which he never more quitted alive."

" What he ?" asked the Disour : " thy wits are wandering, old friend ; sit down and compose thyself."

" No, no," replied the old man, " I am as temperate as thou, but staggered somewhat at the sight I have beheld. Yonder walks, in strength and lustihood, one whom I saw receive his death-blow, and who yielded up his last groans in my arms, four-and-twenty years ago."

" Nay, nay, this is but a fantasy," said the Disour, who felt compassion for what he thought a weakness in the old man's intellect. " The hot crowd has tired thee, and some accidental resemblance has frightened away thy wits."

" But what does he amongst the knights ?" said the old man, not heeding the latter part of the Disour's speech; "why holds he not his rank with the highest barons?"

"Of whom dost thou speak?" asked the Disour more earnestly, as he now thought there was some meaning in the old man's discourse: "I conjure thee to tell me at once what baron thou meanest."

"The Baron Philip de Montaudun, one of the bravest and most courteous nobles that this land ever saw."

"And wast thou present at his death?"

"Ay, in good faith was I," replied the old man, shuddering as the recollection passed through his mind: "I saw him basely and treacherously struck down, in the hall of Montereau, from behind, by a caitiff who dare never have met him face to face."

The Disour's interest was now highly excited; and, in the belief that he should draw from the old man, to whom chance had thus introduced him, some information which might be serviceable to Sir Gui, he encouraged him to proceed.

"When the murderers had withdrawn," continued the old man, "I approached the baron—the only one of all his noble company in whom life remained. I lifted his head, and stanched, as well as I could, the blood which flowed from some of his wounds; and, at his request, I brought to him a holy monk, who received his last confession, and gave him absolution. He

died like a pious Christian and a good knight.
One reflection alone seemed to weigh upon his
heart, and to inflict upon him more pain than the
agonies of death."

"What could that be ?" asked the Disour
eagerly.

"It was," said the old man, "that he left an infant
son, his only child, by an English lady to whom
he was married, but who had not been publicly
recognised as his wife. He charged the monk
who tended him to see his son placed under
proper guardianship, and educated as became his
rank ; but that child is, I suppose, dead, for,
as I hear, the barony is now held by the proud
Bishop of Valenciennes."

"That child is not dead, though a child no
longer!" cried the Disour ; "that is he whom
you just now saw at the head of the knights,
and whose resemblance to his dead father is so
strong that it caused you to believe he was the
baron returned from the grave. In a lucky hour
do I find thee ; for, by thy testimony, the youth,
who is unjustly said to be the illegitimate child
of the late baron, shall be restored to his father's
possessions, and take his place, as thou truly
sayest he ought to do, among the noblest of his
peers."

"I am ready to avouch, before Heaven and in
the face of man, the truth of what I have now
said," replied the old man.

" But by what accident, I pray thee tell me,"
said the Disour, " didst thou happen to be
present at Montereau on the fatal day you
speak of ?"

" Alas !" replied the old man, " I was then
as light and foolish a piece of human vanity as
ever abused Heaven's mercy." I was the jester
of the Dauphin's court, and might have died in
the same thoughtless calling but for the horror
which that base murder occasioned. Immediately after that I renounced ,my sinful profession, and have ever since devoted myself to works
of piety and mortification."

The Disour recollected that, in the relation
which the monk had given of the death of the
Baron de Montaudun, he had mentioned that the
Dauphin's jester was present. That this was the
same individual he could not doubt; and he
was not much astonished at the transition of so
weak-minded a person as the jester was described
to be from the nonsensical profession of a court
fool to one of useless, but unceasing, devotion.
He shortly recounted to the old man the manner of Sir Gui's education, and the urgent
necessity which there was at this moment for
procuring the proofs of his legitimacy. By
pressing the *quondam* jester on that which he saw
was his weak point, and insisting on the religious necessity of his obeying the injunctions of
a dying man, he screwed up his resolution, and

obtained from him a promise to declare, whenever he should be called upon, the tenour of the
late baron's dying declaration.

The Disour now only wanted to find the monk,
with whose assistance he hoped it might be practicable to reinstate Sir Gui in the dignity which
belonged to him ; and he thought, wisely enough,
that no opportunity could be more favorable for
this purpose than the present. The Bishop of
Valenciennes was here, in Ghent, stripped in a
considerable degree of that power which he possessed in his own demesne, and which must have
made a litigation with him extremely tedious, and
even uncertain in its result. The duke, too, was
well disposed towards Sir Gui; and the fame of
his achievements at Varna, with his success
at the more recent jousts, had excited a very
favorable feeling on his behalf amongst the barons, to which his courteous manner and graceful presence had greatly added. The bishop, on
the contrary, was almost universally disliked.
The clergy, over whom he exercised a tyrannical
dominion—the proprietors and tenants of the
lands in his see, from whom he rigorously ex-
acted the uttermost dues for which his craft and
ingenuity could find a pretext—the members of
the duke's council, whom he treated with an insolent scorn, and, amongst these, the chancellor
in particular—all combined in one feeling of detestation against him ; and all would willingly

have contributed to his mortification, and even to his ruin, if that had been practicable.

It was with good reason, therefore, that the Disour—who, from the constant intercourse he held with persons of the highest condition, knew, without seeming to pay attention to, all the political intrigues of the time—thought that, if he could bring the question of Sir Gui's legitimacy before the duke in his court at this time, he should secure its being fairly tried, and by a short process; although the latter was almost as rare in the jurisprudence of the fifteenth century as it is even in our own. The sanguine temper of his mind was also highly excited by his recent discoveries, and he entertained no doubt of the success of Sir Gui's claim.

He consulted the old man, who was of course well acquainted with the city, as to the probability of his finding the monk; and, learning that there was in it a convent of Carmelites renowned for the strictness of their lives, he resolved to hasten thither as soon as the ceremony should be finished. Having arranged a meeting in the evening with the old man, they returned together into the church.

The ceremony was finished, and the procession about to quit the cathedral. On this occasion, however, the order was somewhat reversed: the monks, who had been employed in the holy ceremonies, preceded the duke on his return, bearing the rich reliques which belonged to the cathedral, and the religious banners of their various orders. In this troop of friars, "black, white, and grey," the quick eye of the Disour now discovered the monk of whom he was in quest; and, being unwilling to quit the cathedral at that moment, he whispered to his new acquaintance a request that he would ascertain whither the father went, and bring him intelligence.

The old man readily undertook the commission, and filed out of the cathedral in the crowd of monks.

The duke was now approaching, accompanied as he had been before. Very shortly previous to this the Disour had seen, on the other side of the church, several of the chief burghers of Valenciennes, with whose faces he was familiar. They stood in a crowd, and seemed occasionally to be talking to a man who was in the midst of them, but whose face the Disour could not see, because that person seemed studiously to shun observation by holding up his cap before him, so as to cover his visage.

As the duke reached the place where the burghers were standing, on a sudden they drew open, so as to permit the passage of the man whom the Disour had so particularly remarked, and who now, rushing out, threw himself on his knees before the duke.

He was a young man, well made, but rather slight, and dressed in complete mourning. The Disour, as soon as he saw his face, recognised him to be the youth of whom he had spoken to Sir Gui, and whose intention in thus appealing to the duke he could not doubt.

"Justice, my liege sovereign!" cried the youth. "In the name of the Duke John—in the name of that murdered father whose memory you just now solemnly and piously celebrated—I beseech you to do me justice."

"Justice for what?" asked the sovereign, who was evidently moved by the petitioner's allusion to the fatal event which occupied his whole thoughts, and hardly less by the passionate manner in which it was made. The duke stopped, and the whole of the procession halted.

"Justice on the murderer of *my* father," replied the youth: "his blood yet cries out for vengeance; and here, before your grace, from whom alone I can hope for right, do I appeal his murderer."

"But why do you make this appeal to me?" asked the duke; "the laws are rightfully administered, and they have provided a sufficient punishment for such a crime."

"But the criminal is beyond the reach of those laws, great duke," replied the youth: "a protection so powerful encircles him, that the arm of the law is baffled by it."

" Beware of what you say, knave," cried the duke angrily. " By the power of Heaven I swear that no subject of mine is or shall be beyond the law! Make good what you have uttered, or prepare for the worst punishment."

" May the heaviest tortures fall on me," replied the youth, still kneeling, " if I say aught but that which is true, and which I will maintain."

" Rise then, sirrah," said the duke; " and, albeit neither the time nor the place are fitting for such discussions, yet, for the name which you have uttered, you shall have the justice you crave. Now, tell us what you would ?"

The youth rose at the duke's bidding, and proceeded to relate the cause of his appeal:— " My father," he said, " who was a burgher of Valenciennes, was stabbed by a retainer of the bishop, who now stands beside your highness, in the presence of numerous witnesses. The murderer kept himself shut up in his house, and defied all my attempts to reach him ; else, with my own hand, I had obtained that for which I am now your grace's petitioner. I then appealed to the bishop, who is the supreme judge of the city of Valenciennes. The reverend father examined certain witnesses, by whose testimony he was satisfied that my father had provoked the blow which caused his death, and thereupon decreed the murderer to be fined one hundred marks, to be disposed of in masses for the repose

of the dead.   I will say nothing in this presence
of the justice of the sentence ; it speaks loudly for
itself : but I claim the privilege which is given
me by the laws of Valenciennes, and which provide that the nearest of kin to the person slain
may challenge his murderer to the fight *à
l'ontrance*.   This privilege has been denied to me
at Valenciennes ; but I claim it again here,
where I beseech your grace to grant it me as
you value the memory of your own father, and
by the deep vengeance with which you have
satisfied his murder."

"This sounds fairly and manfully," said the
duke ; " but who vouches for the truth of this
statement ?"

"We do all !" cried the burghers of Valenciennes ; and as they spoke they advanced.

"What say you, bishop ?" asked the duke,
turning to him with a stern expression.

"I say," he replied, " that justice has been
done—full and ample justice, according to the
laws—save in regard to the combat.   That, I
confess, I have withheld in mercy to the youth,
whose strength can in no way compete with that
of the person he accuses."

"And that person is your servant ?" said the
duke.

"He is my tried and faithful servant," replied
the bishop ; " but Heaven forefend that I should

therefore judge him partially ! The death of the late burgher happened in a quarrel, which, as was proved to me by good witnesses, he himself provoked."

" My liege," cried the young man, " for the justice of which his reverence speaks, that may be guessed at when you know that of all these burghers," pointing to them, " who saw the murder, not one was examined by his grace. For the prowess of the caitiff murderer I care not : a good conscience makes me bold, and the righteousness of the cause will supply me strength : if not, I shall die in the attempt to revenge my father ; and I can meet him in the other world without the shame of having suffered his murderer to go unscathed."

" By my soul," cried the duke, " you shall have my good wishes that your cause may prevail !   But is this the law ?"

" It is, my liege," replied the chancellor very promptly—" it is, and has so prevailed in Valenciennes for many years."

" Then let it continue.—Marshal !" he said, calling to an officer, " take this youth into thy keeping, and let him communicate with no one till the trial be over.   Where is the accused ?"

Mahuot, who had been near the bishop, endeavored to steal off ; but, the thickness of the crowd rendering this not very easy, he had been perceived by the men of Valenciennes, who detained him. At the duke's question they dragged him forward.

"Let him also be kept in close confinement," continued the duke. "When shall the combat take place?"

"Now—instantly!" cried the young man, "or as soon as your grace wills."

"To-morrow, then, be it," said the duke: "throw down your glove, boy."

The youth stepped forward; and, casting down his glove, exclaimed "I appeal Nicolas Mahuot of foul murder, which I will prove upon his body—So help me, God!"

Mahuot, who, although one of the worst men, did not want courage, and who thought, moreover, that he should gain an easy victory over the stripling who defied him, picked it up very coolly, and said "I accept the challenge; and will prove, by the blessing of Heaven, that the accuser is a foul liar, and that I am a true man."

"God help the righteous!" said the duke: "now keep them safely," and he signed for the procession to go on.

In a short time the church was cleared, and the Disour went in search of Sir Gui, whom he found with the Bastard of Burgundy. He related in the presence of the latter, whose attachment to Sir Gui he well knew, the discovery he had made; and a council was then held as to the future steps to be taken in consequence of it.

"I have it," cried the Bastard, after several expedients had been suggested and rejected. "You and I, Gui, although we may be able to do somewhat with couched lance and belted brand, can win little profit from crafty priests and courtiers. The duke's old chancellor is as wily as a fox—honest, so to speak, remembering always that he is a lawyer—and an inveterate hater of the bishop. Let our friend here (pointing to the Disour) take his monk and his fool to the chancellor;—a goodly company they will make when they are all met! The old man loves me, or at least he says he does; and I so far believe him as to think that he would not scruple to do me some service, provided it gave him but little trouble, and might be the means of vexing the bishop. I will go before to him with thee, Sir Gui, and prepare him for thy reception, most gentle Disour! Thou art, I know, master of thy craft; and I leave it to thee to tell the chancellor the whole of thy long story, which, I thank Heaven, my brains would never bear. I'll 'gage my knighthood against a monk's virtue—desperate odds!—that he will either make or find some method of bringing their proofs to bear. Like ye my plan, gentles?"

Sir Gui thought it was an excellent plan, and thanked him for its suggestion. The Disour also warmly approved of it; and the Bastard, accompanied by Sir Gui, hastened to the chancellor's house, where he soon succeeded in persuading him to undertake the affair.

Soon afterwards the little mortified remnant of a jester came to the place appointed by the Disour, accompanied by the monk. After they had mutually explained what had occurred since they met at the "Leathern Bottle," the Disour communicated to the friar the proposal of the Bastard respecting the chancellor, whose assistance was just that which the holy man thought necessary to the success of their cause. In a very short time an intimation from Sir Gui was received, in consequence of which the Disour conducted his two witnesses to the chancellor's abode.

The chancellor was not quite so bad as the Bastard, in his flighty way of talking, had made him appear. He was the member of a profession, which, as it familiarizes its members with the worst and weakest moods of the human mind, begets in them a sceptical indifference to the finer sentiments of our nature. He was, moreover, a courtier; and the course of his observations in this capacity had only sharpened his wits, without expanding his heart. The worst that could be said of him—and Heaven knows it is bad enough—was that his virtues and his vices were negative. He, however, entered

warmly into the interests of Sir Gui, and promised to further them by every means in his
power. His chief inducement might be to work
the mortification of the Bishop of Valenciennes ;
or it might be—— But we will leave inquiring
into motives, since they are always of so strange
a nature, that, like counterfeit coin, although
they look well enough to the eye, they often
lose all their brilliancy and their value in the
handling.

He was, in any event, a powerful ally to Sir
Gui ; his legal knowledge, his habits of business, and his influence, were all highly valuable ;
and the Disour, who appreciated these things
better, perhaps, than either the Bastard or his
friend, thought himself blest in the acquisition. The chancellor listened patiently to his
story : he then made his secretary take down the
quondam jester's deposition, after which he dismissed him. He, however, retained the friar and
the Disour, with whom he had a conversation
which lasted several hours.

Sir Gui, in the mean time, visited the house of
the bishop, in the hope of seeing, or procuring
some intelligence respecting, the Lady Maud ;
but in vain. The house was entirely closed, and
every thing about it seemed in perfect repose.
Wearied with long watching, he returned home
and went to bed, having first arranged with the
Bastard the hour at which they would proceed

to witness the combat, which had been appointed for the following morning, between the youth who had made his appeal to the duke and the bishop's steward.

The law by virtue of which the combat was to take place had been rarely exercised at Valenciennes, and was not even known at Ghent. It had, therefore, besides the interest which the circumstance of a son challenging his father's murderer must naturally excite, the additional recommendation of novelty to the people, who are fond of spectacles in any shape, but are beyond all measure delighted with such as are likely to have a bloody termination.

The news was soon spread throughout the city that two burgesses of Valenciennes were about to do battle, *à l'outrance,* before the duke; and at an early hour in the morning a great concourse of people had assembled at the spot where the combat was to take place. This was a round space, closely fenced about with strong barricadoes, of the height of an ordinary sized man's head. The surrounding ground was made to slope towards this fence; a second fence was fixed all round, at the distance of six yards from the inner enclosure; and within were stationed the city guard, in order to prevent the people from approaching any nearer. There was but one entrance to the close lists, which was made only large enough to admit two persons abreast.

Opposite to this entrance, and raised to a level with the top of the fence, was a covered stage, with chairs, for the duke and the civil officers; behind which stood benches for the nobility and courtiers of the duke's suite.

Just before the hour appointed for the combat the duke and his retinue arrived at the lists, and took his seat on the stage, the Count de Charolois, and the Bastard of Burgundy, standing behind him. The two chief judges of the city were placed beside him; and a considerable number of noblemen and knights, among whom was Sir Gui, occupied the back benches.

As the clock struck seven the persons into whose charge the champions had been given on the preceding day presented themselves with their wards at the outer barrier. The person challenged was first admitted; and at the same time two chairs, covered with black serge, were placed opposite each other in the lists. Nicolas was led to one of them, and took his seat. Jacotin, the young citizen of Valenciennes, was then brought in, and placed in the other. The combatants were clothed in dresses of stout leather, which fitted close to their bodies, but left their heads, feet, and hands, entirely bare.

As it would have been considered derogatory from the dignity of heralds to assist in a combat between simple burghers, and for such a cause, the duties usually performed by them were on

this occasion discharged by the chief bailiff of
the city. He read aloud the challenge of Jacotin,
in which he accused Nicolas of having murdered
his father; and concluded by defying him to a
mortal combat, in which he offered to prove the
truth of his accusation on his antagonist's body.
There were no trumpets preceding or following
this ceremony, as in knightly fights; but, when
the reading was finished, Jacotin loudly ejaculated " So help me, God !"

The bailiff then read the reply and defiance of
Nicolas, in which he denied having slain the
father of Jacotin in any other than fair and lawful
combat, and accepted the challenge of the ap-
pellant.

A priest then drew near, and administered to
each of the combatants an oath upon the crucifix,
by which they swore that they had used neither
spells nor magical devices; that they had no secret
arms or poison; and that they would rely upon
nothing in the ensuing fight but the justice of
the cause and their own manhood.

Two bowls were then placed before each of
the champions, one of which was filled with
grease, and the other with ashes. They rubbed
the grease plentifully over their leathern coats,
and then cleaned their hands as well as they
could with the ashes given them for this purpose, and by their roughness to enable them to
grasp the weapons with which they were to fight.

A small piece of candied sugar was then presented to each of them, to enable them to keep
their mouths moist and to hold their breath, for
which purposes it was then considered to be " the
sovereign'st thing on earth."   Of all these things
assay was made before them with as much ceremony as if they had been princes about to fight
for a kingdom. Two shields were then produced,
in weight and shape exactly like those worn in
tournaments; but the holes for the arms were
made so as to cause the shield to be reversed,
the pointed end being next the elbow. When the
champions had put on their shields, they each
received from the officers a stout staff of maple-
wood, nearly four feet long. All things being
now ready, the attendants withdrew, and left the
provost of the city alone in the lists with the
combatants. As soon as the place was quite
cleared he cried aloud " Champions, do your
duty; and God help the righteous!"

They then advanced, and looked at each other
with furious and mortal glances, while each
paused to induce his adversary to make the first
blow. The apparent strength of the champions
was disproportioned. Jacotin was rather slender; and the tightness of his dress showed this
in a disadvantageous light, because it made him
appear meagre, without marking how firmly his
limbs were knit, and how compact were his
muscles. The robustness of the figure of Ni-

colas, on the contrary, was rather improved by the condensed shape in which his close dress presented him. On looking at the two champions there seemed no chance for the younger and slighter; and, although there were many of his well-wishers among the spectators, there were few who did not pity him as a devoted man.

Nicolas looked warily at his enemy, and seemed resolved not to strike the first blow. Jacotin, who saw this, had just made up his mind, that, to induce his antagonist to fight, he must set him the example, when he was surprised to receive a blow which made him stagger. He was, however, quick enough to avoid the next, (which Nicolas intended to take effect in the same place,) and to return the compliment upon his foe, who had overreached himself in the effort. He then attacked in his turn, and pressed Nicolas so closely, that the latter, by his hard breathing, showed he was considerably perplexed at the rapidity with which he was struck. Still, however, he preserved his caution, and parried all the worst blows aimed at him, contriving in return to deal some hard buffets upon Jacotin's shoulders.

This sort of fighting was not to continue long, for the young man had resolved never to quit the lists with life unless he had first taken that of his father's murderer; and Nicolas well knew that there was no safety for him but in the death of his antagonist. Jacotin pressed on him closely, and tried to throw him down. In order to effect this object he even took some blows which he might have avoided; but, at length espying an opportunity just as Nicolas was making a blow at his head, he caught it upon his shield, and, at the same moment thrusting with his staff shortened against the stomach of his adversary, he brought him to the ground, and had his knee upon his breast, while his left hand grappled his throat so firmly that he maintained his hold, notwithstanding the grease with which Mahuot's dress and his neck was covered.

The latter, finding himself thus reduced to a disadvantage, and that all his efforts to disengage himself from Jacotin were in vain, snatched some of the sand with which the arena was strewed, and flung it into his eyes. This manœuvre failed of the effect which it was intended to produce, and only hastened the fate of Mahuot; for Jacotin, wholly blinded by the sand, was enraged by the pain which accompanied it to a state of desperation: his grasp on the throat of his foe became more fixed and relentless, and the agony which he experienced only added force and rapidity to the blows which he rained on the head of his prostrate foe. The posture of Mahuot prevented any effectual defence; and, after a violent stroke which fractured his skull, and beat out one of his eyes, the mangled wretch rolled round upon his face, and cried for mercy.

The provost and his attendants approached, and water was brought by some of them to Jacotin for the purpose of cleansing his eyes, while others tended the dying Mahuot. A leech, who had been brought, pronounced, without hesitation, his opinion that death must speedily ensue from the wounds in his head. The unhappy man, upon hearing this, begged that a priest should be instantly sent for, to whom he might make confession of the sins which burdened his conscience.

At this moment two friars, accompanied by the Archdeacon of Valenciennes, appeared at the barrier, and, informing the provost that they came at the desire of the bishop, requested that Mahuot, adjudged by the issue of the combat to be guilty of the accusation laid to his charge, should be delivered over to them, his life being at the disposal of the bishop.

The provost answered the archdeacon shortly, but civilly, by observing that, although in Valenciennes, and in the duke's absence, the bishop might be considered the liege lord of that city; yet that in Ghent, where the duke administered justice in person, the bishop's power was dormant.

The archdeacon then changed his ground, and begged that he, with the churchmen who accompanied him, might be permitted to receive the culprit's confession, and to bestow on him such spiritual consolation as his case might require.

" This, too, had been provided for," the provost answered; " and the prior of the Augustine monastery of Ghent had already sent some of his community for the purpose."

The archdeacon and his monks, thus beaten from their purpose, were obliged to retire, and the Augustine friars assumed the charge of the mangled culprit, who was borne with all the care which the nature of his wounds required to the monastery.

When the news of his steward's defeat and probable death were communicated to the bishop, although he assumed an appearance of great regret, he was not really so much afflicted as might have been reasonably expected. Mahuot had for many years been his faithful and indefatigable agent. His zeal had never been known to relax ; and it was believed that he possessed the entire confidence of his master, to whom he had become, as was thought, wholly indispensable, for the unhesitating readiness with which he took upon his own shoulders the blame for all those acts of tyranny and extortion, of which he was, in fact, not the cause, but the instrument. For his numerous and valuable services he neither sought nor received any other reward than the immunity which the bishop's protection afforded him against the resentment or revenge of the persons who might happen to think themselves wronged by him. A pecuniary recompense from his master he would have scorned to receive ; for, like all other stewards, he had sufficient opportunities of picking up certain gains —no matter how honestly—which, in the words of modern advertisements, made his " wages no object." Such a servant, then, it would be reasonable to think, must be regretted by the master to whom he had been so invariably faithful and useful ; and, without giving the Bishop of Valenciennes credit for any humane virtues, of which he did not possess a particle, those merely selfish feelings in which he abounded ought to have made him lament Mahuot's ill fate. But there are in all systems, domestic as well as political, secret motives, which, if they were once known, would put an end to the surprise which the actions resulting from them occasion ; and the bishop had, what he thought, very good reasons for not regretting this event. He knew his steward's utility, but he had begun to fear him. Mahuot was so well acquainted with all his master's secrets, some of which were not of a nature to be revealed, that he could, by disclosing them, have done him great mischief—perhaps even have caused his ruin—for he could have furnished the numerous enemies whom he had created by his haughty and tyrannical behaviour with the proofs of his delinquency. It was this knowledge, and the fear lest Mahuot should one day or other turn traitor, that made the bishop now look upon his being killed in the light of a relief, and even to congratulate himself upon it. His rejoicing was, however, very short; and no sooner did he learn that Mahuot was in the keeping of the Augustine friars than his fears were renewed with tenfold strength and magnitude. He had made, as he thought, an infallible provision against the possibility of any disclosure which the approach of death might extort from his steward. For this purpose he had sent some of his own creatures to the lists, in order to secure the possession of the steward's person; and had never contemplated that event which had now happened, and which overturned all his plans.

In the first excess of his rage he uttered a thousand imprecations, all very unseemly for a churchman, on the heads of every one whom he fancied to be the cause, in however remote a manner, of his disappointment. Having calmed the fury of his soul by this most comfortable practice, to which he was addicted even upon slight occasions, his natural astuteness suggested to him that it was necessary to take precautions against the worst event that could now befall. He knew that at Ghent he was surrounded by persons who bore him no very good will; and he felt, too, that his power here was considerably

less than it would be at Valenciennes. For these
reasons he came to the resolution of departing
immediately : he gave directions that all the preparations for setting off should be hastened, and
that the greater part of his household should be
ready to begin the journey homewards at an
early hour of the following morning.

This intelligence was communicated by his
orders to the Lady Maud, who heard it with dismay. She feared, with two much reason, that
if she quitted Ghent it would be impossible to
break the imprisonment in which she was held ;
and for a moment she regretted that she had not
consented to Sir Gui's proposal of flying from
the unjust imprisonment in which she was held
by the bishop. After a few moments' deli-
beration she saw there was no means of preserving her freedom but by postponing her departure from Valenciennes, in order that she
might thereby obtain an opportunity of appealing personally to the duke, which she unhesitatingly resolved to do. She did not doubt
that Sir Gui would be able to effect this point
if she could make him acquainted with her
situation; but it seemed almost impossible to
convey to him the necessary intelligence. She
deliberated for some time what was to be done
in this extremity, and at length resolved to address herself to old Marguerite, the only person

upon whose assistance she could reckon, who might, she thought, be either persuaded or frightened into the necessary measures.

All the blame of the strangers being introduced into the house had been laid upon the old gouvernante ; and, as the sudden appearance of Sir Gui from above stairs, when in his haste he had overturned the bishop, still remained wholly unexplained, poor Marguerite lay under suspicions worse than if the actual extent of her indiscretion had been known. By the bishop's order she had been confined to the suite of chambers appropriated to the Lady Maud, and had been ordered not to quit them until the bishop's further pleasure should be made known to her. The churchman had been so much engaged that he had not yet had time to inquire into the particulars of the mysterious business, and he had resolved to postpone it until he should reach Valenciennes.

Dame Marguerite now sate sobbing and groaning in a corner of the chamber, and praying to all the saints whose names she could recollect to save her from the consequences of the bishop's wrath, which her fears even magnified, and made more terrible than they really were.

" Did you hear the order for our journey tomorrow, Dame Marguerite ?" asked the Lady Maud.

" Oh yes, Heaven be praised !" replied the old woman, " and right glad shall I be to escape from this unlucky town."

" Nay, dame," said the lady, " how can you call it unlucky ? Did you not tell me, but a day ago, that your fortune had been told here, and that a very happy destiny was promised you ?"

" Yes ; but that was all the invention of the accursed sorcerer by whom I am brought to this pass, and whose face I wish I had never beheld," replied Marguerite.

" I think you are unjust to the seer," said the lady very gravely : " I have the firmest faith in his predictions, and I am sure nothing can thwart them, unless, indeed, it be your own want of confidence and courage."

" How can I trust or believe in them, my lady," asked the old woman, " when I am too sure that the stories he told me were all lies, fabricated by the rogue to gain admittance to the house—perhaps to rob it ?"

" Trust in them or not, as you please, dame," replied the lady with an air of indifference ; " it is quite certain that, if we quit Ghent, they never can be fulfilled."

" Why not ?" asked Marguerite.

" Why not ?" repeated the lady ; " I marvel that you should ask. Do you know so little of the bishop as to suppose that he does not reserve you for some very dreadful punishment ?"

" Oh, the mercy of Heaven forbid !" ejaculated the old woman, turning pale, and trembling
with fear.

" Do not alarm yourself needlessly, dame,"
said the lady ; " you should be under no apprehensions while you remain in this city. Here
the power of the bishop is subservient to the
laws, and he dare not commit any outrage ; but,
when we shall be at Valenciennes, then indeed,
my poor Marguerite, I shall feel for you."

" Holy Saint Ursula, save me !" cried the old
woman, more frightened than before, " what
can your ladyship mean ? You do not really
think that the bishop would punish me any further than by some slight penance for having
disobeyed his orders ?"

" I do not wish to terrify you," replied the
lady, " but you know the cruelty and severity
of the bishop's temper as well as I do. You
know that there are vaults under his palace at
Valenciennes, of which horrible tales are told.
You have heard, as well as I, the tragical story
of the nun who was shut up in one of them, and
who never saw the light of Heaven again. You
know, too, that her spectre haunts the cemetery
to this day."

" Oh, for Heaven's sake, Lady Maud, do not
continue ! I shall die with apprehension," cried
the old woman.

The Lady Maud saw that her gouvernante was

so sufficiently frightened that she might do what she would with her. Preserving the calm tone in which she had been talking, she said " There is only one way by which your safety may be provided for, dame; that is, by procuring our stay somewhat longer in Ghent. If this can be managed, I do not despair of effecting my own liberation; and in that case I promise you my first care shall be to extricate you from the clutches of the bishop, who, I sincerely believe, intends to make you feel the whole weight of his vengeance."

" Can we not, then, put off our departure ?" said Marguerite ; " can you not say you are too ill to travel ?"

" The bishop is too wary to be imposed upon by any pretence," replied the lady ; " and, if I were even ill in reality, it would not ensure that delay on which alone your safety and mine depend."

" What, then, can be done ?" asked the old woman, half wild with fright.

" I know not," replied the lady. " If, indeed," she said, after a pause, " we could by any means convey intimation of our condition to a friend of mine, a knight, who is now attending the court, he could, perhaps, obtain the duke's order to suspend our journey. But that is impossible," she added.

" Oh, no !" said the old woman eagerly; " difficult it is—but not impossible. The horrible thoughts which you have suggested to me of the punishment that may await me at Valenciennes will give me courage to encounter any thing. Beseech you, my lady, let me try."

"But, even if you had courage," said the Lady Maud, "what opportunity could you find for quitting the house, watched as we are on all sides?"

"I have the key of the little door in the garden-wall still in my possession," cried the old woman exultingly, as she produced it; "and this ensures me a way out."

"Nay, then, dame, if thou hast both the courage and the means to do the errand I will set thee about," said the lady, "I think I may ensure thee safety from the horrible dungeons at Valenciennes."

She immediately wrote a short billet to Sir Gui, begging him by any means to procure the postponement of the bishop's intended journey, and, if possible, some opportunity for her to appeal to the duke in person. She referred him to the bearer, whom she recommended to his protection, for all the other particulars he might need respecting her situation.

Her billet finished, she delivered it to Dame Marguerite, with one of her. rings which was well known to Sir Gui, and bade her inquire for him of the servitors at the duke's abode. She then urged her speedy departure, to which the old woman, who was thoroughly convinced of the necessity of dispatch, was now quite well disposed.

Marguerite, wrapping her veil about her head, stole silently and unperceived into the garden. The door of which she had the key was at the end of a long alley, and entirely concealed from view by a circuitous plantation which had been made for that purpose. With a trembling hand she unlocked the door, and quitted the garden.

She had not proceeded many paces when some person approached and accosted her.

" Save you, noble madam !" said this person : " may I ask whither you wend so quickly ?"

The old woman drew her veil closer about her head, and pretended not to hear the question ; while she trembled in every limb, lest it was some of the bishop's retainers who had seen her quit the garden.

" Beseech you, madam," said the importunate questioner, " to slacken your pace. I would fain conclude the discourse I had begun with you, and which was so unfortunately interrupted on a late occasion."

Dame Marguerite at this looked round, and saw the Disour, or, as she believed, the fortune-teller. Having nothing else to do, he had strolled towards the bishop's house, for the purpose of trying whether he could pick up any intelligence from the servants which might be useful to Sir Gui. He knew the old woman's figure as he saw her issue from the garden-gate, and had hastened to join her.

"At some more fitting time, good sir," replied Dame Marguerite, (who, although she suspected the seer to be a great knave, thought this was not a convenient opportunity for telling him so, and the more particularly as it occurred to her that she might make him serviceable in her present case) "I will hear the remainder of your spell: now you can do me no service so acceptable as to conduct me to the abode of a knight who is called Sir Gui de Montaudun."

"And I can do none more agreeable to myself," replied the Disour; "for, as he is one of my best and most intimate friends, I shall rejoice in the honour which your visit must confer upon him."

He then conducted the old woman to Sir Gui's dwelling, cajoling and flattering her all the way, for the purpose of keeping in her good graces, and thus, as he thought, securing her influence with the Lady Maud for his friend. Perhaps, if he had known the intent of her errand to Sir Gui, he might not have given himself this trouble; but he would not less gladly have been her guide. He carefully avoided referring any more particularly to the abrupt termination of their last interview, lest he should create in her mind suspicions which, as he flattered himself, did not at present exist.

On his arrival at Sir Gui's quarters he learnt that the knight was closeted with the Lord Anthony; and, having therefore bestowed the old lady in another chamber, he went to that in which Sir Gui was sitting.

On his knocking at the door he was bidden to enter. He obeyed.

" I crave your pardon a thousand times, gentles," he said; " but my excuse must be the news I bring."

" Thou knave," said the Bastard jesting, " thou shalt have no pardon, but instant punishment; and thy doom shall be to listen to my news before thou tellest thine own;—a heavy penalty for one who loves so well as thou dost the sound of his own tongue."

" Say on, then, my lord," replied the Disour, entering into the whim; " I can endure with marvellous fortitude."

" Know, then, though naughty Disour," said the Bastard, " that the chancellor has examined that barefooted monk, and that reformado jester, whom thou didst in thy sagacity unkennel; and that he says thy patron Sir Gui's legitimacy can be proved by them as clearly as the sun's light; which being done, he will no longer be the Knight, but the Baron, de Montaudun."

" Oh, brave chancellor!" cried the Disour in

an ecstacy; " but when shall this proof be made
public ? If we are to go to law with the bishop,
I fear me my exultation was ill timed."

" To-morrow, thou incredulous Tale-teller,"
replied the Bastard—" to-morrow, in the duke's
presence, this claim shall be made, and, as I
trust, allowed. Now what is thy news ?"

" Oh, pardon me," said the Disour, " it concerns a fair lady, and I dare not utter a word in
the presence of a person of your lordship's reputation unless Sir Gui gives me permission."

" A flat calumny, and thou knowest it," said
the Bastard ; " all our Low Countries do not contain a man of a more chastised temper, nor a
more virtuous. Heaven forgive me that I am
obliged to say so much of myself !"

" Nay," said Sir Gui ironically, " what need
of all this amongst friends—and friends, too,
who know thy virtues so well ? You do yourself wrong, good my lord ;—but come," he
added, turning to the Disour, " tell us what
thou meanest."

" I mean neither more nor less," replied the
Disour, " than that I did deliver. There is a
fair lady now below waiting your grace's leisure."

" Prithee let her be brought hither, my good
comrade," said the Bastard : " not that I have
the least curiosity to see thy gentle damsel, but
because I take an interest in thy good fortune."

The Disour had, in the mean time, whispered

to Sir Gui who the lady was, which information induced him to consent—though still with an affectation of suspecting Lord Anthony—that she should be conducted to the chamber.

" But first," said the Disour, " I stipulate that my lord yonder shall stand behind the hangings. The lady is young, inexperienced, and timid; and the sight of a stranger might too much embarrass her."

" Nay, nay, why all this caution?" said the Bastard, in a conciliating tone; " thou knowest, my good friend, that thou mayest depend upon my discretion. Let me but have one glimpse, only one single look, at the damsel, that I may know whether I ought to congratulate Sir Gui or not. Besides, I can convince thee that it is absolutely necessary for me to see the style of her beauty, else I might shock our friend's feelings by praising blue eyes when the lady has black ones, or cry up her auburn tresses to the heavens when her locks are flaxen. Now, prithee, gentle Disour, as thou wouldest save me from such an indiscretion, let me see the lady."

" I am inflexible," replied the Disour; " rocks are not firmer than is my resolution. Could I ever forgive myself for exposing a young and innocent beauty to the gaze of a man like your lordship, who, notwithstanding your vows, are mainly to be feared? Ensconce thyself, or I will not produce my treasure."

The Lord Anthony was obliged to step behind the hangings; and he stood there very impatiently, vowing vengeance against the Disour, while the latter with great ceremony introduced old Marguerite.

The old woman kept her veil closely wrapped around her while she delivered her message in whispers to Sir Gui, after which she gave him the billet of the Lady Maud.

Sir Gui read the letter; and, although he could not but consider with some apprehension the proposed departure of the bishop, he did not doubt that he should be able to prevent it; and he saw, too, that this attempt must complete the disgust which his mistress already felt against her persecutor.

Leaving Dame Marguerite in the care of the Disour, he went to another room for the purpose of answering the letter of the Lady Maud, which he did in such a manner as to quiet her fears, at the same time informing her briefly that a very fortunate discovery had been made with regard to his own affairs.

The Lord Anthony in the mean time slowly crept from his hiding-place, and was advancing to that part of the room in which old Marguerite was seated. The Disour stood before him, and reminded him of his promise: it was in vain. He held his arm, and affected the greatest anxiety to prevent his accosting the supposed fair-one:

this was equally fruitless; and his lordship, fling-
ing the Disour aside, approached Marguerite.

"Fair lady," he said, in a most insinuating tone,
"I beseech thee to unveil the beauties which thou
hast so cruelly shrouded. Heaven never meant
that the gifts which it has so plentifully endowed
upon thee should be hidden from the gaze of
mortals."

Old Marguerite could not tell what to make of
this address. She knew that the gentleman who
spoke to her had not seen the beauties he was
praising; and she could have known, besides, that
all the beauty which Heaven had bestowed on
her might be hidden without doing harm to any
one. But who is there so wise as to be insensible
to flattery? who is there so ugly as to believe that
he or she is wholly without charms? Marguerite
thought only of the fortune-teller's prediction,
and of the glowing anticipations to which it
had given rise. The Disour, in the mean time,
stood aloof, enjoying to the utmost the impor-
tunity of the nobleman and the affected resistance of the old woman.

"Nay," said Lord Anthony at length, "if you
still remain inflexible your cruelty must excuse a
little gentle force—I must once behold your features;" and he removed, as he spoke, the veil from
the old woman's face. One glance was enough—
his impetuosity was at once allayed; and, as he
looked round, he saw the Disour holding his sides,

and attempting to check a fit of laughter which shook his frame.

Fortunately for the relief of all parties, at this moment Sir Gui returned with his letter, which he delivered to Marguerite, at the same time requesting the Disour to escort her safely back again. The latter ushered the old lady out of the chamber, but returned immediately; and, having in a whisper informed Sir Gui of the Lord Anthony's adventure, he went back to Marguerite, whom he took home to the bishop's house, which she was so fortunate as to gain without her absence having been perceived.

When the Disour had departed, and Sir Gui had enjoyed his friend's disappointment a little by good-humouredly bantering him, he communicated to him the contents of the letter he had just received.

"This," said Lord Anthony, "makes it necessary that we should hasten our proceedings. In the first place you must have the duke's order to postpone the bishop's journey. He is now at the palace, whither he bade me bring you to-night. Let us therefore dispatch, and I warrant we shall outwit this old churchman, cunning as he is."

The two friends then proceeded to the duke's residence at the town-hall, which had been prepared with great cost and magnificence by his loving citizens of Ghent for his grace's reception.

During the festival of the Toison d'Or every day
was spent in sports of some kind; and in the
evening the noble persons who formed the court,
with all their retainers of the rank of gentlemen,
were expected to assemble at the duke's banquet.
This prince, who was as much distinguished for
the courtly ease and polish of his mind and
manners in peace as for the energy and skill with
which he conducted his warlike enterprises, was
very fond of assemblies such as these; and he
had the skill, by disencumbering them of a great
portion of that ceremony which then commonly
attended the entertainments of the nobility, to
make them universally agreeable to his guests.
On the present occasion the company was disposed of in various parties : the elders were
employed in chatting or in playing at tables, or
other games then in vogue ; the younger members of the company helped on the flight of the
night by dance and song.

The duke was seated at the upper end of the
hall, playing a game at chess with the chancellor.
The Bastard drew near with his friend, Sir Gui.
The game had just approached a close ; the duke
was check-mated.

" It is always thus when I play with a lawyer,"
said the duke : " you are so cool and calculating,
that there is no hope of taking you by surprise.
Confess now, my lord, you have thought of
nothing but the game since we began to play."

"Nothing is more true," replied the chancellor: "of what would your grace that I should have thought else ?"

"See now," cried the duke; " I knew it must be so. I have been thinking of a thousand different things : the fortifications of this city, and the manner in which they may be strengthened, with a multitude of other matters, have been galloping through my brain; and to them, I believe, you are mainly indebted for your victory, my good lord."

The chancellor shook his head. " Well, well, no matter how it was; you did beat me," said the duke, " but not easily. How now, Anthony ?" he said, perceiving his son; " what news dost thou bring ?"

"No news, an please you," replied the Bastard : "I bring your grace an old servant—young, it is true, in years, but old in renown—Sir Gui, the Bastard de Montaudun."

As he spoke he presented his friend to the duke, who received him with that dignified ease and cordiality which distinguished him from all the princes of his time, and which made him so universally popular.

" We have heard much of you, Sir Gui," he said, holding out his hand to the knight, who knelt to kiss it. The duke raised him; and, continuing for a moment to hold his hand, he gave it a cordial pressure as he added " You

have done good service, sir, and carved for yourself as fair a fame as any knight whom we call
ours.   Fortune, the soldier's bride, has yet been
coy to you: she is, like some other females, fickle
and unreasonable : like them, too, she must be
roughly wooed ere she can be won. But, patience,
sir! she may yet be yours."

"In the mean time," said Lord Anthony, "if
your grace would interpose your good offices,
my friend might obtain another bride whom he
loves nearly as well, and who is somewhat more
kindly disposed towards him than that same
Madame Fortune your grace speaks of."

"What an old man's wooing can do for you,
Sir Gui," said the duke, "you may reckon upon;
but how shall that speed your suit?"

"Sir Gui will not put your grace to such
trouble," replied Anthony with affected gravity;
"the lady he will woo without your grace's aid:
but there is a certain inveterate bishop, the lady's
guardian, over whom the exercise of your authority would have an effect very beneficial to my
friend's suit." The Bastard then went on to explain to the duke the circumstances of Sir Gui's
love for the Lady Maud, the approbation of the
late baron, the refusal of the bishop, and his intention to wed the lady to Sir Jacques Lelain.

The duke's indignation, which was always easily
moved, was roused at this recital. "So help me,
the blessed St. Andrew," cried he, "but I would

rather deal, with the soldan, and all his might, than with one such crafty priest as this same bishop! But we must not let so notorious a wrong be done as that he now meditates. Lelain!" he added: " why, though I know him to be as brave as his own sword, and as honest a man as breathes Heaven's air, he is no more fit to be married than his war-horse. Rest ye content, Sir Gui; we will spoil the bishop's plans, or we shall know the reason."

Sir Gui thanked the duke in the warmest terms that his feelings could prompt for the favorable interest which he displayed.

" My lord," said the duke, turning to the chancellor, " see that the Bishop of Valenciennes be summoned to attend us here to-morrow morning, and to bring the Lady Maud to court also. The same time shall also serve for discussing that other topic on which we have been talking, and which concerns you, Sir Gui, more than you wot of. And, my lord," he added to the chancellor, " lest the bishop should misunderstand my meaning, let orders be given at the gates that neither he nor any of his people be allowed to quit the city."

The duke then changed the subject, and questioned Sir Gui respecting his adventures in the Holy Land—the numbers and discipline of the sultan's army; to all which Sir Gui answered in so clear and soldierlike a manner as increased the favorable opinion which the duke entertained of him. The night grew late ; and at length the duke retired, bidding Sir Gui attend at his court on the following morning, and wishing, as he left him, that his lady-love might soon be his bride.

" That gentleman," said the Bastard, as the duke withdrew, " although he is my father, is as honest and as brave as any in these realms—or in the next, for aught I know ; and in war, or in wooing, would make as good a second as man should desire to have. Now, Sir Gui," he added, " let us home to bed, and to-morrow we shall see if we cannot beat this bishop in spite of all his stratagems."

On the following morning the companions repaired to the duke's palace. It was his grace's custom to hold a sort of open court daily, for hearing such applications as might be made to him, and for the dispatch of all public business. This usually lasted until the hour of eleven, when, at the benighted period of which we are speaking, the people were so barbarously igno rant as to dine. The nobles were in the habit of attending here, and were occasionally consulted by the duke in forming his decisions. The ladies of the court also, although they of course took no part in the serious business which was transacted there, were present in considerable numbers, so that the hall of justice in the morning was often nearly as splendid and crowded as the banquet of the evening.

On the present occasion the court was unusually full. Soon after Lord Anthony and Sir Gui had arrived they saw the bishop enter the hall, accompanied by the Lady Maud. The bishop's usher conducted her to a seat near the duchess, who, accompanied by the ladies of the court, was placed at some distance from the dais, where the duke and the council sate. In this latter place a chair was reserved for the bishop, in which he took his place. The business of the court had already begun.

" My lord bishop," said the duke, " we have waited your coming, because a matter which nearly concerns you has just been urged. It appears that your late servant, the wretched man who died of the wounds he received in the combat with another burgher of Valenciennes, has made a confession"—(the bishop turned as pale as his own stole when the duke uttered this: his grace saw the change of his countenance; but, without noticing it, he went on)—" by which confession he admitted his own guilt; and, as the only reparation he could offer to the son of the man he had slain, he bequeathed to him a house and certain property he possessed in Valenciennes. It seems that this bequest is not valid, until you, as the liege lord under us of that city, shall ratify it. How say you then, my lórd? have you any reason to offer why the dead man's will should not prevail ?"

The bishop was too much relieved by the turn which the affair had taken to dispute a point of such comparative insignificance as this ; and he therefore replied that he consented to it ; not forgetting at the same time to express, in strong terms, the regret which he pretended to feel at having been so much imposed upon'by the dead Mahuot as to believe in his innocence. His ob÷ ject in doing this was twofold : first, he wished to conciliate the duke ; and, in the next, he thought that, by blackening Mahuot's character, he should protect himself against the inconvenient suspi÷ cions to which the discoveries of the steward, if he had made any respecting himself, might give rise.

The duke took the bishop at his word ; and, Jacotin being in attendance, he was ordered to do homage in court to the bishop for Mahuot's lands ; which he did, and, to the deep, though concealed, mortification of the bishop, was legally constituted the inheritor of the property of the man he had been so fortunate as to kill two days before.

The duke then beckoned to Sir Gui ; and, when the latter had drawn near his chair, his grace said, addressing the bishop, " This affair being ended, I have now, in turn, to become a

suitor to your grace, and to pray your consent
that the Lady Maud de Montacute may wed with
this young soldier," pointing to Sir Gui as
he spoke. "You are her guardian, and stand
towards her in the place of her natural father.
That father, it seems, had approved of their
mutual passion ; and you, I trust, will not withhold your blessing and consent from them."

"My liege," said the bishop, rising, and assuming a solemn air, "it gives me pain so great
that I have not the skill to express it at finding
that I cannot comply with your highness's wishes.
My sacred office as a minister of our holy religion, my duty as a guardian, my plighted faith as
a noble, and my feelings as a man, all combine to
prevent my consenting to the union which your
highness proposes. The Baron de Montacute
charged me, on his death-bed, not to suffer his
daughter to wed with any but her equal in rank,
and birth, and fortune ; and I, thinking that to
fulfil these conditions would be the most certain
means of ensuring the maiden's happiness, solemnly swore to observe them. Keeping these
conditions in view, I have selected a gentleman
whom your highness will not, I am sure, think
an unfit husband for the Lady Maud. He is of
high birth, and of unsullied reputation ; his
military prowess and skill have raised him to
the highest rank among the brave knights of
your court ; and his demeanor in peace is not

less honorable and courteous. I mean the noble Sir Jacques Lelain, whose feats in arms have so often excited your highness's admiration."

"Why, zounds, man!" cried the duke, forgetting his state, as he was in the habit of doing when he was moved, "you do not mean that Lelain, although as brave and as honest a warrior as ever wore belted brand, is a fit husband for the blooming Lady Maud, of whom he might well be the father."

"He is her suitor, my liege," replied the bishop; "and, to my poor thinking, his years are not so many as to unfit him to be the lady's consort."

"Then you think, my lord bishop, that fifty and nineteen would make a suitable union. Of all the stretching leather in the world," he said, lowering his voice so as only to be heard by those immediately near him, "commend me to a churchman's conscience! But yonder is Lelain himself. Come hither, Jacques; never stand blushing and biting thy thumb like a schoolboy: tell me, art thou hardy enough to wish to take to thyself a young wife? Couldst thou wed thy December to the Lady Maud's May?"

"I know not," said Lelain sullenly; "what your highness means by December: marry, your enemies have found it hot weather with me many a time ere now, and may do so still.

Surely if a man can fight a battle he can wed a blue-eyed wench."

" For scaling a castle wall, for sacking a city, for stalwart deeds in arms, and for drinking when thou hast done fighting, thy superior cannot be found, and none shall confess thy merits sooner, as none knows them better, than I ; but for wedding——Nay, Jacques, look not so grave—I think thou art the most unfit of all the men in Ghent."

" Your highness may have your jest, and you will ; but, for all that, I have wooed the maiden ; and I should like to see, saving your own royal self, who dare dispute my title to her. For you, my liege, all I have to say is, that I would rather choose you for a champion in the field than for a help in a love-suit."

" Right angrily said, Jacques," replied the duke : " for your challenge, I dare swear, the knight who bewitched you out of your saddle in the joust of yesterday would not refuse to run another course with you if the Lady Maud were to be the prize : but, to leave that for a while, tell me, Jacques, have you the lady's consent ?"

The Lady Maud had been listening with almost overpowering emotions to this public conversation, of which she was the subject, before the noble and numerous company which surrounded her. Her pride was wounded at the cool manner in which Lelain spoke of her, and her indignation roused at the insolent tyranny which, under the pretence of his authority as a guardian, the bishop would have exercised over her. These feelings would alone have been sufficient to rouse her to resent the indignity which, as she thought, had been practised towards her ; but her love for Sir Gui impelled her to a bolder step, and, mastering, as well as she was able, the rising passion which oppressed her, she advanced from her seat beside the duchess, and threw herself at the duke's feet.

" In the name of that chivalry of which you are the honour and the ornament," she cried, " I conjure you, sire, to save the child of a brave knight and true noble from the indignities which are heaping upon her. Is it fitting," she added— rising as the duke extended his hand to her— " is it fitting that the Lady of Montacute should be thus made a prize, to be staked by a priest, and played for by warriors like a captive foe, or like a noteless and worthless person, whose will has nought to do with the choice ? I protest against the authority of the bishop ; I renounce his guardianship ; and here, once and for all, I place myself under that of your grace, vowing solemnly that nothing but absolute force shall ever again put me in his power. For you, Sir Jacques Lelain," she said, turning to the knight,

" who I believe have been duped and set on by
artful contrivance to offer me an affront which
your own generous temper could never have
prompted, hear me say that, although I know
you noble, and believe you brave, I love you
not, and will never wed with you."

" Now what say you, Sir Jacques, to that
frank speech?" asked the duke maliciously.

" I say, my liege," said Sir Jacques, " that it
is said like her father's daughter; and that the
fire in her eye reminds me of that which I have
seen flash in many a stormy moment from the old
baron's. By our lady, but I think I had better
draw off! I do begin to think I have been made
to look like a fool in being wrought upon to woo
a maiden who will not love me. But this is not
my fault," he said, looking at the bishop; "and
they who have led me into this fool's paradise
may thank themselves for the disappointment.—
Lady," he said, turning to Maud, and kneeling
at her feet, " I crave your forgiveness for having
angered you; and beg you to let me lay down
the character of your knight, which I have worn
of late."

" It is I, Sir Jacques," replied Maud—who
wondered somewhat, now that it was past,
where she had found courage enough to get
through the speech she had made—' it is I who
have to beg pardon. As I know you to have

been my father's old and trusty friend, I care not if I confess that I love you as a daughter ; but with this you must be content."

Sir Jacques kissed the fair hand which Maud held out to him, and, rising from his knee, retired to his place.

" This I will say to thee, Jacques," said the duke, " that when thou dost counsel thyself thou dost always right; and it is only when thou listenest to the evil rede of others that thou dost commit follies. But come, old friend, I am glad that thou hast done wisely ; and, since thou hast quitted thy claim, what says his reverence to my proposal ? Shall the youth for whom her father destined this maiden as a bride now have thy consent to wed him ?"

" I beseech your grace to pardon me," said the wily churchman, with an hypocritical air and downcast looks, " if my duty and my conscience forbid me to comply with your grace's commands. I cannot, and I dare not, consent to the heiress of Montacute wedding with a man who, whatever may be his qualifications as a warrior, is of fortune so low and poor as the youthful knight whom your grace protects."

" Nay, for his fortune, that surely matters not, good bishop : the barony of Montacute is large enough, and his sword will probably win more to add to it. While I find him no unsuitable match

on this score, I shall look that you give me better reasons for your refusal."

The bishop saw that the duke's tone began to
grow more serious ; but still, not being a man to
give up his point readily, he thought he might
postpone the marriage, and gain time, in which
he hoped he should be able, by fair or by foul
means, wholly to prevent it.

" My liege," he said, " your grace may, if you
will, change the laws ; for your power is absolute,
and, if you think expedient, you can do so.   I
am but a subject, and my duty is to obey them.
By the laws of the County of Hainault, which
your highness swore solemnly to maintain, the
Lady Maud cannot be married to a man of illegitimate birth ; nor can she be married to any one
without my consent, who am her lawful guardian.   If she should marry such a one, until my
consent is given, her barony and lands are forfeit to the holy church, whose unworthy servant
I am.   I can no more consent to her union with
the Bastard of Montaudun, having a regard to
my sacred function, to my conscience, and to my
character, than your grace can permit it, without violating the solemn compact by which you
promised, before the high altar at Valenciennes,
to maintain the old laws and privileges of the
people of the county of Hainault."

The bishop was silent.   The duke bit his lips,

and twisted his beard about violently—a common practice with him when he was angered or perplexed.

The churchman thought he had made an impression on the duke ; and, not doubting that he should now gain his point, he proceeded in an insinuating tone, and with a mortified air, to say, " I call all the saints of heaven to witness that it pains my very heart thus to thwart your grace's expressed wishes ; but the preservation of a pure religion, the maintenance of moral virtue and good order, depend upon the observance of such laws. But for that of which I am now the champion, albeit an unworthy one, the scandal of illicit connexions would be spread through the land, the holy ties of marriage disregarded, and the pure streams of noble blood, of which our nation is so justly proud, be mingled with and contaminated by the basest mixtures."

The Bastard of Burgundy, who had no great reverence for the bishop, heard this speech with an indignation which he found it almost impossible to restrain. Gui saw his rising passion, and endeavoured to check him by holding his arm, and whispering in his ear that the time for vengeance would come, and that to notice the insolence of the bishop now would be to give him an advantage.

" Scurvy dog of a priest !" muttered the impetuous Anthony ; " if it were not for his frock

I would cram every slanderous lie he has now
uttered down his throat with the point of my
sword."

The chancellor, who had hitherto taken no part
in the conversation, now addressed the bishop.
" You say well and wisely, my good lord ; the
laws of Hainault are as you have laid them down,
and the duke is sworn to observe them. If your
objection to the marriage of the Lady Maud with
Sir Gui is founded upon his illegitimacy, I know
no means of removing it"——

" It is so," cried the bishop eagerly, and without waiting to hear the conclusion of the bishop's
sentence—" It is so : I expected that your lordship would advocate the observance of so wise
and useful a law."

" I say," continued the chancellor, without noticing the interruption, " that I know no means
of removing your grace's objection, save by
proving that the youth is the legitimate son of
the late baron."

" Content," replied the bishop, who believed
that he was quite secure on this point, and who
never dreamt that there was any equivocal meaning in the chancellor's speech. " If the knight
be the son of the Baron de Montaudun let him
wed the Lady Maud."

" Then, with our sovereign liege's permission,"
said the chancellor, " the proofs shall now be
given. Let the witnesses stand forth."

" Room for the witnesses !" shouted the Disour, who had been standing near the chancellor's chair during the whole of the scene, and now made way for the friar to advance.

The monk gave his staff into the hands of one standing near him, and advanced towards the duke's throne, where he knelt. He then rose, and, approaching the chancellor, took an oath which was administered to him to bear true testimony in what he should relate. His face was nearly covered by his cowl, and he stood in such a position that the bishop could not see his features.

" Who are you ?" asked the chancellor.

" My name is Anselm : I am a monk, of the order of Carmelites ; and my abode was at the monastery of Val de Grace."

The bishop was evidently much discomposed by the appearance of this monk, whom he believed to have been long since dead.

" What do you know touching the legitimacy of Sir Gui, commonly called the Bastard of Montaudun ?"

" I know that he is the lawful son of the baron of that name ; and that the marriage of his father and of the Lady Adeline Neville was performed by me, in the baron's own chapel, at Montandun."

" This is an impostor !" my lord duke, cried the bishop. " The Brother Anslem, whom this man thus boldly ventures to represent, was a refrac-

tory member of the church, upon whom, for his
manifold offences, a chapter of my diocese passed
a sentence of imprisonment. He was confined
in the dungeon of the abbey at Valenciennès, and
there he died soon after his confinement. Of
this I have abundant proof."

" In good time, by your reverence's leave,"
said the duke coolly: " we shall talk of the
dungeons at Valenciennes hereafter. Let the
witness proceed."

The monk then detailed, in a simple but striking
manner, the events which we have found it necessary, in the course of our narration, to lay before our readers. He described the death of the
Baron de Montaudun ; his dying injunctions that
the monk would establish the legitimacy of his
child, and carry the news of his death to the ba-
rouess. He then told how the baroness, upon
receiving the fatal intelligence, fell ill ; and that
the shock acted so fatally upon her frame, already broken by sickness and anxiety, that she
survived only a few weeks.

The monk, then feeling it was necessary to provide for the safety of the child, dispatched it by
a trusty messenger to the Baron de Montacute,
and went himself to lay before the bishop the
proofs which he possessed of its legitimacy.

Upon his communicating this intelligence to
the bishop, he said the documents were taken
from him, and he retired to a cell which had

been provided for him in the monastery, and which he was not allowed to quit for several weeks· At length the bishop's steward, Mahuot, appeared, and proposed to him, as the terms of his liberation, that he should solemnly swear never to disclose what he knew respecting the marriage of the Baron de Montaudun with the Lady Neville, nor to set up the claim of this infant. This the monk without hesitation refused to do; in consequence of which he was taken during the night to a range of vaults, beneath the abbey, where he remained for two years, in the custody of Mahuot. His sufferings and complaints at length moved the heart of his gaoler, who consented to his liberation on condition that he would accompany to the Holy Land a levy then about to march, and would swear not to return to Valenciennes nor its neighbourhood for more than ten years. The reason for this condition was, that the report which Mahuot was to make to the bishop of the monk's death might not be doubted.

" I confess," continued the monk, " that I was deeply culpable in betraying the trust which had been reposed in me by the Baron de Montaudun; but the pain and grief of imprisonment were too great to be borne. Penance and pilgrimage have, I trust, atoned for this fault. The state of the Holy Land prevented my returning exactly at the expiration of the period which Mahuot had stipulated for ; and, when I reached this country, I found the Lord Montacute dead—the heir of the Baron de Montaudun absent, no one knew where—and the Lady Maud in the wardship of the bishop. I laboured incessantly to collect the proofs of the legitimacy of the young baron, and for this purpose I have traversed many leagues without success. At length, as I believe, by the interposition of Providence, every link in the chain of evidence which is necessary for that purpose has been supplied in this city, and within the last two days. My trust will now be discharged, and I shall die in peace."

The recital of the monk had been wholly uninterrupted. It was delivered with that earnestness and simplicity which are the invariable characteristics of truth, and every person present was convinced of his integrity.

The bishop alone listened with anger and dismay; and these feelings were heightened as he was convinced of the monk's veracity, and that Mahuout had imposed upon him. He was, however, too great an adept in dissimulation to suffer any outward indication of the storm which shook his bosom to appear. He believed still that Mahuot's death was his security; and in this belief he was prepared to brave the untoward chances which assailed him.

" Now, my lord bishop," asked the duke, " what does your reverence say to this tale?"

" Simply this, my liege," replied the bishop,

" that it is an entire fiction, not of the most ingenious fabrication, advanced by a person of no
note nor credit, and wholly unsupported by proof.
I trust that to such an accusation your grace will
not listen—still less that you will expect me to
answer."

" Nay, my lord, it must be answered," said the
duke ; " I were unfit to be the sovereign of this
realm if I could hear charges so grave against
your holy character, or a tale so deeply interesting a brave young knight, whom I am proud to
call my soldier, without requiring an answer to
them."

The bishop did not like the tone of this speech,
but his self-possession did not forsake him.
" First," he said, " if it please your highness, I
should hear upon what proofs this ribald accusation rests. Or," he added, with an ill-suppressed
scorn, " fits it that I enter into a contest with the
noteless vagabond whose tale is just told ?"

The duke looked indignantly at the proud
churchman, and was about to answer ; when the
chancellor, who had a cooler way of doing things,
said, " His grace's request is most reasonable.
He should hear all the witnesses ; and he will remember that, cheaply as he holds the testimony
of the monk, yet, if it shall be confirmed by some
other, it cannot be gainsaid. Let the other witness stand forth."

The quondam jester now approached, and,

being sworn to give true testimony, he repeated
the story of the murder at Montereau, and the
dying declaration of the baron.

This recital added to the interest which the
duke had already felt in favour of Sir Gui. The
fate of his own father had made so powerful an
impression on him, that whatever was connected
with it was always sure to excite his warmest
feelings. The mere allusion to the subject at all
times affected him ; but, now that the narrations
given by the monk and the jester had brought
distinctly and forcibly before his mind all the
particulars of that bloody event, his grief for
his father's fate, and his detestation of the
traitors who had inflicted it, were renewed
with all the freshness and bitterness which belonged to them. He looked upon Sir Gui as the
offspring of a man who had lost his life by his
fidelity to the late duke, whose heart's blood had
mingled with his ; and he felt that the son of such
a man had claims upon him so strong that they
would perhaps have induced him to strain the
strict rules of law in his favour. Here, however,
the matter was too plain and equitable to need
any such aid. The duke saw that the bishop's
devices must be defeated, and he knew it was
better to let the chancellor proceed in his course,
because his acuteness and ingenuity were more
likely to match the bishop at his own weapons,
than that the duke's blunt passion could be ex-

pected to overcome them. He therefore merely
held out his hand to Sir Gui, and warmly pressed
that which the knight put into it, at the same time
motioning to the chancellor to proceed.

" This then," said the wily old man, who perfectly understood the duke, and turning as he spoke
to the bishop, " is the whole of the evidence respecting the legitimacy of the Baron de Montaudun. Does it satisfy your grace on that point?"

" I marvel that your lordship should ask me
such a question," replied the bishop, who, by a
great effort, maintained his calmness and self-
possession. " You are too good a lawyer to receive such evidence, and I trust you do not think
so ill of my poor understanding as to suppose
that I take one word of it for truth. I have said
before, and I repeat, that your supposed monk is
an impostor; and I dare him to the proof either
that he is the person he represents himself to be,
or that his other assertions are true. The brother
Anselm was for his sins doomed to a short imprisonment, during which he died. The means
of contradicting all that he has said were until
very lately in my power; but it is not because
I am at this moment without such proof that the
unsupported accusations of nameless and suspi-
cious persons shall be allowed to impugn my
reputation. That, as I humbly take it, would be
against all law, as well as against all justice.
Your lordship cannot have failed to observe that

these charges are not brought forward until after the death of Mahuot. That event it is which has encouraged the persons by whom this notable plot has been got up to put it in action, and has afforded the opportunity for venting this tissue of incomprehensible lies. If he were still alive the contradiction would be prompt and certain, and this my enemies know full well. I shall, therefore, under favour of his grace and of your lordship, decline to make any answer to such charges, save by denying them altogether. In this place, and on so sudden an occasion, I might well refuse to do so ; but I abandon all the other reasons, which, if I would, I could urge, to show the justice of my request, and rely solely upon that I have mentioned."

"Upon your being without the evidence of Mahuot?" asked the chancellor.

"Exactly so," replied the bishop.

"Then," rejoined the chancellor, with a gravity which was more cutting than the most malicious tones he could have used, "I am rejoiced that I can relieve your lordship from that difficulty. The evidence of Mahuot is not quite lost to you, for I hold in my hand an ample confession, which he dictated, in his expiring moments, before the Prior of the Black Canons in this city. It discloses many curious particulars, all intimately concerning your grace, but not connected with the present question ; and it contains also a copious corroboration of every particular which has been deposed to by the monk and the other witness respecting the legitimacy of the Baron de Montaudun, the imprisonment of the brother Anselm at Valenciennes, and his release, with the conditions on which it was connived at by your grace's deceased servant."

This was the blow which the bishop had most to dread, but from which, by the turn the investigation had taken, he thought he was quite secure. He saw at once that all was lost, and that his policy, deep and subtle as he had before thought it, was counteracted by persons and circumstances he had not calculated upon. Defeated as he was, still his impudence and self-command did not forsake him; a slight paleness which spread over his face, and an involuntary contraction of the muscles about his mouth, were the only outward indications of the feelings which occupied his mind. He drew himself up with as much dignity of manner as he could assume, and looked with a haughty and indifferent glance on the spectators, whose eyes were fixed upon him, and whose countenances expressed that contempt and indignation which the story of his cruelty and treachery was likely to have excited.

A pause ensued, which was broken by the duke's calling to Sir Gui.

"My Lord de Montaudun," he cried—"for, since your legitimate claim to that rank is now satisfactorily shown to me, and I believe to all present, I bid you henceforward to assume it, and to take the place among our nobles to which it entitles you—As your liege lord, I here give you investiture of the barony late your noble father's, and of which you have been too long deprived."

The baron, Sir Gui no longer, knelt to the duke, who bid him immediately rise, and motioned him to take a place among the peers near his throne.

" And now, my lord bishop," said the duke, " do you still withhold your consent to the baron's marriage with the Lady Maud ?"

The bishop knew that matters had now gone too far for any probability of retrieving them. He would willingly have made his peace with the duke by consenting to the proposal, if that had been practicable; but he knew the temper of his sovereign's mind too well to suppose that, after the exposure which had taken place, he could ever hope to remove the injurious impression which it had made against him. He therefore resolved to give no sign of yielding, but to keep up an air of wounded innocence, as the best means of covering his retreat, and of weakening the effect of the disgrace which had fallen on him.

In as calm a tone as he could command he replied: " Your highness's power is supreme over all but my conscience; my life, and aught else that I possess, is at the command of my sovereign; but the duty I owe to Heaven admits of no compromise, and that bids me still refuse to betray an oath solemnly pledged. Assailed as I am by the foul conspiracies of hidden enemies, I will not do myself so much wrong as to countenance in any way their nefarious attempts. Until I shall have had an opportunity of showing the wickedness and falsehood of those attempts, or until by more competent witnesses this matter shall be proved, I do withhold my consent."

" Nay, then, I know not what shall be done," said the duke. " It were a grievous wrong that the Baron de Montaudun should be deprived of a bride for whom he has waited so long, and whom he has so fairly won. It were the most discourteous thing in the world that the Lady Maud should be disappointed of two suitors in the same day ; and that, having dismissed Sir Jacques Lelain, who seems not to take his disgrace much to heart, she should be restrained from marrying the man of her choice. It were also highly unjust to our court, who have been led to expect that the celebration of this noble marriage would be added to the festivities of the solemn ceremony of the Toison d'Or, that they should be disappointed. There is only one way that I can hit upon by which we may hope to overcome this difficulty ; and that must depend upon the Lady Maud's acquiescence. The guardian appointed by her noble father refuses his consent. Now, I am sometimes called the father of my people."

"And not without reason," muttered the Lord Anthony, loud enough to be heard, and in a tone which caused a general smile throughout the assembly. The duke looked round with the intention of reproving him; but he could not withstand the arch expression of his son's face, and his own features relaxed into a smile.

"No matter," he said, composing himself as well as he could; "I will, upon this occasion, exert the authority of a parent, and, if the Lady Maud will take my consent instead of the bishop's, there shall be no further obstacle to her union. How say you, lady?" he asked of the blushing Maud, who found it difficult to utter the ready acquiescence which her heart prompted.

"What would your grace have her say?" replied the duchess, who saw and pitied her confusion: "a maiden's blushes speak distinctly enough to all who can read them, and your grace is wont to be tolerably clear-sighted on occasion."

"I am schooled, my good lady," said the duke, as he took from the duchess the hand of the Lady Maud; and then joining it in that of the Baron de Montaudun, who stepped forward to receive it, he said "May you be happy!"

The pair knelt at the feet of the duke, while

a joyful shout rang through the assembly, in which the voice of the Disour was heard above all others. When this had subsided, and silence had been resumed, the duke, assuming an air of severity, and turning to the bishop, said to him—

" My lord, we permit your grace forthwith to depart to Valenciennes ; but we think it not right to do this without intimating to you that the confession of your steward, with the other particulars which have this day come to our knowledge, shall be dispatched immediately to Rome. You know best whether you will be able to manifest your innocence ; but we would have you told that there are heavy accusations against you—so heavy, that, if but a tithe part of them be true, you are in a perilous case. We are glad that your holy office takes from us the necessity of investigating those accusations, and to his holiness and his council we remit the judgment of a matter in which we cannot trust ourselves to decide. In the mean time we bid you to withdraw from all interference with the possessions both of the Lady Maud, over whom your guardianship now terminates, and of the Baron de Montaudun ; and we order that you prepare to account to the latter for the long stewardship you have exercised over his barony. See that these things be done, my lord, for the Baron de Moutaudun will not want friends to enforce his rights, if need be ; and, if you fail to obey the command we now give you, it may chance that some troops of our soldiers, who, as you know, are not very reverent even to churchmen, may be quartered upon your fat bishopric."

The prelate did not wait for a second bidding to depart, but withdrew hastily, burning with confusion and mortification, and followed by the reproachful glances of the numerous company which filled the hall. He hastened immediately to Valenciennes, where the fear of disgrace and the pain of his defeat put a hasty period to his wicked life, and prevented all opposition, if, indeed, he had meditated any, to the duke's bidding.

The wedding of the Baron de Montaudun and the Lady Maud was celebrated with great magnificence, and, after the festival of the Toison d'Or was finished, they retired to Montaudun, where they lived in the practice of those virtues which deserve and ensure happiness, and transmitted their wealth and honours to a numerous and illustrious progeny.

The monk became the baron's almoner, and an inmate of the family; and the Disour, when, after a few years, he got tired of wandering, took up his abode in the castle-hall, where he continued to tell tales, and to tease old Dame Marguerite (who became the baroness's housekeeper) to the last hour of her existence.

The history of his patron's marriage was always his most favorite relation; and it was from the traditional account of his version of that story, which is still remembered in the house of Mont-audun, that I have been able to compile this tale of

The Knight and the Disour.

By the time my grandmother had finished her tale, the supper hour, usually observed with so much punctuality, had passed; and I knew the regularity of the old lady's habits so well, that I saw the story-telling must be finished for the night.

" The conditions of our sport have been performed now by every body present, with one exception," said Harry Beville ; " I hope it is not intended to permit him to escape."

The certainty of my departing early in the morning made me bold, and I disclaimed any wish to escape.

" But, if you are allowed to execute your intention of setting off to-morrow morning for town," said Harry, " you will evade the terms of our agreement."

" And pray whose fault will that be?" I asked. " If some of the persons concerned in that agreement have kept their faith so ill that they have been compelled to tell two stories instead of one, and have thus excluded those less ambitious individuals who are content to fulfil only the letter of the compact, let the blame rest upon them alone. I should have taken my turn fairly but for the double stories told by you and my grandmother."

" Now, if any one gives you credit for a single grain of sincerity, notwithstanding your very plausible look," said Elizabeth, " they do not know you so well as I.   But I hope you will not be allowed to laugh at us in this manner."

" Why, indeed," said my grandmother, " I think it would be unjust to every one to let Harry Slingsby off so easily ; it would, besides, be disagreeable to himself to be dismissed thus ingloriously, without having taken any other part in our sport than that of listening."

" You are too good, my dear grandmother," I replied : " I have no taste for glory ; it suits better with the quietness of my temper to remain in the back ground, than to share in a contest for honour amongst such expert story-tellers as are here assembled.   I assure you I shall be quite content with the gratification I have already enjoyed in hearing your tales."

" It goes to my heart that he should be allowed to go scot-free," said Harry Beville.

" I have a proposal to make," said Mr. Wharton, " by which he will not altogether escape ; and, if it shall be approved of, we shall convince him that we know how to do justice to ourselves as well as to him."

" Let us hear the proposal" was unanimously called out.

" It is this," said the attorney :—" Among the stories which we have listened to with so much pleasure are some which, unless I am deceived, other folks would not altogether disdain. In this tale-telling age I cannot but suppose that the united labours of our fancies would look mighty well in the shape of a book; and I really think the experiment worth trying. I suggest, therefore, that we shall each of us hand over our several contributions to Mr. Slingsby, and that he shall be charged with the care of revising and editing them. When he shall have reduced them to such a shape as he thinks most advisable, he shall have them published, and we will boldly try the taste of the public. All the world are authors, and why should we not try? Is my proposal agreed to ?"

A loud assent was immediately pronounced; the several MSS. were delivered into my hands; and thus, without my being at all aware of the honour which it was intended to confer upon me, I became at once installed in the office of editor of " The Tales of My Grandmother's Guests." All my attempts to relinquish the charge were unavailing; and, when I was convinced of this, I set about executing my task with as good a grace as possible.

Gentle reader, the result is before you. To your indulgence I commit " My Grandmother's Guests and their Tales," with a very sincere desire that they may prove agreeable to you ; and, for myself, I have only to say, that

" I tell the tales as they were told to me."

FINIS.

J. ROBINS AND CO. ALBION PRESS, LONDON.